QUICK AND THE DEAD

QUICK AND THE DEAD

An Alex Quick Mystery

Susan Moody

This first world edition published 2016
in Great Britain and the USA by
SEVERN HOUSE PUBLISHERS LTD of
19 Cedar Road, Sutton, Surrey, England, SM2 5DA.
Trade paperback edition first published
in Great Britain and the USA 2016 by
SEVERN HOUSE PUBLISHERS LTD

British Library Cataloguing in Publication Data

Moody, Susan author.
  Quick and the dead.
  1. Women private investigators–Fiction. 2. Detective and
  mystery stories.
  I. Title
  823.9'14-dc23

ISBN-13: 978-0-7278-8588-3 (cased)
ISBN-13: 978-1-84751-691-6 (trade paper)
ISBN-13: 978-1-78010-751-6 (e-book)

Typeset by Palimpsest Book Production Ltd.,
Falkirk, Stirlingshire, Scotland.

ONE

That year, the weather changed overnight. Fast and hard. On Saturday afternoon, there were blue skies and the weak pee-coloured sunshine of mid-winter. By Sunday morning, it had turned gut-wrenchingly cold: heavy clouds, pavements sparkling with hoarfrost, bone-chilling winds driving in straight from the Russian steppes.

Shivering in my woollen bathrobe as I got ready for bed, I sat in front of the dressing-table mirror. I'd spent the last week hunched over my desk, all day, every day, putting together pictures and text, ready for tomorrow's meeting, my only exercise the removal of the cork from a bottle of red and the subsequent lifting of a glass to my lips. Probably bad for me, but I was careful not to overdo it, and it helped to keep some of my chronic sadness temporarily at bay. Now, pitilessly examining my grey-faced reflection, as one does, especially if one is on the wrong side of thirty (oh, all right then, thirty-three), I catalogued my assets. No double chin, so far. Rather glamorous red hair, but usually pulled severely back from my face so it wouldn't get in my eyes. Good cheekbones. Not too many crows' feet around the eyes. Not too much flab on the hips. Breasts . . . well, not exactly pert, but then they never had been. I was in good shape, though I knew I ought to go to the gym more often.

But would lifting a few more weights, spending fifteen minutes on the running machine instead of ten, swimming sixty lengths of the pool instead of fifty – would that seriously make any difference to my weight or shape?

I thought not. I was already pretty fit – I kept myself in good nick by jogging. Perhaps I was having a bad day, but something in me rebelled as I stared out at the whipping clouds and the dreary grey sea. Okay, so most of my body parts were moving inexorably southwards or sideways, but I decided that I could not bear the thought of spending even one more minute at the gym. Not today. Not ever. The smell of the changing room, the damp trainers and damper towels, the ghastly cosiness of the other women and their feminine chat about children, menfolk, *periods*. If there's one thing I do not want to discuss or hear about, it's other women's periods, thank you; I have enough problems coping with my own. And I *hated* the way they didn't really mean their grumbles about their husbands, secure because at least they had one, their smug alliance as they slagged off their menfolk – *He still hasn't worked out how to switch on the washing machine, like I was born with an instruction manual in my mouth! Send him to the shops and he'll always come back with the wrong item! He never leaves the seat down after he's peed, however many times I ask him to!* Choruses of *Yes, yes, typical, men, tell me about it!* – and only me wondering aloud if they would leave the seat *up* for him if he asked them to. Cue hostile stares, as though I'd suddenly revealed that my (un-pert) breasts had turned gangrenous and were about to leak all over their leotards.

The Maiden Aunt, I thought suddenly. I stared once more into the mirror. Even though neither of my siblings had so far enlarged the gene pool, I was in danger of becoming a Maiden Aunt. Put me in a gingham apron, hand me a pitchfork, and I could picture myself clearly: Mrs American Gothic, severe face, lips set in permanent disapproval. I needed to laugh again. I needed a man in more ways than one. I needed a fuck.

My mobile buzzed. 'Quick here,' I said.

'Alex, darling.' It was Dr Helena Drummond, my collaborator. My friend. And, in several ways, my saviour.

'Hi, Helena.' I couldn't help smiling. It was the effect she always had on me.

'I'm just touching base, because I'm actually on my way out the door, or at least standing *at* it, waiting for my lift. So what time are we supposed to meet this guy?'

'I've already told you three times. Ten *thirty*. In the *morning*. *Tomorrow*.' I spoke slowly and clearly, as though she was not only mentally challenged, but also deaf. Neither of which was remotely true.

'I hope to God this publisher person keeps his place warm, because if not, I'm staying wrapped up at home.'

'No you're not. In any case, you'll never know how high he keeps the heating unless you show up there, will you? And I'm telling you, if you're late, I shall have to start the meeting without you.

And. You. Will. PAY! We cannot afford to risk giving the impression that we don't care. That we are anything but professional and on the ball.'

'Oh, God.' Helena groaned. 'It's *so* cold.'

'Are you listening to me, dammit?'

'Yes. But can't we postpone it?'

'No,' I said firmly. 'Because first of all, I set this up weeks ago, second of all, Cliff Nichols is expecting us, and third, and most important of all, he is almost certainly going to commission us. So tomorrow we are going to work. *Work*, Helena. If you know what that means.'

'Darling, so severe! Chee-rist, look at the time.'

'Where are you off to?'

'I'm going to a concert in the cathedral, and then having dinner with some friends, including the owner of that antiques shop just off the High Street, the one who has antiquarian books as well as mahogany breakfronts. He's one of our fans and always keen as mustard to talk us up to his customers. I don't know *how* many copies he's sold for us so far, so I have to be nice even though he's a frightful old grump. At least he hasn't tried to get me into bed.'

'Not yet,' I said. 'Don't get pissed, will you?'

'Pissed? *Moi?*'

'You need to be on full alert tomorrow. Have fun.' Pointless advice: Helena always had fun. I suppressed a sigh. I liked my own company, which was just as well, but sometimes I wished I had a more vivid social life.

'You know me, darling, don't I usually? Anyway, back late tonight – unless I get lucky – sleep like a baby and up betimes to drive – oh Gawd, do I really have to? – all the way to Billingsgate House or whatever it's called.'

'Barnsfield.'

'I suppose I'd better get my stuff for tomorrow sorted before I go to bed.'

'Excellent idea.' Although Helena often appeared scatter-brained and out of it, in fact she was usually pretty well organized. As someone on the part-time teaching staff of three different universities, she had to be. 'And don't forget to bring your portfolio with you.'

'It's already in the car, Bossy Lady. I'll be setting off around eight-thirty tomorrow, to leave myself plenty of time, given the latest weather forecast. Snow, groan. Sleet and frost, double groan. But I ought to reach the place just about on time, unless the traffic's bad. So fingers crossed and see ya tomorrow, babe.'

'Right. And don't be late.'

'I won't be – unless I'm kidnapped or something.'

'Any possibility that you might be?' I stared again at my reflection, wishing I could be more like Helena. More carefree. More insouciant.

'Well, I've told you I'm being stalked, haven't I?'

'Several times.' I had never taken her seriously. Not after the time I had digested with horror the dramatic news that Helena had stomach cancer, only to be airily informed later that it was just a mild attack of food poisoning after all.

Her tone changed. 'You think I'm joking or making it up, don't you?'

'Of course I don't,' I lied.

'Well, I'm not. I've seen him standing outside in the dark, watching the house, trying to spook me. But what if,' Helena said, 'tonight's the night he decides to get proactive?'

'Tell him to come back the day after tomorrow.'

Afterwards, of course, my flippancy haunted me, filled me with guilt of the worst kind. If I'd taken her seriously, if I'd only listened, asked more questions, how differently things might have turned out. But to what was likely to prove my eternal regret, I had not.

The following morning, I looked out at the rime-frosted communal lawn in front of my second-floor flat, each grass blade edged with ice, at the hard-packed soil of the flower-beds, dead leaves hanging brown and lifeless from withered stalks whipping to and fro in the raw breeze. Beyond the garden wall was the promenade, and then the stony beach. Beyond that, the sea churned restlessly, bleak and drab, waves crashing occasionally against the shingle, throwing up high curtains of white spray.

Mrs Gardiner, from one of the ground-floor flats, was walking along the seafront, bent forwards against the buffeting wind, her whole posture indicating cold and discomfort. Her three hairless dogs skittered along beside her, their little paws click-clacking gingerly across the frosty tarmac. Each one was wearing a grey tweed coat edged with red or holly-green, already anticipating Christmas. At Easter, their coats would be bordered with yellow and lime.

Even inside the flat, with the central heating cranked up, I felt cold. I groaned at the thought of having to go out into the freezing air, get my car started, then set out on roads that the weather forecast had already warned would be treacherous. But business was business . . . Yet again I checked the papers lying on my bed, including the roughs for two further picture-and-text compilations, then placed them carefully into my leather briefcase, a gift from my sister.

I had gasped with pleasure when she gave it to me. 'It's *beautiful!*' I said, stroking the satiny leather.

'I know. Now that you've set up your own company, you need to look like a professional,' Meghan said. 'First impressions are one of the most important parts of your pitch, if not *the* most important. Leo says that if a would-be client can't be bothered to create a good impact right from the get-go, then what else won't he bother about? In other words, he's probably not someone we want to work with.'

Meghan and her husband lived in Florence and ran a small and very exclusive leather-goods company, which supplied Harrods and Fortnums and, behind the scenes, Mulberry. They had recently secured contracts with Bloomingdales and Saks in New York.

Perhaps I should add that Meghan is not her real name, any more than mine is Alexandra. Thanks to the proud heritage handed down from my ancestor, Elaward de Cuik, generations of Cuiks had given their children ludicrous Anglo-Saxon names. When I was ten, my sister had called a council of war for the three of us. 'I absolutely refuse to be called Ethelburgha for a single nother second,' she'd stated. 'They've started calling me Cheeseburger at school. It's the last straw.'

'I rather like being Hereward,' said my brother.

'Well, I *hate* Frideswide,' I said. 'What a terrible name.'

'Loaded with history,' my brother pointed out.

'This is what I'm going to do.' My sister spoke loudly. 'I'm going to tell them twice – because they won't listen the first time – that from now on my name is Meghan, and I won't answer to any other name. What about you?' she said to me.

'Alexandra,' I said promptly. 'That's what I'm going to be called.

There's all sorts of famous people called that. Athletes and princesses and stuff.'

Now, I glanced at the clock on top of the bookcase. Cripes! I would be running late if I didn't leave in the next fifteen minutes. And I wasn't even dressed! I rushed into the navy-blue business suit I'd retained from my Detective Inspector days, the white silk blouse, the navy tights. I clasped the pearls my parents had given me when I turned twenty-one round my neck, stuck matching studs in my ears, and ran down the stairs. Power dressing. Equipped for battle.

Before I left the house I telephoned Helena again. I could just imagine her swearing loudly as she hopped about her bedroom, trying to get into a pair of tangerine-orange or peacock-blue tights, dragging a brightly patterned dress over her head, shrugging into a quilted satin jacket covered in stars, flinging a multi-coloured scarf round her neck, shoving her feet into cabbage-green ankle boots in need of a good clean. That was if she had even bothered to get out of bed.

There was no answer. She must be on time for once; must, indeed, already have set out. Good. The coming meeting was of particular importance.

Driving carefully over treacherous roads, I reviewed the steps which had brought me to this point. At university, I had joined various leftist groups and come out after my three years with a reasonable degree and, although not a liberal idealist, a vague desire to do good in some form or another. Someone had mentioned the police, which seemed to tick all the right boxes. *Do you have the ambition, deter-mination and vision to accelerate into the senior ranks of the police service?* the literature had asked, and, feeling that I did, in spades, I joined the force on a fast-track programme, rising rapidly through the hierarchy to become, after six years, one of the youngest Detective Inspectors in the country. I discovered from practical experience how to run a team, how to keep it together, when to chivvy, when to sweet-talk, when to praise and when to admonish. Although it was supposed to have been wiped out, there was still plenty of lingering misogyny in the police force, but I was lucky enough not to experience anything worse than the odd sexist remark or the occasional show of resentment from some disgruntled junior officer who felt it was inappropriate to be taking orders from a woman. I ignored the *Playboy* images of spread female legs placed centrally on my desk, countering them by pinning up raunchy shots from gay magazines, not giving a toss if that brought me down to their level. If you can't beat 'em, join 'em. The minor harassment stopped soon after that.

Above all, I learned to observe, whether it was picking up tensions between the members of my team, or an overlooked detail at a scene of crime. I also learned that not every officer is equally dedicated to truth, justice and the rooting out of evil. But all my hopes and ambitions, my dedication to the job, and, yes, my real ability, came to an end when I got married.

I had fallen in love with Jack Martin, a colleague as aspirational as I was myself, and for nearly three years I had been completely happy. I had truly loved him. Like W.H. Auden, I thought that love would last forever, and like him, I was wrong. Two life-changing events occurred. Firstly, I found myself pregnant. Secondly, I discovered that Jack was having an affair – had, in fact, been involved with the same woman since very shortly after our wedding. I had confronted him, saying it was either his pregnant wife or his mistress, and had been both humiliated and completely heartbroken when he'd chosen the mistress, adding that in any case, he wasn't ready yet to be a father, couldn't guarantee that he ever would be. I wondered how I could have once been so deluded as to believe that the sun shone out of his backside.

There was still the baby. Determined not to display my mortification at being rejected, I resigned from the force, hating the possibility of running into Jack the Love Rat, Jack the Shit, almost as much as I hated leaving a job I cared passionately about and wanted to go on doing until I retired. And then a month after Jack had moved in with his lover, a beautician with her own salon, I woke in the night, my back aching, dull cramps in my stomach which gradually morphed into a severe abdominal pain. I had been experiencing discomfort, especially in the lower back, for the past three or four weeks, for which my GP had prescribed a mild painkiller. So that night, I took two tablets and went back – eventually – to sleep. I woke to find my bed drenched with what I at first took to be perspiration but – on pushing back the covers – saw, with horror, was blood. I knew at once what it was. I called the hospital and an ambulance was sent immediately. They took every possible care but they couldn't save the baby. They told me he was a boy. I was completely crushed. Emotionally broken.

So there I was, in my late twenties, unemployed, unmarried and childless. And very unhappy. The maisonette flat I had once shared with Jack and from which I could not afford to move (at least I had been able to keep it as part of the divorce settlement) was almost too strong a reminder of happier times. I changed. I grew a cynical carapace over my vulnerable heart, determined that I would never again be hurt the way Jack had hurt me. My friends and family wondered aloud where the real Alex had gone. I shrugged. Murdered, was the answer. Dead and buried. Burned in the ashes of a faithless love.

With nothing much else to do, I decided to carry on putting together a book similar to one I had been given by a godmother when I was ten. It had contained paintings by famous artists, with a fictional story woven around the people inside each picture. I'd been trying to produce something similar for my coming child. When I lost him, it gave me a purpose, something to concentrate on, something to divert my mind. I called it *Tell Me a Story*. A small local publisher took it and had a gratifying success with it.

I started another book, along the same lines. Given the wealth of material out there, I decided to concentrate on pictures of babies, or parents and babies. I talked about it to the man in the local bookshop, who was very encouraging. 'It's a terrific idea,' he said. 'And unusual. You shouldn't have any difficulty selling a concept like that.' He'd smiled at me. 'I'll order a dozen for the shop.'

I called it *Baby, Baby*. A way of easing my pain. Distancing myself from Jack's defection. The man at the bookshop – Sam Willoughby – was right. Months later, when the book was finally put together, the same small local publisher who had produced *Tell Me a Story* had enthusiastically taken it on, offered a reasonable advance, and asked for more of the same, perhaps losing the fictional element and gearing it towards adults. 'Gorgeous painting on the right-hand side,' he'd said. 'Beautifully presented text on the opposite page.' His face had gleamed with fervour. 'Oh, I can see it clearly.' Unfortunately, shortly after I'd signed the contract, his company went belly-up and he disappeared to Scotland to take over his father's farm.

But at least I had finally felt a lifting of the murk which had surrounded me since my divorce and subsequent miscarriage. And then I came across Helena.

Barnsfield House, headquarters of ArtWorld Books, lay down a rural lane deep in the Sussex countryside. It was an unassuming country house, surrounded by woods and fields. I pulled up in front of the place, heart sinking a little as I registered the fact that Helena's ancient black Humber wasn't there. I shook my head. Typical Helena.

'*Please* don't be late,' I said aloud. 'At least, not *too* late.' Through the windscreen I could see a piece of crumbling wall, not connected to anything else, which I judged to be pretty ancient. I could also see a small burial ground along one side of the house, complete with yew trees, mossy headstones and carved granite crosses. Kind of gloomy, I thought. I remembered a visit to Haworth and the Brontë family's Parsonage, and the way they practically lived in a cemetery. *When I have fears that I should cease to be . . .* I hoped Mr Nichols would not turn out to be some lugubrious Dickensian character with a high stiff collar, a dark suit and a waistcoat embellished with egg stains.

After checking my appearance in the mirror, I climbed out of my car, thanking the weather gods that the rain-snow-sleet had abated for a few seconds. I ran across a courtyard of sandy yellow gravel into a porch with gothic windows and oaken seats on either side. I was just about to press the brass-encircled bell at the side of the front door when it opened.

'Alex Quick! How very nice to see you.' Hand out, a man stepped forwards. 'I'm a huge admirer.'

'I take it you're Mr Nichols.'

'Indeed. But I must insist that you call me Cliff.' He stepped back. 'Do please come on in.'

'Thank you.'

He stared beyond me. 'And your partner?'

'Helena's coming across from Canterbury. I'm afraid she's not the best timekeeper in the world, but she should be here any moment,' I said, as confidently as I could. We stepped into a panelled hall with various doors giving off it.

'This way.' Nichols ushered me into a library full of books and ancient oriental carpets. A plump woman stood at a large round table in the middle of the room, with a heavy silver tray in front of her which held coffee pots and cups and jugs of warm milk.

'This is Elaine, my . . . uh . . . chief assistant,' Nichols said.

And what else . . .? I nodded at her. Smiled.

'Weren't there supposed to be two of you?' she asked.

'There were, but my collaborator may be a few minutes late.' Inwardly, I cursed Helena. This meeting was *so* important. It could determine the next few years of our lives.

'Let's have coffee while we wait,' Nichols said.

The three of us settled at another table, a long rectangular one of centuries-polished oak, with papers laid out as though for a board meeting.

'And let me explain about this place,' he said, 'before you start wondering . . .'

About what?

'. . . I inherited this house from my godfather, lock stock and barrel, five years ago, and it seemed the ideal place to run a small business from, with London rents and house prices getting more and more absurd. So down we came. Me, Elaine, our secretary Shan . . .'

'Old Uncle Tom Cobley and all,' put in Elaine. She laughed loudly. I laughed too, though I couldn't see it was all that funny.

'And it suits us down to the ground,' Nichols finished.

Again I nodded. There was something about the two of them which I couldn't put my finger on. Something off-kilter – so much so that I wasn't even sure whether it was a positive something or a negative one. If I had been interviewing him as a witness in a crime scene, I wondered what questions I might have asked him.

Over the rim of my coffee cup, I studied him as he chatted to Elaine about a book they were in the middle of producing. Nice-looking, youngish, somewhere in the mid-forties, wearing the standard country-dweller's uniform of corduroys, a checked shirt and a sweater. Short-cut brown hair, hazel eyes, some kind of dark birthmark beneath his left eye. I tried to analyse what exactly had set my antennae quivering but failed to come up with anything convincing. Was it because he had greeted me by name, when he'd not met me before and I might easily have been Helena for all he knew? That didn't hold water. He looked like a man who did his homework, so he could have found our photographs from various sources. Was it because he'd insisted that I call him Cliff? There was no need for him to *insist*, since I was quite ready to call him anything he pleased. And why should he presume that I might wonder about his house – why offer any explanation at all when it was none of my business in the first place?

I wished that Helena would get here. Even though I was the practical one who dealt with contracts and negotiations, drove bargains, hard or otherwise, demanded concessions I knew we wouldn't get, in order to be conceded ones we might not otherwise have been offered, I also suggested paintings, researched pictures. But I wanted my collaborator at my side. Especially since Helena was adept at coming up with the pertinent question which could make all the difference to a contract.

A grandfather clock in one corner of the room wheezed and puffed and finally chimed twice. The half-hour. Where on earth was Helena?

'Would you mind if I tried to call my partner?' I asked apologetically, wishing that the word hadn't now taken on the suggestion of Significant Other. 'My business partner, that is. She should be on her way, but perhaps there's been a pile-up on the motorway. And she did mention she was suffering from a bit of an upset stomach.' Not a lie, not really. She'd certainly mentioned such a thing a week or three ago.

'Or maybe she's stuck behind a herd of cows.' Nichols laughed. 'Happens quite a lot round here. Drives our staff mad.'

'Or the road conditions are too difficult, thanks to the weather,' said Elaine.

'Yes, we did kind of wonder if you would ring to cancel or postpone.'

What? And lose the opportunity to strike while the iron was hot? No way. I pressed in the numbers of Helena's mobile and listened to it ring until the answerphone message came on. I tried her home number, too, just in case she hadn't yet left for some reason. Again I was sent directly to her answerphone. What on earth was the wretched woman up to? I looked across the table at the other two. 'Look, I'm terribly sorry. I hate wasting your time like this, so shall we just get on with it?'

Over the next couple of hours, we hammered out an agreement for three (*Yay!* I thought) more anthologies. Nichols even mooted the possibility of a TV series. 'I've got contacts,' he said. 'And I think it could go. Like that nun who did a series on art. Very popular . . . the Singing Nun, was it?'

'Something like that,' I said vaguely.

'You're confusing Sister Wendy talking about art, and the Singing Nun from the Sixties, dear,' Elaine said crisply. 'Probably before your time.' She gazed at him fondly.

'The point is, we're thinking of maybe creating a subsidiary company . . .'

'Barnsfield Enterprises, something like that,' said Elaine. 'Which would handle screen projects for us.'

I could immediately visualize it. 'A TV series sounds really great,' I said.

'Fronted by Doctor Drummond,' Cliff said. 'Not that you yourself wouldn't be good, but she's got the academic reputation. And the voice.'

'It could be a real success for us,' said Elaine.

'People really do like to think that they're getting something a bit classy,' Nichols continued. 'Not all the time, mind you. And let's face it, *Coronation Street* is always going to win out over Corot. But the idea definitely has legs. Elaine . . .' He turned to her. 'Find out what you can about the possibilities, if there's any chance at all.'

Another slightly off-piste remark from Clifford, since they must already have done so. Elaine made a note on her electronic pad. I thought that if anyone could swing a TV deal, it would be her. I wondered if by any chance she was the mother he had mentioned on the phone when setting up this meeting: she was certainly the right age. And I was by no means the only person to call my parents by their Christian names.

I had stopped feeling embarrassed about Helena's absence. Instead, I was starting to worry. What could possibly have happened to her? Asking permission first, I called Helena's phone numbers again, with the same results as before. Where the hell was she? However hard I tried, I could no longer prevent my cool professional persona from starting to slip.

Eventually I stood up. 'This has all been very exciting and, I believe, productive. Please let me have a summary of what you feel we've achieved today, and I'll do the same and send it to you. An extremely useful discussion all round.' I tried for a rueful smile. 'All I need to do now is track down my vanished partner and find out what she's been up to. I know she'll be as enthusiastic as I am.'

I said goodbye to Elaine and followed Nichols back to the tiled entrance hall. He retrieved my coat, gave me a polite buss on the cheek, watched as I climbed into my car, turned on the ignition and, making a wide circle on the gravel, drove off. Turning left at the stone gate posts, I continued down the lane until I reached a lay-by, where I pulled in. What the hell was Helena up to? I'd given her the address several times, and she knew my mobile number. I used my phone to locate the numbers of the hospitals which lay along the route Helena would have taken from Canterbury, then started to call them. Half an hour later, I had established that none had admitted a Helena Drummond that morning. Nor any other fifty-year-old female.

TWO

The sky grew darker as I drove back to my flat. Bursts of sleet spattered the windscreen from time to time; gusts of wind rocked the car. I grew increasingly steamed as I drove, so much so that instead of carrying on, I impulsively turned off the M25 towards Canterbury. More and more enraged, I was conscious too of feeling aggrieved. I had worked hard for this meeting, been sweet when I didn't feel like it (I don't do sweet). I had smiled, nodded and subdued my personality, something I hated to do. And then Helena, for whatever reason, had bloody well failed to show up, leaving me to handle the whole deal on my own. Which I had done pretty well, in my humble opinion, so much so that Cliff Nichols had not only accepted my explanation of Helena's absence (possible food poisoning), but had more or less promised to send Drummond & Quick a three-book contract within the next two weeks, on distinctly favourable terms.

I drove around the outer ring-road of the ancient city. Through the gloomy afternoon, the floodlit spire-crowned blocks of the cathedral stood above the grey roofs, invoking, as always, the ghosts of Chaucer and his Canterbury pilgrims on their way from London, the robust Wyf of Bath forever banging on about something, the parfit gentle Knight and his son the Squire, chivalrously paying attention.

Helena's house was in a pretty village two or three miles outside the city. As I drew closer, fury continued to build inside me. When she hadn't answered her phone early that morning, I had taken it for granted that it was because she was already on her way to our appointment. But maybe she had seen the call was from me and decided not to answer. The lazy cow had probably just stayed in bed with a book, or with the hangover she was undoubtedly nursing after eating out with her friends last night. Or maybe she'd gone home after the concert with some man and not yet surfaced. If that proved to be the case, I wasn't sure I could answer for my actions. And of course I dismissed without a second's thought her lurid stories of kidnappers and stalkers.

I screeched to a stop in the fortuitously empty space in front of her place, parking erratically just behind her big old Humber. Seeing it there, reinforcing my assumption that she hadn't even left the house that morning, I tore off one of my gloves and furiously jabbed at the doorbell, holding my finger in place. My other hand curled into a fist as I waited. 'Come on, bitch,' I muttered, through gritted teeth. 'Open the fucking door!'

But there was no response from inside the house. I stepped back into the road and looked up at the bedroom windows. As I had suspected, the curtains were still closed. Long ago she and I had exchanged keys to each other's places, in case one or other was away and access to papers and books relevant to our joint work was needed. So in the end, after more fruitless knocking and ringing, I fished out my key ring, found the key to Helena's front door and stepped into the narrow red-painted hall. Everything looked as it normally did: the tall Chinese vases on either side of an antique console table set below a huge gold-framed mirror; the coat-rack laden with fur-lined jackets, rainbow-striped ponchos, knitted coats in brilliant colours; the stag's head hanging crookedly above the door into the sitting room with a tam o'shanter dangling from its antlers; the vividly coloured rugs on the floor, for once lying flat and undisturbed on the Victorian cream-and-terracotta tiles. No obvious signs of anything out of the ordinary.

'Helena!' I screamed. I listened, but there was no answering call. She couldn't seriously still be in bed, could she?

'Helena,' I yelled again, 'I'm coming up, ready or not.'

As I mounted the stairs, my ex-copper instincts were beginning to kick in. Despite the apparent calm of the hallway, the lack of any signs of disruption, I was feeling uneasy. As I climbed the carpeted stairs, past piles of books, an overflowing work-basket, clean, folded laundry, a red shoe with a four-inch-high glitter heel, I became more and more convinced that something was desperately wrong. Had Helena had some kind of seizure? Had she slipped in the shower and cracked her head against the edge of the bath? Had she tripped while getting dressed? The hairs at the back of my neck rose in a primeval awareness of danger. Three steps down from the upper landing, eyes level with the floor, I stopped. I smelled the unmistakable, all-too-familiar metallic whiff of blood. *Dried* blood. Peering through the banister rails, I looked straight into Helena's womb-like bedroom: rose-pink walls, an armchair covered in cherry-coloured linen, dark-red carpet overlaid with several more bright rugs, a cerise-swirled duvet dragging from the bed to the floor, a bulb still burning under a strawberry-patterned shade, even though it had now gone four-thirty in the afternoon.

And . . .

I grabbed the railings . . . oh, my God! Oh no! I could see a naked foot dangling over the end of the bed. The manicured toenails were painted with gold polish, which glinted in the glow from the bedside lamps. For a moment I stood paralysed, then I ran up the last three steps, past the gilded life-size Fu Dogs, Chinese sentry lions which stood on snarling guard outside the room, snatching up a heavy wrought-iron candlestick set just inside the door as I ran, in case . . .

'Helena,' I said quietly, and was met by silence. No tortured breathing. No sighing gasps. Just a stillness that made me bite my lip.

Of course I knew all about contaminating the scene of crime, but sod that. Priority had to be given to finding out what state Helena was in. Was she dead, or still alive and breathing? As I hastily crossed the room and stood above the bed, I was thinking *heart attack*. At least I knew the procedures to follow while waiting for the paramedics to arrive. Because what else could it be? She had been perfectly fine when I rang her last night. And then I was looking down at a half-naked body lying on its side, its back to me, a tangle of ringletted blonde hair, a skull obviously stove in by a colossal blow to the back of the head, blood and brains mixed in with the hair, dried blood coming from the ears. An uneven red line encircled what I could see of the neck, as though she had been part-throttled prior to death.

I reached down and gently touched her shoulder. Cold. Smooth as clay, and chill as stone. I would need time, and resilience, to take it on board. Whatever had taken place must have occurred last night. And given her fairly relaxed attitudes towards sexual partners, I could all too easily imagine her returning home with some unsuitable and ultimately homicidal pick-up.

'Oh, Helena,' I said sadly. 'What the hell kind of a mess did you get yourself into?' Horror and guilt weighed me down, so much so that for a moment my legs almost gave way. This was not an anonymous corpse, to be treated with concerned but brisk impartiality. This was my dear friend Helena. And I had been cussing her out while she lay dead – murdered – in her bed.

There was movement, as though the corpse had previously been unbalanced and my touch had caused it to shift. I hastily drew back my hand, but too late. An air bubble forced itself from between the puffed-up lips, sounding like an enormous burp. The body rolled stiffly onto its back and I saw, with a massive sense of shock, that there were bloody holes where the eyes had once been; they appeared to have been pierced by the awl which was still protruding from the left one. Blood mingled with a jelly-like substance that welled from the wrecked eye sockets. There was a squelching sound, something I had heard before when attending other violent deaths. The bloodied face had been brutally battered into near-unrecognizability before death: nose and mouth were swollen to three times their normal size and streaks of blood, now dried and flaking, ran from the damaged eyes and clearly broken nose down the engorged upper lip.

Perhaps most horrible of all was the fact that the nipple had been sliced cleanly away from her left breast, leaving a hole full of congealed blood. Dark stains had seeped from under what remained of the former human being, and darkened the sheets. More stains had dripped onto the floor, a darker red than the damp carpet. I bent and brushed my forefinger across them and brought it up to my face. I wrinkled my nose. It was blood all right.

One look had been enough to make it clear that the woman was no longer alive. But the body on the bed was not Helena's. It belonged to a younger, slimmer woman than my friend, though even her parents would find it hard to recognize her, whoever she was. Relief made me feel almost euphoric. Admittedly any man's death diminishes me, but, to be brutally frank, somewhat less so if it is not Helena's.

And then I noticed something protruding from between the woman's spread legs. It looked like rolled-up paper, once covered in typing, now bloodstained into illegibility before being rammed into her vagina. Without moving my feet, I bent closer. I could see two things. One, the genitals had been viciously disfigured, as though someone had tried to pull them open by sheer brute force, torn apart almost like a spatchcocked fowl. Secondly, here and there I could

still make out a word or two on the paper: *dei Branca. bute Mon.*
There were the straight edges of picture reproductions, the swirl of
an apostolic robe, a monastery arch, all heavily besmirched with
dried blood.

My God! What kind of a sick pervert . . .? But that was for the
police to determine. For a couple of moments, I stood quite still,
trying to maintain my composure, then turned slowly in a full circle to
survey the room, trying to note as many details as possible. Were
there any clues as to who this dead person was? Or why she was
lying semi-naked and brutally dead on Helena's bed? Or where
Helena herself had gone? No answers leaped out at me. No clues,
apart from a flat gold circle, much too large to be a ring, which lay
on the carpet, half-hidden under the bed. Was it something of
Helena's, or could it have come from a necklace or chain wrenched
from around the corpse's neck – which would explain why the marks
did not completely fit the standard impression usually left by a
ligature? Knowing my friend's chronic untidiness, I guessed it was
the former. I don't know what prompted me to commit what was
undoubtedly an indictable offence, but I took a paper tissue from
the box on the bedside table, bent down and picked it up, a memento
of my friend, before sliding it into my pocket.

Carefully, I trod my way back to the landing, trying to place my
feet exactly where I had stepped before. Then I pulled out my phone
and dialled Emergency Services. I wanted to search the house, but
my police training told me I should not disturb the scene any further
than I already had. However, while I waited, I went out to Helena's
car. It was unlocked, as I guessed it would be. Using another tissue,
I inched open the door and peered inside, front and back, lifted the
boot and checked it out, but nothing in the muddle of old shopping
bags, yellowing newspapers, boxes which had once held beef toma-
toes or strawberries, struck me as significant. The portfolio she had
mentioned during our phone call the previous night lay on the back
seat.

While I sat in my car, waiting for the police to arrive, trying to
remain calm, I thought back to my first meeting with Helena, nearly
four years earlier, shortly after the defection of my husband and the
loss of my unborn child. I'd been invited to a publisher's party,
having contributed some picture editing work to a couple of their
productions that year, and was standing by a tall, uncurtained

window, looking out at the mist-shrouded lights of Trafalgar Square as the sky slowly faded behind Nelson on his column. I was wondering, as I so often did, whether leaving the police force had been a wise decision.

Whether, in fact, to continue living was a wise decision.

Someone came up behind me. 'I can't read what your label says, and I can't be bothered to fish my glasses out of whichever pocket they've hidden themselves in, but you look interesting,' said a Scottish voice as warm and seductive as melted caramel. 'Are you?'

I turned. 'I'd like to think so.' The voice said Confident, Humorous, No Longer Young: I registered all this in the time it took to focus on the woman who was standing in front of me, peering at the name badge pinned above my right boob. She was wearing rose-pink tights pushed into blue suede ankle boots, a green flower-printed summer dress and a shiny purple quilted jacket. I admired her eclectic dress sense as much as the gush of golden dreadlocks which streamed Medusa-like from her head. 'I'm Quick. Alex Quick. And you?'

'Helena Drummond. Art historian. Professor at the University of Kent at Canterbury, Visiting Fellow at the University of Melbourne. Consultant here and there.'

'You sound very high-powered.'

'I suppose I am rather.' She said it so matter-of-factly that it didn't sound in the least conceited.

I liked her at once. Hoped to see more of her. The feeling was mutual. Discovering how near to each other we lived, we met several times over the next months. Despite the fact that we were a generation apart, we formed an instant friendship. When we had time to spare, we often spent it together, talking, talking, covering shared enthusiasms or joint dislikes. Helena came down to my parents' house or lounged about on the long sofas in my flat on the edge of the sea on the south-east coast, devouring my large collection of crime novels; I often hung out in Helena's house, a space as eclectically coloured and patterned as Helena herself. Sometimes she would telephone me to put off some arrangement we had made; her voice would assume a silky note and I would know that some man was in the offing. How I envied her. And how impossible I found it to go in for casual pick-ups the way she did.

'I've been married twice,' Helena told me once, 'but never again.

One of them was a bit of a shit but a lovely feller all the same, and we still do stuff together – but he likes his own space and so do I. I want to be silent when I choose, I want to have a bath at three o'clock in the morning if I feel like it, I don't want to lie awake at night listening to someone's snores. I don't want to explain myself, I don't want to have to . . . ask *permission*.'

'What about the other one?'

She was uncharacteristically silent. Then she said: 'He was extremely charismatic, and an absolute bastard. The nearest thing I hope I ever come to a psychopath. Without feelings, without emotions . . . I don't know how I survived three years with him. I think I was flattered that he chose me, when he could have had anyone. Or so he often told me – and I have to say women were always flinging themselves at him.'

Compared to Helena, I often felt as staid and dull as a grocer. I very rarely went out on a date, not from lack of invitations but because I felt a reluctance, almost a fear of getting seriously involved with anyone in case I was dumped again. Sometimes colleagues from my days on the police force would invite me to functions with my old friends, but increasingly I turned them down.

'I know what you mean,' I had said, when Helena came up with her thesis on marriage. But truth to tell, I didn't go along with all of it. Put quite simply, although I was perfectly able to manage my life without a man in it, I nonetheless longed to have someone to cherish. Yet it sounded too girly and wimpish to say so.

It was eight months into our friendship that Helena picked up a copy of *Tell Me a Story*. 'What a brilliant idea,' she said, flicking through the pages. 'Done any more?'

I showed her the second one, *Baby, Baby*. 'This is marvellous!' she exclaimed. 'Ever thought of expanding this idea into other artistic fields? I mean, with other themes?'

'Yes. Often. But I've done nothing about it.'

'Well, you should,' she said firmly. 'I'll come on board, if you like.'

I did like. Very much. We gazed at each other and laughed.

As easily as that, Drummond & Quick Ltd was born. We set ourselves up as a company, producing high-quality art book anthologies of pictures and appropriate text. And away we went.

Eventually, we published two for very little more than expenses and a few free copies, and we both felt that some kind of turning point had been reached when our publisher offered exactly the same measly terms for our third effort.

We knew that we deserved more. A lot more. Nonetheless . . . 'Maybe it's a case of better the devil you know?' I'd said nervously, as we sent off our turn-down of the offer from Tyson Lowell, CEO of a small niche publishing house based in Amsterdam. 'And he does do a terrific job of presentation.'

Watch This Space, our most recent publication, putting together pictures of famous rooms with illustrative texts that were like miniature stories, had hit the book market just before Christmas, and thanks to Helena's contacts and its suitability as a gift, had been a big success.

'Granted.' Helena was firm. 'But eighteen months of research and writing, and that's all they can come up with? Especially when they're fully aware that *Space* was a minor bestseller. Fuck 'em, say I.'

Tyson Lowell had phoned back immediately on receipt of our email of refusal. 'That's my best offer, ladies. Times are really hard,' he whined accusingly.

I had switched on the speaker-phone. 'Not only for you, Tyson. Especially with what you're offering.'

'He means if he pays us a living wage, he won't be able to afford that luxury yacht he's set his heart on,' snorted Helena loudly in the background.

I frowned at her. 'Mr Lowell, I'll be quite frank. Your offer is ridiculous. You're taking us for a pair of suckers. We're both highly trained professionals, we both have a living to earn, we have multiple expenses to fork out for in the course of our research, which are not repaid until you accept the book and produce a contract.' *Highly trained professional* was a bit of a stretch in my case, though not in Helena's. I'm more of a highly trained amateur. 'So all in all, we'd prefer to look elsewhere.'

'And the best of fucking luck,' Tyson had said malevolently. 'I can make things very hard for you, by the way. I have contacts all over the publishing world. One word from me and you'll never sell another book.'

'*Two* words from me, you little creep,' Helena had shouted, 'and neither will you!' She pressed the OFF button on my phone and made a face. 'That's not nearly as satisfactory as banging down a receiver, is it?'

'Well, that's one bridge burned good and proper,' I said. 'What do we do now?'

'We wait.'

And then, fortuitously, had come an expression of interest from Clifford Nichols, MD of ArtWorld Books, leading to this morning's appointment to discuss *Ripe for the Picking*. 'I loved the book you did a few years back, on paintings in the National Gallery, written for young people,' he had enthused down the phone at me. 'Such a clever idea. And with plenty of follow-up.'

'*Tell Me a Story,* yes.' My concept had been to take twelve pictures from the National Gallery and produce stories about them in a way that would engage the attention of children aged anywhere from eight to fourteen, make them really look at the paintings.

'My mother picked up a copy in our local bookshop and said I must get in touch with you immediately, which I regret to say I didn't do. Then she bought *Watch This Space* and more or less forced me to contact you before somebody else does.'

'Somebody else already did.'

'I'm aware. Your current publisher. With another insulting offer.' How did he know that? 'Well, we haven't accepted it . . .'

'Insulting is the only word to use.' He echoed Helena's words. 'Especially when *Space* was so good.'

After the phone call, I'd checked him out on the internet and been impressed by his track record. In the past three years, he had published specialist books on subjects as varied as the Napoleonic Wars, the cult of voodoo in Haiti, vintage motor cars and, most recently, Japanese woodcuts. It looked as though he might be moving into art book production, and I very much hoped that Drummond & Quick could be part of it.

'What I want, what I reely reely want, is this contract,' I'd told Helena. 'Reely reely.'

'You and the Spice Girls?' Helena had raised her eyebrows. 'How far would you go to get it? Are we talking womanly wiles?'

'If you mean batting my eyelashes, smiling winsomely, lightly touching his hand from time to time and laughing girlishly? Oh, all the way.'

'Batted eyelashes might not be enough.'

'If you mean yielding up my body to his coarse embraces, then no.'

'Ach, weel. So then we'll have to go back to Tyson Lowell and beg for favours.'

'No way. Even if the bastard would take us back. And don't forget there's always self-publishing . . .'

'For our kind of book? I don't think so.'

'We'll just have to keep our fingers crossed and see how it goes.'

THREE

Inspector Alan Garside stared at me, his expression unsympathetic, his forehead wrinkled with hostility. 'Let's go through it once again, Miss – um – Quick. You say you arrived at this house – belonging to Mrs Helena Drummond – just after four thirty this afternoon.'

'I don't just *say* it, I *did* it.' I sighed. 'As I've already told your sergeant, twice. And it's *Doctor* Drummond, not Mrs Drummond.'

'Whatever, take me through the sequence of events once more.' He opened his mouth to say something else, then stopped.

I did so, trying to keep the impatience out of my voice. I knew that witnesses were usually exasperated by having to tell the same story over and over again. But I also knew, from experience, that it was often on the fourth or fifth telling that some small and significant detail might be mentioned for the first time. I had not yet informed him that I had once been on the force, had in fact decided that I would keep the information to myself, if he didn't bring it up. Although I knew all about him, I had resigned a couple of years before he was transferred to our local CID.

'And when you let yourself into the house this afternoon,' he said, 'there was no indication that anyone had been here last night except Mrs Drummond?'

'*Doctor* Drummond? None whatsoever.' Apart, I thought, from the mutilated body of the still-unidentified woman, now being extensively photographed and examined by the pathologist and scene-of-crime officers. 'Everything seemed as it always was. Mind you, I didn't go into any other rooms, only straight up the stairs and into her bedroom.'

'Not even while you were waiting for the police to arrive?'

'While I waited for the SOCOs, I sat outside in my car. Apart from going upstairs and across the carpet to the bed, then retracing my steps, I did nothing that could have contaminated the scene.'

He looked slantways at me, as though wondering how I knew the jargon. Civilians usually did not, apart from a few phrases learned from the watching the television. I didn't say that these days, most police-procedural crime novels are word-perfect in the language used in situations where the police are called in. 'And the . . . uh . . . victim: did you recognize her?'

'Considering her face had almost been obliterated, no, I didn't,' I said. 'However, I can tell you that she is *not* Doctor Drummond, the house-owner. Who seems to have gone missing. Could she have been abducted by whoever did this? And if so, shouldn't you have some kind of APB out, looking for her? The murder obviously took place while it was still dark outside, since all the lights were on when I arrived.'

'Which was when?'

'As I've already said, somewhere between four and four-thirty this afternoon.'

Again he narrowed his eyes at me, as though this in itself was an admission of guilt. Maybe someone had told him he looked like Sherlock Holmes when he did that. 'Quick,' he said. 'How do I know your name?'

'Are you an art-lover? Because in that case, you might have seen one of the anthologies I've produced with Doctor Drummond.'

'Yes, well, I don't have much time for that sort of thing.' He looked smug about this piece of information. He smoothed his forehead, as though hoping to iron out some of the hostility. It didn't work. 'Have you considered the possibility that Doctor Drummond killed this woman herself, perhaps not intending to, and then took off in a panic?'

'Of course I have. But this is just not her style.' *Style*? Even as I spoke, I realized that with murder involved, the remark sounded unsuitably offhand. 'I mean, I simply cannot imagine Helena indulging in this kind of violence. Especially when you consider that the victim had been stripped more or less naked, and her eyes had been obliterated. Not to mention the papers which had been stuffed inside the body. In my book, that points to some kind of kinky sexual crime. Has to.'

'Not necessarily. Maybe she stripped willingly. Maybe Doctor Drummond, you know, dances down the other end of the ballroom.'

'Bollocks.'

He leaned back, smiling with self-satisfaction. Inspector Alan

Garside, the latest in a long line of perspicacious hawk-eyes, up there with Philip Marlowe and Nero Wolfe, Lincoln Rhyme and Jack Reacher. 'So Mrs Drummond didn't have any tendencies towards . . . uh . . . the other direction, if you see what I mean? Play for the opposite team, as it were?'

'If you're asking if *Doctor* Drummond was a lesbian, then the answer is a resounding no,' I said, again emphasizing Helena's title. 'I've been her close friend and collaborator for some years now and I can assure you that she is totally straight. Heterosexual,' I added, seeing a faint look of incomprehension on Garside's face.

'There's always the possibility, of course, Miss Quick . . .' He coughed into his fist. '. . . that much as one hesitates to accept the fact, there *is* such a thing as pure evil. Sadistic psychopaths do exist.'

'And spend their time lurking around houses in rural villages in the hope of finding a victim? I don't think so.'

'The person responsible for this might have been stalking the victim for days.'

Again I was flooded with guilt. I hated to hear this. Stalker, kidnapper, psychopath: why had I taken so little notice of Helena? Though I don't know what I could have done to protect her. Unwillingly, I told Garside what Helena had said to me just the evening before.

'Hmm,' he said. 'It needs investigating, of course.'

'She also told me that this stalker might have a motorbike, since a couple of times she'd heard an engine revving or a machine roaring away down the street. So the neighbours might have seen or heard something. She told me she saw him across the road sometimes, watching her house after dark, waiting for her. Like Nemesis, she said.' I didn't tell him how Helena had shuddered as she told me this.

'Nemesis?'

'The spirit of divine retribution. Another name for her means "The Inescapable One".'

'Any description of this possible stalker?'

'Nothing specific. Tall, slim, wearing what looked like black leathers. That's all she said.' Once more I castigated myself for not asking for more details.

'Not a lot to go on, is it? Meanwhile, Doctor Drummond will have to remain our prime suspect until we have reason to believe otherwise. Unless you have any ideas about who else might have been responsible for this killing.'

'Since I still don't know who the victim is, any more than you do, it would be difficult to say. It's always possible that the dead woman came to visit Helena last night and the two of them were ambushed by a third person who entered the house after that.'

'Or,' Garside said, with a knowing look, 'had already secreted himself inside the house.'

'In that case, though far be it from me to tell you your business, it might be a good idea for you to search among her students, see if anyone resented a grade she'd given them, or whether she'd had some kind of falling out with a colleague.' I thought back to the scene I had stumbled upon in the bedroom. 'Though as I said, the death seems to have a clear sexual component, implying that the victim was the intended target, rather than Doctor Drummond. Not that she isn't sexy enough in her own right. And she did mention this black-clad stalker more than once.'

Garside seemed vaguely discomfited by all this talk of sex. He straightened the notes in front of him. 'What, if anything, do you make of the words . . .' He looked down. *'dei Branca*? Or *bute mon*?'

'Just off the top of my head, I would guess them to be part of the name *Cappella dei Brancacci* – that's the Brancacci Chapel in the church of Santa Maria del Carmine,' I said. 'Plus a reference to a fresco by Masaccio called *The Tribute Money*, which is in that same chapel. In Florence. In Italy.'

He looked irritated at the implication that he didn't know where Florence was. 'You said Doctor Drummond had been married twice. Has she told you anything about her former husbands?'

'She hardly ever mentioned them. I have a feeling that one of them was Australian or Canadian, or that she met him in Australia – among other things, she's a Visiting Fellow at the University of Melbourne. He may be the one she called an absolute bastard, but I don't know for sure because she didn't expand on him.'

The Inspector wrote something down. 'What about the other one?'

'Nothing at all, really, except that she referred to him once as a lovely fellow, but a bit of a shit. In an affectionate sort of way.' Repeating the words, I felt a sudden sharp pang. *Oh Helena, where are you?* I thought. *What is being done to you? Are you safe, or are you lying somewhere, trussed up and in abject terror?*

'Doesn't sound all that affectionate to me.'

'Her idea of a joke,' I said.

'Can you give me names? Occupations?'

I shook my head. 'As I said, she rarely speaks of either of them. I don't even know if Drummond is her own surname, or whether it belonged to one of the husbands. As for occupations, my best guess would be that they were somehow involved in the world of academe, or art. Or both.'

The two of us sat without speaking as footsteps went bumping heavily past the closed door. The body being removed, I assumed.

Garside resumed his interrogation. 'Have you ever had reason to believe that Helena Drummond was in any kind of trouble? Did she do drugs? Or owe money to some criminal gang, the sort that might have sent an enforcer to break into her house and murder her as a warning to others?'

'Are you thinking mistaken identity?' The possibility occurred to me for the first time. Helena wore her hair in a similar style to the victim and it was more or less the same blondish colour. It seemed perfectly feasible that a commissioned enforcer, not acquainted with either woman, might have killed the wrong one.

'At the moment I'm not thinking anything. Or, rather, I'm keeping an open mind. But certainly mistaken identity is a possible answer. Which is why I'm asking you so many questions about the home-owner, this Doctor Helena Drummond, who is, as far as we know, alive and well and possibly drinking a latte or espresso in the nearest coffee bar, even as we speak.'

'That's quite an assumption.' And although I didn't say so, a bloody stupid one. If Helena had discovered a mutilated body on her bedroom floor, ditzy as she could sometimes be, she was hardly likely to head out to the nearest Costa coffee shop without informing the police.

He shrugged. 'So what's your answer?'

I had to think for a moment to recall his question. Then I said, 'I've never heard her say anything at all which would indicate that she was worried about anything criminal. Students, yes. Publishers, sometimes. Tracking down a painting she was certain would be perfect for one of our books, yes. She used to get really frustrated if she couldn't remember where she'd seen it. Granted she's eccentric. But under the eccentricity, she's pretty much on the ball. About everything.'

'No money troubles? No problems with family or boyfriends?'

'Not as far as I'm aware. As for drugs, she didn't touch them. She often told me she'd seen too many of her most promising students frying their brains with toxic substances, turning into zombies, and completely dropping out.'

'Very interesting.' He placed his palms flat on the table and stood up. 'Well, thank you for your help, Ms Quick. Perhaps you would give one of the uniforms as comprehensive a list as you can of Helena Drummond's associates, insofar as you know them.'

'Including myself?'

'Of course.' He grimaced, which might have been intended as a smile. 'The person who telephones the police often turns out to be the one who perpetrated the crime.' He paused, then added, 'As I expect you know. But for the moment, we shall be giving priority to finding Doctor Drummond.'

'I can tell you categorically, here and now, that whoever it is lying dead upstairs, Helena Drummond is not responsible for her death. It's absolutely out of the question.'

'People always say that after the event, don't they?' He adopted a high-pitched sing-song accent. '*I can't believe it, he was always so quiet, always had a nod and a smile, always nice to the kiddies when we walked past.*' He gave his grimace of a smile once again. 'But who am I to be telling you that?'

I raised my eyebrows at him. Had I been rumbled? I rather thought so, not that it mattered. As I left the room, I heard his voice behind me informing me that he might have to question me further and if I heard from Dr Drummond I was to contact him immediately.

Seated in the chilly shelter of my car, I considered the overriding question: what was Helena up to? And why was she not answering her phone? I tried to imagine what could possibly have happened in the house the previous evening. Helena must have been picked up by friends, since her car was still outside. She had presumably attended the concert with them. She'd then gone out to some restaurant for dinner. Then what? Had she come home?

I found the number for the antiques and antiquarian bookshop Helena had mentioned and pressed the digits, wondering if they would still be open this late on a winter's day. They were. A female voice answered the phone.

'This is Alex Quick here,' I said. I swallowed. 'Uh . . . Detective Inspector Alex Quick.' I felt uneasy about the deception. I knew it was a crime to impersonate a police officer, but I had been one once and rules sometimes have to be broken when needs must. With any luck, I would get away with it.

'Oh . . .' The woman sounded worried. 'Is anything wrong, Officer?'

'No, no. It's just a routine enquiry.'

'Paul's in the office. He's terribly busy, though. I don't know if he'll be—'

'I only want a minute of his time.'

'All right. I'll just put you through.'

There was the usual clicking, dead pauses, buzzing. Then a bad-tempered male voice said, 'Paul Sandbrook here. What seems to be the trouble?'

'I believe you joined Doctor Helena Drummond last night for dinner?'

'That's right. In Prego's.'

'And how did she seem?'

'Her usual gung-ho self.'

'Did she mention anything unusual?'

'Such as what?'

'A . . . uh . . . new man in her life? Something abnormal or out of the ordinary?'

His voice changed. 'Look here. What's this all about? Has something happened to her?'

'Not as far as we know.' I attempted a small laugh. 'It's just that we can't locate her at the moment.'

'How did you even know I had dinner with her?'

'She told me.'

There was a pause, then he said, 'Hang about, don't I know your name? My assistant mentioned the name Quick . . . aren't you Helena's collaborator?'

'That's ri—'

'And, I believe, *ex*-DI Quick.'

'Very ex.'

'You do know that it's an indictable offence to impersonate a—'

'They said you were busy, and I couldn't think how else to get you to come to the phone.'

'Hmm.' Another pause. 'Let's start again,' Sandbrook said. 'What exactly are you after?'

'Helena was supposed to join me this morning for an important meeting with a publisher, but she never showed,' I explained. 'And when I went to her house this afternoon to find out why she hadn't turned up, there was . . . well, she wasn't there. But . . . someone else was.' I wondered whether it would matter if I mentioned the body and decided it would not since it was bound to hit the local news media any moment now.

'Someone else?'

'Not to put too fine a point on it, Mr Sandbrook, there was a body.'

'*What*?' I waited while he digested this information. 'There's no suggestion that it's Helena, I hope.'

'No, no. It was somebod—'

'Nor that Helena is responsible,' he said.

'Not from me.'

'Because she's the very last person I would have thought—'

'But I can't speak for the police. Which is why I want to get hold of her as quickly as possible. Except I don't know where she is.'

'Good God.'

'Did she say anything last night about expecting visitors after supper? Or mention that someone had arrived to stay with her?'

'Nothing whatsoever. As I said, she was on good form, looking forward to your meeting this morning, hoping it would lead on to contracts and so forth. And, if I may say so, very well-deserved they would be.'

'Thank you. Meanwhile, where might Helena have gone?'

'Give me your number, and if I think of something, or remember anything else, I'll let you know.'

'What about the others who were there last night?'

'They were mostly Helena's friends. I don't think I even caught their names. There was a Fergus, I seem to remember. Or maybe it was Angus. Yes, Angus. And there was a Mona, with her husband Guillaume. A couple of others. Some man she was flirting with – but she always does. Peter Someone.'

'No surnames?'

'Nothing that springs to mind. Except the Angus person was MacSomething. I'm not very good with names, I'm afraid. The Guillaume guy runs some kind of art gallery somewhere local. But before you ask, I've no idea where.' He paused, then added, 'Oh, and then there was some woman at another table who came over. A former student, I believe, who was in town to deliver a lecture today to the art department.'

'Name?'

'I haven't a clue. Didn't catch it, I'm afraid.'

'If you talk to any of them, I would suggest you don't mention the . . . uh, the body to anyone. Not until it's public knowledge.'

'See what you mean. I'll do my best.'

'And what time did this gathering break up?'

'Close to eleven, I'd say.'

'So when would Helena have got home?'

He thought about it. 'She'd have had to walk to the multi-storey car park. Find her car. Drive out into the street. Her place is fifteen minutes or so from Canterbury. So provided she didn't stop anywhere on the way, she should have got there before midnight. But not much.' He paused. 'Except come to think of it, I don't think she drove herself into town last night. She was picked up by a neighbour, I believe.'

Ending the call, I had to ask myself how I would have reacted if one of my former colleagues had behaved as I had just done, giving false ID. No getting away from it, I would have been livid. But until I found Helena, this was personal. The end justifies the means, I told myself. Nonetheless, I was uncomfortably aware of rules breached, of principles betrayed.

Back home, I parked in my allocated space outside the former convalescent home which ten years ago had been converted into a dozen comfortable flats overlooking the sea. Jack and I had been lucky to be able to afford to buy one of them, which we had done with help from my parents and his, plus a small lump sum from my godmother, a rich and chilly friend of my mother's. Reluctantly handing over a reasonably sized cheque, she had added, 'And don't expect anything further in my Will.'

Hot coffee in hand, I stared out at a wintry sea, mulling over the names I'd been given by Sandbrook. Angus was a Scottish name, and Helena was originally from a small town outside Edinburgh – not that it made any difference, beyond the fact that this Angus might be a close enough friend to be aware of places she might go to earth if she needed to. Guillaume was French – which wouldn't stop some poncey middle-class English parent giving the name to his or her child. The first name, Angus, produced the faintest tinkling in my brain; the second, Guillaume, I had no recollection of ever hearing before. How soon would I be able to get back into Helena's house and poke around? The police would almost certainly be taking her computer away for examination; after all, she must be considered a person of interest, with a body found in her house, and she herself missing.

The worst-case scenario would be that some maniac had killed the first woman and abducted Helena with a view to murdering her at his sadistic leisure. But I felt instinctively that this was not the case. Why, I could not have said. But if I was right, I had to come up with an alternative – and plausible – set of circumstances to explain Helena's vanishing act.

First of all, though, how and why had the dead woman got into Helena's house? That might offer some clues as to her disappearance – but then again, it might not.

Staring out of the windows at rain which was rapidly turning into serious sleet, my thoughts were still dominated by Helena, trying to imagine where she might be. Was the stalker she had mentioned several times a reality after all? She had spoken with such over-exaggerated melodrama that I had never taken her seriously. Now I wished with all my heart that I had not been so sceptical. Is that what had happened? A deranged stalker had broken into the house, seen a naked woman on the bed, bashed in her head, mutilated her eyes, forced pieces of paper into her body, only to discover, too late, that it wasn't Helena at all?

It was a hypothesis which only led on to further questions. Why was the dead woman in Helena's house in the first place? Why had she removed her clothes? Had it been a consensual act, or had she been forced to? And if so, why? It was inconceivable that she and Helena had been having sex; nonetheless, I tried to visualize a scenario where this had happened, a jealous husband or partner forcing his way in and finding the two women in the midst of lovemaking, seized with rage and striking the nearest one with a heavy instrument of some kind.

I frowned, my stomach clenched, muscles knotted. My overriding feeling, over and above the questions, the impact of violent death, the sight of flesh from which the life had been brutally snatched, was fear.

I longed to know whether the victim had been identified yet. I hesitated, finger above the relevant buttons, then pressed ahead.

A voice said, 'Detective Inspector Fairlight here.'

'Fliss, it's Quick here.'

A silence. Then, 'Quick as in former DI Alexandra Quick?'

'The very same.'

'Tell me you're going to come back to us.' Felicity Fairlight had been on my team, back in the day, a bright and extremely perceptive copper, seeming almost psychic on occasion.

'I can't.'

'If I told you that Jack the Love Rat has applied for a transfer to Wales, would it make any difference?'

'I doubt it.' Nonetheless, I did feel a faint rousing of interest, small shoots of curiosity stirring beneath what I liked to pretend was total indifference to my previous career. With my former husband gone, it might alter how I felt about rejoining the force.

'I shan't give up trying to persuade you,' Fliss said. 'So . . . how can I help?'

'There was a homicide last night – or possibly this morning – in a house near Canterbury, and I'm wondering if they've identified the vic yet.'

'I don't think so. It was Alan Garside's team who copped the call, not mine – but I think we would have heard. I can make enquiries, if you like. What's your interest?'

I explained the connection. 'And now Helena's disappeared. I feel like I need to find her because although she has lots of friends, she never seems to have anyone looking out for her.'

'And if you knew who the vic was, you might be able to track her down?'

'That's the idea.'

'And you're certain your friend isn't the perp?'

'About as certain as anyone can be.'

'In that case, I'll do my best.'

Early the next morning, logging onto the internet, I found a site which listed all the art galleries in the British Isles. Narrowing my search down to the south-east, refining further to the area round Canterbury, I was dismayed at how many there were. It seemed as though every tiny community had its own gallery, selling not just original art, but prints, etchings, cards, handmade paper, even pottery and glassware. At first glance there was nothing which indicated a place run by either a Mona or a Guillaume. That meant I would have to telephone every one of them, unless I could narrow the search. Anglo-French Gallery would provide a good clue, I thought. Or GuilMon. Or Monguil. Or something. But most of the places on the list were called things which indicated the village or small town where they were situated.

After what I presumed would be opening hours, around ten o'clock, I called the first one. No answer. The same at the second. The third one yielded a voice that would have sounded just right for Rip van Winkle on his awakening from a twenty-year sleep. 'Yeah?'

'I'm looking for Mona or Guillaume,' I said.

'Dunno nobody by that name, mate.' A huge yawn.

'That *is* the Woodsbourne Gallery, isn't it?'

'Yeah.' Another yawn.

I ended the call. Talk about dozy. Literally. The next three calls yielded nothing, but the one after that provided the information I wanted. 'Mona and Guillaume? They're out at Upper Horton. The Horton Arts Centre. Nice people.' The voice hesitated, then added, 'On the whole.'

What the hell did that mean? 'Do you have a number for them?' I asked.

'I'll get it for you.' The voice went, and came back, recited the number, wished me good luck.

I dialled the number, listened to it ring a dozen times and was about to abandon the call when it was answered. 'Hello, yes? Horton Arts Centre. Mona speaking. How may I help?'

'I don't know if you can, but I hope so.' Once again I explained that I was supposed to meet Dr Helena Drummond the previous morning but she hadn't shown up, that I was now trying to find her and understood that Mona herself had been with Helena the evening before that, and I wondered if she had given any indication of where she might be going?

'I don't think so, no,' Mona said doubtfully. 'She mentioned a meeting she was going to the following day – that's yesterday, of course – and that she was expecting it to be productive. Nothing else. We were talking mostly about the concert – and the cathedral itself, of course. Guillaume – my husband – is on the Cathedral Appeal Fund committee and people always seem delighted to hear how it's all going. So much is needed, as I'm sure you know. Bell Harry Tower, the precious stained glass, Christ Church Gate – oh, I wish I was a multi-millionaire, what more worthwhile project could there be than to pay for all the necessary repairs? Especially when you consider that it's the mother church of the Anglican community worldwide, of course, as well as the seat of the Archbishop himself.'

'Absolutely,' I said. Ironic that God should have such need of Mammon. 'But you can't think of anywhere at all Helena might have gone?'

'It was some place in Surrey, I believe. Bathurst Manor or something similar.'

'Barnsfield House?'

'Oh, yes, that's right.'

So, another dead end. Thanking the woman profusely for precisely nothing at all, I managed to get away. Damn. I still had no idea where Helena was.

FOUR

I sat slumped in front of some mind-numbingly moronic quiz programme (*'Which Shakespeare play is set in Denmark?' 'Uh, Richard the . . . uh . . . Fourth?'* – cue triumphant look at the audience) while the successful contestants squealed with hysterical excitement over winning some small amount of money and the studio audience cheered. Switching over, for ten minutes I watched a drama featuring skeletal women emoting in an emaciated plot until I felt like sawing off my own head with a nail file. There was nothing else I could bear to watch for even a couple of minutes. Two or three layers of emotional insulation seemed to have been flayed from my brain, leaving me ultra-sensitive, prey to unname-able terrors. It wasn't just the horrific sight I had endured in Helena's bedroom yesterday afternoon: the blood, the wounds, the attempt to rip the body apart. *Where on earth was Helena?* I was haunted by hideous images of tasers and jugs of bleach forced down throats, of fingernails pulled out with pincers and broken bottles rammed into anuses. I've always read too many misogyn-istic thrillers.

Eventually I ran myself a bath and lay steeping in it, trying to scour away the vile images swamping my mind. I was particularly bothered by the bizarre remembrance of the bloodied papers pushed into the dead woman's body. Why would someone do that? Did it have some wider psychological significance or was it only mean-ingful to the murderer?

Although I was sure I would be unable to sleep, I got into bed and opened a book, until the words danced and blurred across the page, making a mockery of the story. I was about to turn off the light when the phone rang.

'Sorry it's so late, but you asked me to let you know.' It was DI Fairlight.

'What've you got?' Newly alert, I sat up further against my pillows.

'Your body: so far, they haven't been able to identify her. No clues at all as to who she is. Best guess, she'd been dead for anywhere between six and twelve hours when you found her.'

'So it could have happened between Helena leaving the house in the morning and me arriving there that afternoon – except no, it couldn't, because Helena's car was still outside her house, ergo, she left the night before, but never made it home.'

'You sound doubtful.'

'Well for starters, the lights were still on, curtains closed, implying it happened the previous night, rather than in the morning. And how did the victim get into the house in the first place? And why?'

'Doctor Drummond must have invited her in, I suppose.'

'What do we know about her so far?'

'She's forty plus, slimmish, blonde. Her prints aren't on record. There was no handbag found at the scene of crime, so no means of identifying her. No car which might have been hers was found unaccounted for in the vicinity. They're hoping someone will call in a misper, but so far nobody has.'

'She must have had a bag.'

'No sign of one.'

'So the killer probably took it away with him.'

'Seems logical to assume so.'

'Strange, isn't it, that you can't establish identity.'

'Is it? If you're not in a relationship with someone – family, marital, flat-share, whatever – and if you've never come to the attention of the authorities, you're very unlikely to be in the system.'

'What about work? If she hasn't shown up at the office or wherever today, won't they start wondering where she is? Especially if she hasn't rung in to say she's sick or whatever.'

'Maybe she hasn't got a job. Or she's self-employed, or works from home. There wouldn't be any work colleagues to call you in as missing, or to arrive at your door wondering why you hadn't shown up for work.'

'What about – God forbid – kids waiting at home for her?'

'Kids are pretty savvy these days. I'm sure by now they'd have contacted someone if Mum hadn't come home, even if it's only the next-door neighbour.'

'Suppose they're too young.'

'Then they wouldn't have been left alone.' Fliss sighed. 'Probably.'

I sighed too. 'Tell me about it.'

In my years on the force, I had seen any number of instances of careless parents leaving their young children alone in the house while they went off to the pub for several hours, occasionally with tragic consequences, as happened with little Madeleine McCann, though in her case her parents were only gone for thirty minutes, which in my opinion was twenty-nine minutes too long. Sometimes, unbelievably, I'd even seen parents go off on holiday abroad, leaving their young kids behind to fend for themselves. Fliss and I had worked together on a case where the parents had gone away for a week, leaving girls of eight and six alone. The elder girl had decided to make chips for supper and managed to tip a pan of boiling fat all over her little sister. The damage to the child was horrific: she'd been reduced to little more than raw hamburger, her face melted into her chest, limbs fused to her body. The worst thing was that when we arrived, she was still conscious, though mercifully not for long. The parents seemed bewildered at being arrested and subsequently given prison sentences, protesting that they'd left plenty of food for the children. My colleagues and I had never been able to comprehend such levels of stupidity, combined with such complete indifference to the children's welfare.

After finally switching off the light beside my bed, I lay sleepless, staring up at the darkened ceiling, while every now and then the headlights of a car ran across it from one side of the room to the other. I should have been indulging in a feeling of satisfied triumph after yesterday's meeting with Clifford Nichols, which I was ninety-five per cent certain would result in a fulfilling contract. Instead, I was trying to imagine what circumstances would have led Helena to abandon her home and her routine. And maybe – though I couldn't conceive of the possibility – even be complicit in some way in the death of the woman discovered in her house.

Another scenario presented itself: Helena leaving in the morning for the appointment with Clifford Nichols, and being snatched off the street by some maniac, without even knowing about the corpse in her bedroom. But that was surely impossible. If she had been abducted, it would have to have been the night before, after the concert and the restaurant meal, possibly before she got home. In that hypothesis, she would probably not even have got inside the house. Because surely, finding a dead body in her bedroom, she would immediately have called the police. It seemed proof enough to me that the corpse had materialized without Helena knowing anything about it. Unless the killer/abductor was inside, waiting for her. But none of that made sense. Which implied that we were dealing with a killer clever enough to close curtains, switch on lights, in order to deliberately mislead as to the time of death. New scenario: Helena leaves for the evening, victim arrives, followed very shortly by enraged killer, who sets about his grisly work with blunt instrument and awl, before driving off again, taking the victim's handbag with him. So what happened to Helena after she said goodbye to her friends?

And there was no means of identifying the victim, with her gold-painted toenails . . . which was when an idea struck me. The more I considered it, the more possible it seemed. And even if I was wrong, and I could actually see no reason why I should necessarily be right, it was a suggestion warranting someone looking into it. The fortyish, slimmish blonde woman might be, as I myself was, someone who worked from home. Someone who knew Helena, had been one of her students, and therefore might quite legitimately have called at her house. Someone who had recently produced a book on Masaccio. Someone called . . . Amy Morrison.

Worth a try. Excited, I got out of bed and hurried along to my office since I didn't have Fliss Fairlight's number on my phone. I brought it up on the screen and made a call.

'Fliss,' I said, when the DI picked up. 'This is just a wild shot off the top of my head, and I know it's not even your call, but I'm wondering if the vic found in Doctor Drummond's house could possibly be Amy Morrison.'

'And she is . . .?'

'An art historian and author. I know nothing about her except that she had a book published two or three months ago. And back in the day, she was one of Doctor Drummond's students. And frankly, she's a prize bitch. But she fits the physical description you gave me.'

Fliss digested this. 'Thanks, Alex. If it *is* this woman, I'd say things don't look very bright for Doctor Drummond, do they?'

'Who*ever* it is, it's not looking very bright for her.'

'True.'

Back in bed, I switched the light off again and lay looking into the darkness. The sea was calm tonight; through the open window I could hear the swish, swish of waves, the crunch of shingle.

I thought back to the one occasion I'd met Amy Morrison, about two months ago. Helena and I had been working on *Ripe for the Picking*, which we thought would go down well with the Christmas market, when she said, 'Have you had an invitation to the launch of the new Masaccio book?'

'No.' I studied a Flemish flower-piece. 'Should I have?'

'Not necessarily.'

'Who's publishing it?'

'Lewis & Barton.'

'I've done some work for them in the past. Picture editing and stuff. But nothing to do with Masaccio.'

'In the dim and distant past, the wretched Amy Morrison was one of my students,' Helena had said, picking up a reproduction of one of Cezanne's apples. 'Oh, the appleness of these apples, Quick!'

'"*The golden apples of the sun*",' I quoted.

'Exactly. Anyway, I imagine I've been invited so La Morrison can gloat. She was a right little cow back then, and I very much doubt that she's changed. Tell you what: the invitation is for me and a guest, so why don't you come with me?'

'Love to,' I said.

I bought a copy of the biography before we went up to London to celebrate the publication of this definitive study of Masaccio, his life and works. It was amazingly good, a tremendous undertaking, and would have involved years of research and labour. 'You must be an inspiring teacher for this woman to have produced such a great book,' I said, as Helena and I stood together in the crowded room, waiting for a few words from publisher and author.

'Huh! As far as Amy was concerned, nothing could be further from the truth.' Helena lowered her voice but not enough to be discreet. 'Frankly, she was as poor a student as I've ever come across in twenty years of teaching. Lazy and unmotivated. Possessed of an entirely unoriginal mind. Mind you, she's had a complete makeover since those days. Totally reinvented herself. Outwardly, at least, though I'd lay a hundred to one on that she's the same cold-hearted bitch on the inside.'

'In what way?' I glanced over at the woman for whom we were gathered here.

'It's not just her appearance, it's her attitude, her manner,' Helena said. 'She used to be brash and vulgar, unashamedly on the make.

Now, you'd think she'd come out of the very toppest of top drawers
– though I'm sure she's still not exactly a beacon of truth and
honesty.'

'Meaning what?'

Helena raised sardonic blonde eyebrows. 'More than once I
suspected her of stealing work from other students. Especially if
they were male. Such a pity men tend to think with their dicks. Talk
about honey-traps! It was all very subtly done, of course. Nothing
that anyone could prove – not even the poor lads she stole from!'
By now, people nearby were turning to look admonishingly at the
two of us.

'How could you tell?'

'Well, sometimes she came up with insights and ideas which I
simply couldn't believe were her own. Especially when some of my
brighter students offered the same hypotheses. To tell you the truth,
I'm absolutely staggered that she could have produced this book
– which I understand is actually very good indeed. I haven't had a
chance to read it yet, but when I do, I hope I haven't read it all
before, under someone else's name.'

'I'm a great fan of Masaccio's,' I said. 'And I'm telling you it's
a great book.'

'Then Madame over there definitely didn't write it.'

She really was amazingly tactless. Or just amazingly forthright,
which amounted to much the same thing. I looked across the room
to where a group of thin, young publishing assistants, dressed mostly
in black, stood like members of the *Schutzstaffel* in a protective
semi-circle behind another woman.

Amy Morrison. Star of this launch party at the National Portrait
Gallery. Slim as a knife-blade, in a fitted scarlet dress and a lot of
silver jewellery. A mass of blonde curls. And drop-dead gorgeous.
Author of *Masaccio: The Magic of Illusion*. I knew her to be some
years older than myself, but from this distance, she looked to be no
more than eighteen or twenty.

'Who's the man salivating down the front of her dress?' I asked.

'Gillon Drew. Owns a small private gallery in North London.
Not that there's a lot there for him to drool over.' Helena glanced
down at her own generous frontage.

Someone tapped on a glass, and gradually the room fell silent.
A tall man in a shabby Prince of Wales check suit stained yellow

around the crotch area (obviously not a man who had been taught to catch the drip), a Tattersall-checked flannel shirt, a bow-tie and a red waistcoat liberally dusted with either dandruff or snuff, it was hard to tell which, spoke. 'Good evening, everybody. I'm Donald Lewis, Amy's editor at Lewis & Barton, and I want to say that we're really thrilled to be launching her Masaccio book here tonight. It's already received rave reviews from the critics, and we anticipate that it's going to be a huge success.'

He looked down at Amy who stood beside him, looking tiny and vulnerable. 'Amy?'

'I do hope so,' she said shyly. She looked up at him and smiled, producing a pair of dimples as big as potholes.

'We feel that Amy has a great future ahead of her,' continued Lewis, while Amy did the dimpling thing again.

Beside me, Helena whispered in a childish falsetto, 'What, little me?' which had people turning round again, this time to shush her.

Amy clasped her small hands together, diamonds sparkling on her fingers as she spoke. 'It's been a wonderful journey,' she said. Her voice was soft and high-pitched, part little girl, part aristocrat. 'Ever since art school, I've wanted to write about Masaccio, to research his short life and gaze at his paintings. He died at a tragically young age, only twenty-six, as I'm sure most of you here know, and the marvel is that he produced so much outstanding work in such a brief time.' She dimpled again and raised her glass of white wine. 'I only hope I've done him justice. Here's to Masaccio!'

'Huh,' grunted Helena scornfully.

'Does she know how you feel about her?'

'I doubt it. We've barely been in contact since she left college.'

Standing against the wall with two or three others I noticed a motherly-looking woman in a brown velvet dress under a magnificent jacket of fine embroidered silk. Her abundant grey-brown hair was piled untidily on top of her head and precariously fixed with a number of tortoiseshell combs, many of which seemed about to fall onto her shoulders.

'Who's that?' I motioned with my chin.

'Sadie Johns. I can't imagine why she bothered to come. Unless she's planning to drop a cyanide pill into dear Amy's glass. Cheers!'

'Why would she want to do that?'

'I'll tell you later.' Helena drained her own glass and made a face. 'Christ, why do they serve such tooth-rottingly ghastly stuff at these events?' She gazed round the room. 'Oh, look . . . there's dear Pieter Salzmann, and Hermann Braun.' The two men were well-known art critics. 'They must have flown over from Munich.'

'Who's the couple they're talking to? They seem familiar.'

'Bob and Mercy Lamont. Americans. Great collectors, both of them.'

'Of course! Didn't he pay a record sum at auction quite recently?'

'They're the ones. For a rare Leonovsky, one of the Russian Impressionists. Two and a half million dollars. Just walking-around money for him, though, since they're both rolling in it!'

'Isn't there a son?'

'That's right. A very promising artist. And a good academic mind as well. Not sure what he's doing at the moment. I taught him for a semester, some years ago, when I was a visiting prof in New York. He and La Morrison were actually an item at one point.' She hoicked another glass of wine from a passing tray. 'Must catch those two.'

'I may just quietly leave, Helena. Thanks for bringing me along.'

'My pleasure. See ya, babe.' And she swirled off into the crowd like a peacock on acid.

I slowly made my way over to Amy Morrison, stopping here and there to talk to friends and acquaintances. It seemed like the whole of art-connected London was there. Finally there was a space in the crowd around her, into which I inserted myself. She turned cold eyes on me and raised an uninterested eyebrow.

'I'm Alexandra Quick,' I said. 'Freelance picture editor – I've worked for your publishers from time to time.'

'Oh, yes?' Amy's eyes rested on me without curiosity.

'You've done a great job, and I'm sure the book will—'

'Thanks.' Her silver chains, lockets and necklaces jangled against her almost-non-existent bosom as she turned to someone standing beside her. 'Isn't that Pieter Saltzmann over there? I'd better go and be sweet.'

Consider yourself dismissed, inferior person. *Non*-person . . .

What a bitch! I could hardly believe that anyone could be so ill-mannered. Working in picture editing, I had heard other tales about the Morrison woman: temper tantrums, failure to show at programmed meetings, ridiculous demands insisted on. I just hoped she would get her come-uppance one of these days.

I felt bad when she did – but perhaps not as bad as I should have done.

I stopped to introduce myself to Bob and Mercy Lamont, whom I'd met before, though briefly. A handsome couple, they were both in their sixties, tall and distinguished-looking, with the impeccable manners, displayed in that blue-blooded way that only well-bred American Yankees can truly produce.

Mercy grimaced sympathetically, indicating that she had witnessed my comprehensive rejection by the star of the evening, and that she sympathized. We chatted for a while, mostly about the world of art. 'We both love your compilations,' she said. Her voice was low and husky; I imagined that in her young girlhood, it was incredibly sexy. Still was.

'They're hard work, but great fun to do,' I said. 'The trouble is that often the production costs don't match with the profits they bring in to the publishing houses.'

'My wife and I have been talking for some time of setting up our own company,' Bob Lamont said. 'Unlike other commercial publishers, we wouldn't have to make the books balance overall.'

'It would be a labour of love,' Mercy said. Her eyes briefly glowed.

'Look, do you have a card?' Bob asked. 'We should keep in touch.'

I delved into my shoulder bag, found one and gave it to him.

He glanced at it. 'We must talk some more.'

'Sounds like an excellent idea.' And I meant it. With backers like the Lamonts, Drummond & Quick could really take off. Helena had a host of other jobs bringing in money, but I didn't. I had refused any kind of alimony payment reluctantly offered by Jack the Rat. A little financial security would most definitely not go amiss.

Meanwhile, there was Helena to worry about. As DI Fairlight had pointed out, things were not looking good for my friend. In fact, they were looking exceedingly bad. It was far too easy to come up with some kind of scenario which involved the arrival of Amy – if it was Amy, of which I was more and more convinced – at Helena's place (for whatever reason, to be determined later), a heated altercation, during which Helena had swung at her former student with something heavy, such as the candlestick (maybe the one I had picked up as a defensive weapon without even thinking about it), then, panicking, tried to make the scene look like some crazed sexual psychopath's battleground (Helena loved crime novels, the more gruesome the better), before fleeing for a hiding place somewhere. Or crossing the Channel on an early ferry. Maybe even flying out to Oz.

But two minutes' rational thought gave the lie to this supposition. First of all, if there had been an argument, why would it have taken place up in the bedroom with at least one of the protagonists more or less naked? Second of all, it might not even be Amy Morrison. And thirdly, although it was relatively easy to imagine Helen losing her cool, it was absolutely impossible to imagine her stripping the body, or ramming some sharp instrument into the woman's eyes, setting a false trail by closing curtains and switching on bedside lights.

In the twisted mind of the killer, did the fact that Ms Morrison spent so much of her professional life gazing at pictures (as Helena and I did) take on a new significance? Only someone filled to the brim with hatred and anger against humanity, especially women, could possibly indulge in such macabre behaviour.

But if Helena wasn't the perpetrator, why had she disappeared? And perhaps more pertinently, given the fact that her car was parked outside her house, *how* had she disappeared? A trawl of local cab firms might be in order, if the police had not yet got onto it. In the morning, I knew I would need to do some intensive work running down facts, contacting her colleagues, chasing down even the slightest lead. And all the time anticipating the feeling of being an idiot, because Helena was going to waltz in at any moment, with some rational excuse for why she had gone AWOL.

Wasn't she?

My heart began to sink as I contemplated the possibility that the police were correct in assuming that she was responsible for the murder.

'Still haven't a clue who she is.'

Off-duty the following morning, DI Fliss Fairlight had telephoned again. 'I passed on your hypothesis to Garside and his team, but so far no nearest and dearest have shown up. We haven't got due cause to go into Morrison's house to get DNA, but the pathologist has taken scrapings from the body and we're thinking of sending them off to the lab. Trouble is, to get the tests done will cost a fortune, stretch the budget tighter than we'd like, and after all that, it might not even be her.'

'So what do you do?'

'We play the waiting game for another twenty-four hours, in the hope that someone will miss her and start making enquiries.'

'When can I get into Doctor Drummond's house?'

'Why would you want to do that?'

'It's work-related.' I had never minded telling useful lies.

'I suppose under supervision . . .' Fliss said doubtfully.

'Are you actively looking for her?'

'Of course. A corpse found in someone's home, the owner vanished? Of *course* they're actively looking for her!'

'And where are you looking?'

There was a silence. After a moment, Fliss said, 'I expect someone will be coming round to interview you some time soon.'

'Again? I've already told Garside and his team absolutely everything I can.'

'But last time they were concentrating on the victim, not the possible perp.' Fliss yawned loudly. 'Anyway, it's been a long night. I'm off to bed.'

FIVE

Over coffee in Willoughby's Books, I asked myself what I actually knew about my friend and collaborator. The answer was remarkably little, I discovered, although we had been working closely together for over three years. I knew something of her professional life, but apart from the two husbands, almost nothing concerning her personal affairs, though I was well aware that she was keen on men, especially those younger than herself. Nor did I know where to start looking.

The police were after her as a possible murder suspect, whereas I myself simply wanted to find out what had happened to her and to offer help if it was needed. Did she have children? If so, she had never mentioned them. Or siblings? It was unlikely her parents were still alive, but they might be, if only I could track them down. If I knew where to start looking. But Helena wasn't the sort to run home to Mummy when in trouble. Or Daddy, for that matter. What other leads could I try?

In my bag I found a notebook and pen.

Colleagues at U of K @ C, I wrote.

Colleagues at U of Melbourne

Should I add the name of our current publisher, the vindictive little Tyson Lowell? But we had comprehensively dissed him. If he had any information in the first place, he was unlikely to pass it on to me, out of spite, if for no other reason. Anyway, why would he be offering help and succour to Helena?

The University of Melbourne was an expensive phone call away, even supposing that in the last couple of days Helena had managed to evade the police, fly out of England and land up in Australia. So a line went through that item too. Helena's husbands I knew nothing about. Which left the faculty in Canterbury. To which it would be better to drive than try to telephone. I smiled at the bookshop man, gave him a little wave and went outside. I shivered, got into my car and set off.

I'd had occasion to visit Helena on campus the previous year and knew it was built on several hundred acres of green parkland, over-looking the city. Very pleasant, if you liked modern buildings, which I didn't particularly, with plenty of open green spaces between them. Courtyards, gardens, ponds and woodland, with stunning views of Canterbury and the Stour Valley – okay, so it wasn't Oxbridge, nor was it meant to be, but as contemporary campuses went, it was up there.

At this time of year, with the students gone for the Christmas vacation, parking was easy. I got out, shivered again – damn, I *really* didn't like being cold – and started walking towards the Jarman building, which housed the School of Arts. Once through the doors, I could hear a lot of distant wavery shouting, rather like the sounds you get in a swimming pool, but there was no one around to ask. What would happen if I shouted myself? Would anyone come? I saw directions to Studio 3, which Helena had mentioned in the past, and started to make my way there. I was in luck. A youngish man in a paint-stained T-shirt and jeans which gave new meaning to the word 'threadbare', was standing in front of an abstract painting full of swirls of pink and green, with his hands on his hips and his head on one side.

'What do you think of that?' he said, without bothering to see who had just come in.

'Not much,' I said.

'You know, I think you're right.' He turned round in a single fluid movement. 'I'm Perry Nutley, and you are . . .?'

'My name's Quick. Alex Quick. I work with—'

'Oh my goodness, yes, I know exactly who you are. You work for Helena Drummond, *n'est-ce pas?*' He flung out an expressive arm, fingers flexed.

'That's one way to put it.'

'And how is she? We haven't seen her for a couple of days.'

'I was hoping you could tell me. It's a long story, but . . .' I swallowed. '. . . She seems to have gone missing.'

'And you're bothered about it?'

'Of course I am. Especially since we were supposed to go to a meeting two days ago and she didn't turn up.'

'That's not like her.' Light grey eyes, unkempt eyebrows, hair in need of a trim, his movements a sort of ballet dance. He was some-what older than I had first taken him to be. Despite his feyness, his expression was kind and he displayed an obvious sympathy for whatever dilemma was bugging me. 'Come and have a coffee,' he said.

He showed me into an office the size of a freezer chest, plugged in a kettle and made two mugs of instant. 'Now,' he said, handing one to me, 'tell me what's happened.'

So I did. 'And now I have no idea where she could possibly be, and the police are after her, and to be honest I'm worrying that she's been abducted or worse.' I sipped at the disgusting coffee. 'The thing is, I've only just realized how little I know about her, even though we're working colleagues. She comes across as so open and let-it-all-hang-outish, but in fact she gives almost nothing away. So I don't know anything about her background or her family situation. Nothing. Apart from the fact that she's been married twice.'

'To Liam, and of course, to dear Ainslie,' said Perry. 'Ainslie's a painter, lives in France, in the Dordogne. Liam's—'

'Do you mean Ainslie Gordon?'

'That's the one.'

I literally felt my jaw drop. 'Are you seriously telling me that Helena was once married to Ainslie *Gordon?*' I couldn't believe what I was hearing.

'Yes, I seriously am.'

'But . . .' I didn't know what to say. 'Why didn't she *tell* me?'

'She plays her cards very close to her chest, does our Helena.'

'Yes, but even so . . .' I had to admit that I was ruffled by this news. Not too long ago, I had even suggested one of Ainslie Gordon's paintings as suitable for inclusion in a possible future collection of pictures of woods – *Lovely, Dark and Deep* – but she had turned the suggestion down flat. 'Especially when she knows how much I admire his work.' It was spare and powerful stuff, blocks of colour, almost impressionistic, but symbolic rather than representational, suggesting that things bleak and sinister were taking place just out of sight. I was always reminded of Lyonel Feininger or Howard Hodgkin when I saw Ainslie's work.

'Anyway,' I said. 'Do you have any idea where she might have gone?' My phone vibrated in the pocket of my coat, but I ignored it.

'Not really. I know she's been a visiting professor somewhere Down Under, but otherwise . . .' Perry spread his hands wide and shrugged.

'What about family?'

'I think there might be a daughter somewhere, but no idea where. I have a feeling that they don't get on.' He frowned. 'Or am I mixing her up with another work colleague? Yes, scrub the daughter – it's not Helena I'm thinking of at all.'

'What about siblings?'

'If she has any, she's never mentioned them to me.'

'Friends? Somewhere she might feel safe?'

He frowned, holding his mug against his face. Pursed his lips. Shook his head gently from side to side. 'Funny thing: I've never thought about it before, but I don't think Helena has a whole heap of friends. Apart from you.' Head on one side again. 'I assume you *are* friends . . .'

'Of course.'

'But it's kind of surprising how, well, *lonely* she is, considering how in-your-face she comes across. How . . . *joyous*.'

Joyous . . . it summed her up precisely.

Was I joyous? Had I ever been?

'She does have friends,' I said, defensive for Helena. 'She was out with some of them a few nights ago.'

'Of course. So she was. She invited me to come along but I had a previous engagement.'

'Well, thanks.' I stared bleakly at Perry Nutley, beset by images of my friend locked into a home-made coffin, or kept in a wheelie bin, or hanging upside down in some sadistic pervert's cellar.

No! Don't think such thoughts. Back in my car, I drove to my parents' house. Despite their peculiarities, I felt in need of their common sense take on life, after the events of the past couple of days.

And what about Ainslie Gordon? He was one of the Bright Old Things of the current scene, famously eccentric, reclusive, eschewing any event which could be described as arty, rarely giving interviews, refusing all invitations to speak, to teach or to accept awards and prizes. Why had Helena concealed this relationship from me?

I was aware that he lived in the south of France. Was it possible she had gone down there? If there was no alternative, and other lines of enquiry had petered out, I thought, with a guilty frisson of pleasure, that a trip to the Dordogne might be called for.

SIX

Arriving at my parents' red-brick Queen Anne house, I walked up the path, rang the doorbell, at the same time letting myself into the square hall and calling out. The objects, the pictures, the furniture had not changed appreciably since I was a child. Some watercolours of flowers painted by my grandmother. A small set of shelves holding books. A hideous vase which looked like melted vanilla ice cream with chocolate sauce on top. A fine, if battered, inlaid walnut drop-leaf table. An illuminated family tree, showing my father Edred's lineage as far back as a thirteenth- or fourteenth-century knight of Norman extraction called Elaward de Cuike.

I walked into the kitchen, where my parents were seated in creaking basket-chairs on either side of a wood-burning stove. Something in the kitchen was either charred or had been.

'Have a productive time at your meeting the other day?' Mary Quick – my mother – asked perfunctorily, glancing through the *Guardian* as she spoke. Tall, angular, unfeminine, and detached to the point of disengagement as far as her family was concerned, she was the least maternal mother that could be imagined. Nonetheless, all three of her children knew that if it came to it, she would swim piranha-infested waters for them, crawl across broken beer bottles, face down any number of rabid panthers armed only with an umbrella.

'Good in parts.' I could do detachment as well.

'Curate's egg stuff, eh?' said Edred, shuffling through the *Daily Mail*.

'What's the bad bit?' Mary, a sufferer from a terminal drop at the end of her nose, sniffed, noisily turning the page of her paper.

'Helena has vanished.' To my dismay, I felt weak tears at the back of my throat.

'Has she done this before?'

'I doubt she makes a habit of it,' I said drily. 'She's certainly not gone missing since we've been working together. But it's worse than that . . . on my way back from the meeting, I stopped in at her house and . . .' Voice shaking, I outlined my discovery in Helena's bedroom.

'How frightful!' Attention caught, both my parents stared at me. Over time, they had struck up a close friendship with Helena, who was nearer to their age than she was to mine. 'How appalling!'

'You must be extremely . . .' My father struggled judiciously to find a word that would convey sympathy alongside common sense. '. . . concerned.' He got up and fetched a glass, which he filled with Cabernet Sauvignon from a box, and passed across the table. 'Tell us the whole story,' he said.

So I did, alternately sipping from the glass he kept refilling, and wiping my eyes.

'Where can she have gone?' my mother asked.

'I can't imagine. I'm not sure I want to imagine.' I sniffed. 'Actually, I thought she might have come here.'

Both of them shook their heads.

'Any idea who the dead body belongs to?' my father asked.

'Last night, they still hadn't identified it,' I said. 'But maybe they have by now.' Belatedly remembering the unanswered call on my mobile while I was talking to Perry Nutley at the university, I fished out my phone. DS Fairlight had sent me a text: *You were right!* 'Oh goodness . . . yes, they know who it is.'

'And are you going to tell us?' My mother dabbed at the end of her long aristocratic nose with a screwed-up piece of tissue.

'If they're right, it's Amy Morrison.'

'*What*? The art historian whose launch you went to a couple of months or so ago?'

'I'm not quite up to speed here.' Edred frowned. 'You're saying you let yourself in to Helena's house because she hadn't shown up at a business meeting you'd set up, and then you found this Amy Morrison woman lying murdered in Helena's bedroom?'

'Exactly. Though I didn't know it was Amy at the time.'

'Forgive me for asking,' Mary said, 'and you know how very fond we are of Helena, but is there any likelihood that she could be responsible for this death?'

I shook my head vigorously from side to side. 'Absolutely none whatsoever.' If there was one thing I could be firm about, it was this.

'I agree with you,' my father said. 'I can't imagine her mixed up in murder.'

'Do you think she even knows about this body in her house?' asked Mary.

'It's quite possible that she doesn't,' I said. 'But the police aren't going to believe that. In fact, I know that they *don't* believe it.'

'So they're making every effort to find her.'

'Unfortunately, yes. As a matter of urgency. Completely ignoring the fact that it could be— that it *must* be someone else entirely.'

'On the other hand, maybe she was in the house when this woman was killed, and the killer then abducted her.'

'That's actually what I'm afraid of,' I said.

I looked at them both with approval. As a child, I might have lost out on the smell of home-baked cookies, the hand-sewn zombie costume for the Hallowe'en party, the swimming and bike-riding lessons. On the other hand, I had parents who were always keen to discuss and evaluate any proposition or problem that I laid before them. Not only to evaluate, but very often to come up with some sort of resolution.

'If we assume that Helena is innocent – and I too cannot imagine her getting violent to the degree that you've described – then it seems to me that what the police need to do is establish who might have wanted to get rid of this Amy Morrison,' said Mary. 'Thus letting Helena off the hook.'

'I've already decided that's the best thing I can do.'

'Even though you'd probably be covering some of the same ground as the police?'

'If that's what they're intending to do, then yes. But it looks as though they're concentrating most of their efforts on finding Helena so that they can arrest her for murder, rather than on the victim. At least for the present. So if I can get in first . . .'

'There's nothing in my paper about this woman's death,' said Mary, sipping coffee. The steam from her cup made her nose turn an almost translucent red.

'Nor mine,' added Edred. Stanley, his mangy old cat, jumped onto his knee and he stroked it, murmuring sweet nothings.

'So it doesn't look like the Press are on to it yet,' Mary said.

'And there was nothing on the radio about it, either.' I frowned. Not that it was likely to hit the headlines, since the average punter on the street probably wouldn't be all that interested in the death, however violent, of some obscure art historian who wrote about an even more obscure (to the uninitiated) Quattrocento Italian artist. Nonetheless, I would have thought that given the circumstances of the murder (pretty woman, been on the telly, found semi-naked with punctured eyes and her face beaten in), the down-market newspapers might have found room somewhere for a salacious paragraph or two. So my mother was right: it looked as though the police were still sitting on it and had not yet released the details.

More worrying – and a cold chill of apprehension crept across the back of my neck at the recollection – was Helena's conviction that she was being stalked, and my own light-hearted response to what I had considered little more than her drama-queen posturing. Perhaps she really *had* been stalked, and the guy had now snatched her off the street in order to act out his sick sexual fantasies. I didn't want to go there. If only I had made Helena tell me more, instead of cutting her short.

'So what's your next step?' my mother asked.

'I'm going to make some enquiries in London. Stay with Hereward.'

'Hereward?'

'Your son.'

'Oh, *that* Hereward,' said my father. As though the streets of London teemed with men called Hereward.

'Does he know?' my mother asked.

'Not yet.' I shook my head affectionately as I looked at the two of them. Edred had been a journalist on one of the nationals; Mary had taught chemistry and physics at a local girls' school. Warm and loving, in the traditional sense, they were not. But both had a keen interest in things cultural: art, music, literature, for which I was deeply grateful. When I was a child in this huge cold house, there were always books lying about the place, particularly books of paintings, thick catalogues of exhibitions, studies of individual painters, all of which I had read and reread as I grew up, and which had undoubtedly steered me towards my current career.

Back in my own flat, I put in a call to my brother. 'Herry, it's your little sister,' I said.

'What do you want?' Like my parents, there was no beating about the bush with Hereward Quick.

'I need to spend a few days in London.'

'Yes, the basement flat is empty, if that's what you mean. When do you want it?'

'Immediately. Well, this evening, anyway.' Briefly I outlined my reasons.

'It's yours for as long as you want it. You've got the key. Go in and make yourself at home. Lana's in Morocco for the week.'

'Herry, you are a star.'

'I know.' He put down the phone.

I called him back. 'What now?' he asked.

'Do you know someone called Lamont?'

'The art-collector guy? No, never met him.'

'What about Gillon Drew?'

'The gallery man? Matter of fact, Lana and I were at a rather exclusive bash he threw last week.'

'What's your opinion of him?'

'An arse-licker. But got his finger on the pulse . . .'

'An unpleasant image, I must say.'

'He mentioned you when I told him my name, asked if I was any relation. It was in connection with one of your anthologies. Seemed rather impressed when I said you were my sister.'

'A man of taste and discernment.'

'Obviously.'

'So you won't mind if I use your name to weasel my way into his confidence.'

'If it'll do you any good, be my guest.' Again the call was abruptly ended. Herry didn't do chat.

I sat at the table and thought. In my years as a senior cop, I had often found that twenty minutes of concentrated thinking was worth several hours of faffing about. Eyes closed, hands relaxed in my lap, I reviewed the time Helena and I had attended the Morrison launch party. Some of the attendees were completely unknown to me, though not, apparently, to Helena, since I'd watched her drifting purposefully from group to group, always greeted with the obligatory mwah-mwah kiss, the friendly arm-rubbings.

The fabulously rich Lamonts were one couple it might be useful to contact. Another was Gillon Drew, owner/director of a small private gallery in Chelsea. There was the guy from Amy's publisher, of course, Donald Lewis, if I remembered his name correctly. And a strange woman with a US-army-inspired haircut and a red leather onesie, who had been hovering proprietorially round Amy, like Bo-Peep who'd just recovered her sheep and didn't want to lose them again. An art critic, if I remembered rightly. Or was she the one from Rome who was mentioned in Amy's extensive list of acknowledgements: Senorita Graziella Montenegro? I couldn't see that any of them were likely to have murdered Amy in Canterbury, or have any clue as to where Dr Helena Drummond might be, but I wrote their names down.

The more I thought about it, the less likely it seemed that Helena could have vanished voluntarily. And with that fact in place, my earlier tentative conclusions crystallized. If Helena was aware of the body in her house, she would have notified the police. If she wasn't, it could only mean that she had not seen it and, very likely, was now somewhere she had not intended to be.

Before I left for London, I walked down to Willoughby's bookshop. Even though Christmas was fast approaching, it was quiet in there, close to the end of the day, mums gone to pick kids up from school, such students as were still around already preparing to go clubbing or down the pub. Sam Willoughby's assistant had gone home for the day and he himself was at the till, reading a book which he shoved into a drawer when I came in.

'Don't mind me,' I said, waving a hand.

'Indeed I do mind you,' he said. 'It seems far too long a time since you were last in here.' He glanced up at the clock on the wall behind him. 'How about a cuppa?'

'Sounds good. A mugga would be even better.'

'Workman's tea, isn't it? Coming right up.'

Over tea, he asked how my wacky friend, Dr Drummond, was. I bit my lip. 'I'd tell you, if I knew.' Once again I briefly outlined such details as I had about Helena's disappearance.

'So now you're trying to find out more about Madame Masaccio.'

'That's right.'

'Where are you going to start?'

'By talking to people.' I lifted my mug, which was labelled KEEP CALM AND BUY A BOOK. 'I don't know anything about the woman.

As a matter of fact, I realize I don't know much about Doctor Drummond, either.' Was this because I had become as detached from other people as my own mother, something I had always vowed would never happen, or because Helena didn't give much information away?

'As it happens, I was reading the foreword to Morrison's book a couple of days ago,' Sam said. 'But it wasn't big on autobiographical detail – though you wouldn't expect it to be. It mentioned her professional career – which was extremely short, I must say – and that was about it. I even looked her up on the internet. You usually get something in the front or back of a book, a small paragraph headed "About The Author". But there was nothing about her personal background. Mysterious origins, I would say.'

'In other words, origins she wished to conceal. Though we do know she was at art school, because Doctor Drummond was her tutor, for a semester, at any rate.'

'And that she got an MA, according to the back flap of her book, though it doesn't say where.'

'I wonder what she did when she wasn't writing about Masaccio.'

'Went hither and yon – wrote columns for the arty-farty journals, gave lectures, that sort of thing. Got married and moved away. Who knows? But this book will certainly have put her back on the map.'

'And now it's all too late, poor woman.' I lifted my mug again. 'Thing is, somebody wanted her dead, and it wasn't my friend Helena.'

'So who was it?'

'That's precisely what I need to find out.'

A customer pushed open the door of the shop, sending the old-fashioned bell fixed to a spring above the door into a frenzy of clanging. Sam got up. 'Best of luck with the hunt, Alex. Keep me up to speed, won't you? And if there's anything I can do . . .'

What could he do? What could anyone do? From the way Helena had spoken of her, there might be plenty of people who had cause to dislike Amy Morrison. But to want to butcher her . . . that argued a pathological hatred. And much as one might dislike another person, however often one might say, *Oh I really hate him or her*, genuine hatred, segueing into violence was something rarely encountered. So, unless I was being unduly optimistic, the field of suspects should be small. All I had to do was eliminate those who couldn't have done it and the last one standing would have to be the perp. Once he was found, Helena could come back, assuming she was still a free individual.

I walked to the station, my bag slung across my shoulder. Change of underwear, minimal make-up, toothbrush, alternative outfit. No way did I intend to take a car into central London.

Once I reached my brother's house in Oakley Street, I trod carefully down the treacherous frosty steps to the basement flat and let myself in. Not luxurious, but pleasantly furnished with the kind of fittings that students couldn't damage – though Hereward and Lana only took PhD students from the LSE, preferably the older married ones, in order to minimize the wild parties and all-night drinking sessions.

Someone (Herry's Portuguese housekeeper?) had thoughtfully turned on the heating and put fresh milk, bread, butter and marmalade on the counter in the galley kitchen. I made tea, then sat down at the telephone which stood on a small table.

'Drew Gallery,' a voice said.

'My name is Quick and I'd like to see Mr Drew as soon as possible,' I said.

'May I ask what it's in connection with?'

Which name would have the greatest effect: Amy's, Helena's, Hereward's? Remembering Drew's behaviour at the launch party, I went for the first one as more likely to yield a positive result. 'It's to do with Amy Morrison,' I said.

'Mr Drew's very busy. Can I help?'

'I'm afraid it's personal.'

'Hold the line and I'll see if I can get hold of him for you.'

A minute passed. And a second. Then Gillon Drew was on the line. The man with his nose stuck between Amy's boobs at her launch party, I remembered. 'What's all this about Amy Morrison?' He sounded like a man trying to assert authority and at the same time hide a prurient curiosity.

'I'd rather not discuss it on the phone,' I said. 'I'm not far from you. Could I buy you a drink after work? Or now, even.'

'Let me think . . . Yes, I could spare half-an-hour or so this evening. How about meeting me at the Cock and Bull at five forty-five?'

'I'll be there.' I disengaged before he could ask any further questions.

In spite of the chill, the patrons of the Cock and Bull had overflowed onto the pavement outside. The noise level was high enough to be heard two streets away. Most of the clientele were Hooray Henry city-types: stock traders, bond salesmen, arbitrageurs and the like, with three or four bar-flies in grubby shirts perched stubbornly on high stools up at the bar, resolutely ignoring the in-crowd. A few tourists were grimacing over their warm beer but happily soaking up the atmosphere, feeling that they were seeing a slice of genuine English culture.

I shoved through the crowds to the bar, but couldn't see Gillon Drew. I ordered two double single-malt whiskys, and thrust my way back to the entrance, hoping there wasn't a side access. A table beside me suddenly became free and I sat down swiftly, ignoring the couple who had been waiting for it, who stared at me indignantly. Luckily, Drew arrived very shortly afterwards. I watched him standing at the door as he tried to find me, and shouted his name across the hubbub, raising a glass to indicate that I had a drink for him.

'Very kind.' Standing at my table, he loosened a canary-yellow cashmere scarf and undid the buttons of his British Warm to reveal a Young Fogeyish three-piece suit of green tweed. 'God, it's cold out there, and getting colder by the second,' he said. Although comparatively young (compared to what, I wondered, the thought having flashed across my mind: Methuselah?), he had a headful of thin white hair, and eyebrows in need of a trim.

He started to toss back a slug of the whisky I offered him, then hesitated. 'Just a minute. You *are* Ms Quick, I take it.'

'Indeed.'

'Glad I'm not drinking someone else's drink. I believe I met your brother recently. And of course I know your work. How is Doctor Drummond?'

'Well, I hope.'

He had his eyes fixed on the small TV above the bar, and as he raised his glass again, he stiffened, so suddenly that whisky slopped onto his scarf. He brushed absently at it, at the same time exclaiming, 'Christ on a bicycle, isn't that Amy Morrison? What the hell is going on?'

By the time I had turned round to look up at the soundless screen, the picture had given way to Inspector Alan Garside mouthing silently at the camera.

'That's a policeman . . .' Drew knocked back the contents of his glass and turned to me. 'Does this make any sense to you?' Before I could respond, another thought struck him. 'Is this why you wanted to meet up with me?'

I nodded.

'What's happened to Amy? Is she . . . she's not . . . *dead*, is she?' His eyes remained fixed on the screen, which now showed the front of Helena's house near Canterbury, cordoned off with police-tape.

Again I nodded.

'My God! How? What happened? That's impossible!'

'I'm afraid not. The police seem to think they know who's probably responsible, but I disagree with them. And it occurred to me that someone like you might have more information about Ms Morrison than I – or they – do. Because as I see it, that's the best way to find who really killed her.'

'I can't say I was that close to her,' Drew said hastily, avoiding my eye. 'And of course, I only knew her on a purely professional basis. She came into the gallery from time to time, in the course of doing research for this Masaccio book, and of course we talked.'

'Is that all? I understood you knew her quite well,' I said, taking a punt.

'Well, when I say professional . . .' Drew wriggled uneasily.

'Assuming her death wasn't either accident or suicide, what I need to know is whether you're aware of anyone who might have had it in for Amy.'

'Oh my Lord, where to start?'

This was the sort of information that I had been hoping for. 'How do you mean?'

'The woman isn't – *wasn't*, I suppose I should say – exactly Miss Congeniality. She must have got across half of London's male population – and I don't mean just figuratively speaking. Extremely attractive, of course, but a first-class bitch with a heart of ice would sum her up, in my opinion.'

I was guessing that in spite of the wedding-ring on his hand, Gillon Drew had tried it on with Amy Morrison and been rudely and comprehensively rebuffed. 'So you would definitely see yourself lining up alongside the possible suspects?'

'Me? *Me*?' He almost screamed the word. 'What are you, crazy or something?' He pulled out a handkerchief and pressed it to his upper lip. 'Apart from anything else, I can't stand the sight of blood.'

'She could have been strangled. Or poisoned.' I was rather enjoying this. 'But to be serious, could you point to anyone in her world who might have a reason to kill her?'

'Apart from just about everyone who knew her,' he said sulkily.

'Anyone in particular that you can think of?'

'I feel a bit like the tell-tale-tit at school, but there *is* someone else who loathed her more than the average person. A woman called Sadie Johns.'

'And what did Ms Morrison do to her?'

'I know Sadie quite well. A sweet woman, wouldn't hurt a fly. Teaches art at one of those exclusive London girls' schools, St Paul's or North London Collegiate, somewhere like that. She's something of an expert on Italian Renaissance painters, contributes learned articles to the relevant journals.'

'So what's her beef with Amy?'

'Claims that she not only used Sadie's research without acknowledgement or even permission, but was also instrumental in blocking a book deal with Amy's former publishers which was already in the pipeline.'

'Why did they agree?'

'The sex factor. Obvious, isn't it?' Drew looked pityingly at me, as though I were a particularly dense student. 'Trouble is, if you've got something to promote, publicity-wise, the gaudy peacock is going to win out every time over the brown sparrow. Not to mention the age difference between the two of them. But Sadie with a knife in her hand? No, I can't see it.'

'Who says Amy was knifed?'

'Just a figure of speech.'

A billow of raucous laughter gusted in through the door as someone opened it to leave. I debated offering Drew another whisky but quailed at the thought of pushing through the crowd, which showed no signs of thinning out.

But Drew was right there. He stood. 'Another?'

'Yes, please.'

He brought back refills and sat down again. 'Well,' he said. 'I'm shocked, of course. But I can't say I'm all that surprised. If ever there was a woman who was likely to get her come-uppance one of these days . . .'

'Do you think this murder has to do with her professional life?'

'If I was investigating her death, that's certainly where I'd start looking.' He drew a deep breath. 'Dear oh dear. Amy Morrison dead. It's hard to take in.' He didn't sound as if he was all that bothered.

'So you have no inkling at all of who could be behind her death?'

'None at all. I know she'd made enemies in the business – your colleague Helena Drummond among them – but to take another person's life . . .' He shook his head. 'Quite a step, really. And not one I can imagine anyone I know taking. Sorry not to be more help.'

SEVEN

Later that evening, there was a rapping of fingers at the basement door. I recognized my brother's knock and let him in.

'Got everything you want?' He looked round the flat. 'Discover the whisky?'

I had indeed found it, had even poured myself a small dram and savoured it so appreciatively that I was eventually tempted to have a second one. I wasn't about to say so. I shook my head in feigned bewilderment. 'No?'

Hereward delved into the recesses of one of the beneath-the-counter kitchen cupboards and pulled out a bottle of the twenty-five-year-old Macallan. 'Here.' He thrust a glass at me. 'So, what are you up to?'

Yet again I explained. 'Amy seems to have been universally disliked,' I continued. 'The perp could be one of hundreds, far as I can gather. But you'd have to narrow it down a bit more than that. So since I've got to start somewhere, I'm starting with her professional life.'

'Anyone she's known to have had a recent altercation with, you mean?' Herry wrinkled his rather noble brow, which made him closely resemble our father. 'At that do of Gillon Drew's I mentioned, I did hear someone offering unflattering remarks about the woman. And when I say unflattering, I mean downright vindictive.'

'What did they say she'd done?'

'Stolen other people's work, if I heard right.'

'It seems to have been a speciality of hers. Do you remember the person's name?'

'The one they particularly alleged she'd ripped off was an academic of some kind. Susan? Sarah? Sophie? Something like that.'

'Sadie?'

'That's the one. Sadie.'

'Sadie Johns. Was she at this gathering?'

'Someone pointed her out to me. Untidy-looking woman with a nice face.'

This was the second mention of Sadie Johns. Tomorrow I would make an appointment – or maybe not: nothing like surprise for winkling out the truth – and flog down to Epsom, current home of North London Collegiate School for Girls. I had no serious worries about finding myself closeted with a mad murderer intent on not being found out and prepared to kill again to preserve her freedom. But someone with a real beef about Amy Morrison might shed further light on the woman . . . and the sooner light was shed, the sooner Helena would be in the clear.

I refused to contemplate for a single moment the possibility that Helena herself was in any real danger, outside my thriller-fuelled imagination. Nonetheless, the thought of her chained, gagged and terrified was hard to dismiss. So much so that I wondered if going after Amy Morrison's connections was a futile waste of time, compared with the urgency of finding my friend. But where to start?

For the moment, I had no idea in which direction to go, who to interrogate, where to start looking, whereas, as far as Amy Morrison was concerned, at least I had some leads to follow up.

'Big favour to ask you,' Hereward said suddenly.

'Ask away.'

'I want Anton to live here while we're away.'

'Who's Anton?'

'The dog.'

'You know I don't like dogs.'

'Anton is a rescue dog.' Herry carried on as though I hadn't spoken. 'An Airedale terrier. You'll like him.'

'I won't.'

'I'll bring him down tomorrow morning before I go to the airport.'

Sunlight sparkled off the frosty lawns and playing fields surrounding the wedding cake building of the famous girls' school. I was directed to the drawing school and design technology block, where Miss Johns was said to be currently working. The building was modern – brick, wood and glass – pleasantly situated by a pond where in summer there would be water-lilies and shrubs.

Inside, I asked directions from a group of girls in brown sweaters over blue shirts, and found my way to an office containing drafting tables, desk, several adjustable drawing boards. The unassuming woman seated at a desk looked up when I knocked at the open door. 'Yes?'

'Excuse me for not making an appointment beforehand.' I explained who I was, and indicated that we had met at Amy Morrison's party.

'Oh, yes,' Johns said. 'I remember seeing you and Doctor Drummond there.'

'Very sad about poor Ms Morrison,' I said, when Miss Johns didn't grab the bait.

'I suppose it was.' The response was about as perfunctory as it could be.

'Murdered,' said I, with a fake shiver. 'I wonder who could have been responsible.'

'Any of a dozen people, I should imagine.' Johns reached for one of the several pencils pushed into the wild nest of her hair. 'Excuse me . . . I need to make a note of something.'

'Goodness. Odd that it happened in Helena Drummond's house, don't you think?'

'Not particularly. As I understood it, Doctor Drummond had once been her tutor; perhaps she was passing and decided to drop in.'

'Kind of unlucky to have chosen the very evening that a killer also decided to drop in.'

'Unless they were together.'

'Are you suggesting that Amy and her killer might have arrived together, and then . . . then what?'

'I've no idea. Helena was always a bit of a gal: maybe he was Morrison's boyfriend and Helena came on to him. There's a bit of an altercation between the two women, he tries to break it up and—'

'And what? Accidentally smashes Amy's head in? It doesn't seem very likely. Especially as that evening Helena happened to be out with friends and couldn't have arrived home much before midnight, if she came home at all.'

'And I'm bothered because . . . as my students like to say?' Johns shrugged. It was a disturbing gesture, indicating total indifference. It didn't sit well with her motherly image.

'Each man's death diminishes me, and all that,' I said.

'Not Amy Morrison's. It doesn't diminish me in the slightest.'

Her tone was so harsh and aggressive that I seriously began to wonder if Miss Johns could have travelled to south-east Kent and killed Amy herself. 'Moving on,' I said, 'I've heard here and there that Amy was in the habit of – shall we say – "borrowing" other people's work.'

Johns stuffed the pen she was holding into her hair, and looked directly at me for the first time. 'Stealing,' she said. 'Say it like it is. She *stole*. She turned plagiarism into a fine art. Academically, she was like a magpie, hopping about, picking here and there at other people's research, and then turning it in as her own work. While I still taught at the art school she attended, I had several students complaining bitterly about it, especially the men.'

'Why the men?'

'That was her preferred *modus operandi*. She would target the brightest guys, give them the best sex of their lives, then steal their ideas, their words, their research. She was fairly blatant about it, too.'

'Why wasn't anything done?'

'I tried once to have her answer for her sins, but she simply insisted that the other party was the one who was stealing, taking her own original stuff and trying to pass it off as their own. And you were there at her launch party. You saw how she was. The arch-manipulator. She just gave her inquisitors – ninety-five per cent of them men – the full force of her dimples and boobs and they actually, the stupid idiots, bought it.'

'So could you perhaps nominate someone who hated her enough to kill her?'

'As I said when you first arrived, any one of a dozen people. But if you think I'm going to nominate anyone in particular, finger someone as a murderer, well, that's simply out of the question.'

My mind moved on. There was still the possibility that Helena didn't come home at all that evening. Since it was late, I could easily envisage her deciding to stay in Canterbury overnight, perhaps with the man Paul Sandbrook had told me was called Peter, especially as she was over the limit. The more I thought about it, the more sense it made. Amy and the boyfriend wait up, Helena never arrives, they decide to indulge in a bit of rumpy-pumpy, they have a quarrel, he bashes her over the head and when he realizes she's dead, he runs for the hills.

'Look, Miss Quick,' Sadie Johns said. 'You probably think me cruel and callous for not showing more concern over Amy Morrison's death. I couldn't give a flying – if you'll excuse the word – fuck about the woman. I loathed her. She was cruel, arrogant, petty. She hurt a lot of people, especially those who could least afford to be hurt. If she's been killed, it's not before time. And if you're wondering, I wouldn't demean myself to have any hand in the woman's death. And what's more,' she half-turned in her seat so she was looking out at the lawns in front of her, 'I hope she suffered, the way she made so many other people suffer.'

'Well,' I said. 'You can't say fairer than that.'

'Close the door when you leave,' she said, and bent back to the papers in front of her.

On the way back to Chelsea, I stopped the car by a municipal park and fished out Anton, who was lying mournfully on the back seat, paws stretched in front of him, looking undeniably cute. 'Sorry, guy,' I said, 'you're okay, but you won't win me over.'

I let him off the leash and watched as he bounded away, stopping to sniff at rubbish bins and the legs of concrete picnic tables before lowering his hindquarters to the grass.

Mouth in a moue of disgust, I went over and picked up his droppings in a plastic bag and dropped it into a red-painted box set on a metal stalk. 'You are revolting,' I told Anton.

Not everybody shared my view. I was stopped at least half a dozen times by people wanting to tell me how lovely he was and asking where he came from. 'He's a rescue dog,' I said, not sure whether that was a brand of dog or not, and people nodded sagely.

Back in my brother's basement flat, I opened my briefcase and pulled out the text and pictures for the next Drummond & Quick anthology, stuff I had been accumulating for several weeks. If Cliff Nichols stayed true to his word and came up with a definite contract, I wanted to be prepared. *Eat, Drink & Be Merry*, our next book, was well advanced but still needed work. Should we include Da Vinci's *Last Supper*? A melancholy image, it was not strictly compatible with the expectations set up by the jolly title we had chosen for the anthology. All the more reason to include it as an antidote to all the bucolic Peasant Weddings and Arcimboldos, Helena argued, while I felt that incorporating it would demean the spirit of a great iconic painting. I set it to one side. Ralph Going's *A1 Sauce* was iconic too, but in a different way. Livelier and with much more heart than Warhol's vastly overrated soup cans. That was definitely going in.

Time passed. Although it had been a bright day, the weak winter light gave way early to the thick black clouds of advancing night. At my feet, Anton moaned, bringing me back to the reality of a dog needing to be walked. I glanced out of the window up to street level, and saw a figure standing on the pavement staring down at me. Man or woman? It was impossible to be sure. I frowned. How long had whoever it was been there? Was it just a nosy passing stranger, or someone spying on me? And if the latter, how would they have known I was there? I briskly tugged down the blind, then rattled the curtains across the window. I pulled on a warm jacket and attached Anton to his lead, locked the door securely behind me and climbed the basement steps to pavement level. I stared up and down the street, but could see no one lurking in the shadows. Reminding myself that this was one of the best neighbourhoods in London, I set off towards the Embankment. Bare trees rattled in the darkness above my head; dried leaves scuttled along the pavement. Anton the dog had evidently been trained to do his repulsive business in the gutter, which I took to indicate that, unlike earlier in the park, I didn't have to pick it up.

The houses on either side of the street were settling into early evening. Lights had been switched on in book-lined rooms, soft lamp light illuminated high ceilings and elaborate plaster cornices, walls in sage green and Chinese red served as admirable backgrounds to pictures which needed no price tag to inform viewers (including the sneaky ones like me, standing outside on the street) that here were some serious paintings.

I heard footsteps behind me and turned quickly to see a man coming up fast at my rear. I bent unnecessarily to adjust Anton's lead, ready to launch myself like a coiled spring at the guy, should he attempt to attack me. Anton growled low in his throat, as the be-scarfed and be-hatted man, features almost invisible under the brim of his headgear, came up level with me, tipped his hat, said 'Good evening,' and walked rapidly on.

Wreaths of fog trailed across the river as I reached the Embankment and looked down at the murky water. There were lights on the other side, and a party boat was moving slowly upstream, discharging brightness and laughter into the night.

A pang for the lost days of my marriage darted through my heart. I kicked it away. Perhaps the worst aspect of Jack's betrayal was the realization that all the happy times had been a sham, like a toadstool found hidden under dead leaves which had been hollowed out by woodland creatures. The single discovery of his infidelity had undermined and tainted my entire perception of the time we had been together. We had always enjoyed spending a few days in Hereward's flat, walking hand-in-hand along the river, visiting galleries and museums, admiring the splendour of London's monuments, getting tickets for the theatre. Happy times.

At the end of his lead, Anton moaned and tugged, wanting more freedom than he could be allowed on these Chelsea pavements. When I got back to my brother's house, I would let him out unleashed into Herry's back garden for five minutes. And if he did anything on the little lawn, Herry could pick it up when he came back.

A new idea struck me. Was it possible that Amy's killer had in fact been after Helena, which would be one explanation for Helena's disappearance? Perhaps I was wasting my time, trying to pinpoint those who might have hated Amy strongly enough to kill her. Possibly I should be trying a different tack altogether, concentrating my efforts on someone who had it in for Helena. But the well-developed sixth sense which all good coppers possess told me that I was looking in the right direction. It was a pity I didn't have the slightest idea which way it was.

EIGHT

Donald Lewis belonged to the old school of publishing. So did his publishing company, Lewis & Barton, housed on many creaking levels of a narrow building fronting a Georgian square near Soho. Lewis was wearing the exact same clothes he'd worn at Amy's launch party; I hoped he'd washed the shirt in the interim.

'I recognize your name, of course, and have met your collaborator, Doctor Drummond, on a number of occasions,' he said. 'And of course the two of you were at Amy Morrison's launch party not long ago.' He sighed out some tobacco breath. 'I wish we could have afforded to take Drummond & Quick on. Thing is, the kind of books we publish are expensive to produce, and frankly, don't make a lot of profit for us. We're in it for the love of it, rather than in the hope of retiring early as millionaires. So quite often it's a toss-up: do we undertake an attractive compilation like yours, or a more learned tome like the Morrison book on Masaccio.' He heaved a deep sigh. 'Poor Amy,' he said. 'She always was her own worst enemy.'

'Looks like she just came across an even worse one,' I said.

'True, true.' He leaned across his desk, reaching for one of the pipes which sat in a teak rack in front of him. 'Now, Miss Quick, what can I do for you?'

Once again, I explained the situation: my visit to Helena's home, my discovery of Amy's body, the disappearance of Helena. 'And according to my sources, Doctor Drummond is now the main Person of Interest,' I said. 'And if you knew her at all you would be aware that she could not possibly have killed Amy Morrison.'

He sucked on his pipe and assumed a professorial mode. 'Can one ever really tell what another human being is capable of?'

'I suppose not, but—'

'Don't the neighbours, or the friends or families, always say that it's impossible to believe when their son or uncle or work colleague is carted off to the police station and charged with murder? *He was*

*so quiet. Always had a smile for you. Drove old ladies to church
. . .* You know the kind of thing.'

Just what Garside had said. 'Helena didn't take old ladies to
church, or anywhere else,' I said. 'But I would stake my life on her
not being a stone-cold killer.'

'Hmmm . . .' Lewis picked up a box of matches 'So what information are you hoping to get from me?' He tapped the upside-down
bowl of his pipe with the matchbox until various bits of dried-up
tobacco fell out of it, then found a waterproof packet from some
inner recess of his clothing and unwrapped it. A rich smell of
oranges, nuts and sherry flavoured the air above his desk as he
stuffed tobacco into his pipe.

'Were you aware of anyone at all who might wish Amy Morrison
ill?'

Again he sighed. '*Nil nisi bonum* and all that, but there's no
denying that Amy was a difficult woman. I should imagine that she
alienated quite a lot of those with whom she came into contact. My
assistant, for example. Miranda. Couldn't stand the sight of her.
She'd hide in the stationery closet whenever she knew Amy was
expected.'

'What did Amy do to her?'

'For starters, she behaved as though Miranda were an incompetent
flunkey, whose role in the company was to wait on Amy hand and
foot, with a large dose of brown-nosing thrown in. I can tell you
Miranda didn't take at all kindly to it, refused to play ball. Amy
even tried to get her sacked for insubordination. Miranda took a
first at Oxford and is one of our key staff members. Naturally we
refused.' He shook his head. 'Quite extraordinary.'

'Was there a husband?' I tried not to cough as Lewis set a match
to the tobacco, sending a plume of scented smoke puffing to the
ceiling and swirling round his office.

'Indeed there was. Mark . . . but he's only the current one.' Lewis
brushed at the burning shreds of loose tobacco which had fallen
from the bowl of his pipe and were now smouldering gently on his
waistcoat.

'Mark?'

'Sheridan, son of General Sheridan who played a big part in the
Kosovo conflict.'

'Any idea where I might find him?'

'If he's got any sense, he'll still be occupying the marital home. I've no idea how Amy planned to dispose of her assets, whether she'd even made a Will, but he would certainly be in the running. She wasn't a pet lover, so unlikely to have left the lot to some animal charity. And if she has any other family, we have no idea who or where they are.'

'What about previous husbands?'

'Before Mark was Jason, a body-builder and judo expert – Fourth Dan or something – she met at her gym. And the first one, Seamus, was a handsome brute from County Cork, who enjoyed beating her up when he'd drink taken. I'm extrapolating a bit, you understand. I only ever met Mark.'

'What did he do?'

'Worked at the local supermarket, I believe.'

'Were these happy marriages?'

'God, no. Violent, vicious and tear-filled, as far as I could make out. Amy was always partial to what my mother would have called "a bit of rough". Sometimes she came in to the office in sunglasses to hide a nice shiner.'

'Why on earth would she want to marry men like that?'

He leaned back and steepled his fingertips across his chest. 'The in-house theory was that Amy was too moral for her own good.'

'*Moral*? Can you clarify that?'

'Selfish though she was, somewhere deep down she felt that having slept with them, she had to make honest men of them. I don't think they quite realized what was happening until they found themselves saying "I do" at the nearest registry office. Some of us went to her last wedding and the thing that struck us most was the piteous look of bewilderment on poor Mark's face.' Puff, puff . . . 'It really was rather comic.'

'Would any of them be likely to come and smash her head in?' I asked. 'Were there grudges held? Vows of vengeance? Threats uttered?'

'I never heard of any.' Lewis puffed thoughtfully at his pipe. 'But given what might be deemed their anti-social tendencies, I should imagine any of them might be capable of it – certainly the first two – though I only have this from Amy herself. On the other hand they're all – how shall I put this? – simple men. Hollow between the ears. I can't really see them planning to bump Amy off, in the sense that I can't imagine them organizing anything as sophisticated as following their former wife in order to kill her in someone else's house. Why not do it in the comfort of their own home? Spur of the moment men, all three of them. Or so I gathered, from the things Amy let drop.'

'So they weren't marriages of true minds?'

'True bodies, possibly, but minds? Absolutely not.'

I hastily repressed an unbidden image of Amy wrestling sweatily with one or other of her husbands, sheets tangling under their bodies, grunts of pleasure or squeals of orgasmic delight. I wondered if the neighbours on either side of Helena's house had heard anything the night Amy was killed and reflected that, by now, the police would surely have made enquiries, and in any case, the Forensic Scenes Investigators would have picked up any remnants of sexual activity and been able to extract DNA from the bed linen. There would have been various body hairs: pubic, facial, head. Not to mention semen or vaginal secretions, saliva, skin traces . . . it must all be there.

'Strange, for such a scholarly woman,' I said.

'And she *was* scholarly, no question about it. The Masaccio book is a masterpiece of meticulous research.'

'You'd think she'd go for someone of her own calibre.'

'You would, wouldn't you?' A flame shot out of the pipe bowl, causing Lewis to start back, and scattering red-hot debris over the papers on his desk. 'Damn thing,' he said.

'Did you like Ms Morrison?' I asked.

'Like Miranda, I couldn't bear the woman. Arrogant, ill-mannered, conceited. A frightful snob – though God knows she had nothing to be snobbish about, except possibly academically – and extremely unpleasant with it.'

'When you say she had nothing to be snobbish about, what exactly do you mean?'

'She never talked about it, but I understood that her origins were . . . uh . . . not of the highest.' Lewis looked furtively from side to side as though worried there might be a member of the PC brigade lurking in the corner.

'Where did you understand that from?'

'I'm not quite sure.' He pondered. 'Something we picked up from somewhere, but I couldn't tell you from where.'

'Is that why she was attracted to these rough types, do you think?
A return to her roots?'

'You could be right.'

'Is it possible that someone from her earlier days might have
held a murderous grudge?'

'My dear Miss Quick, *anything's* possible.'

Of course he was right: anything *was* possible. But you couldn't
include the entire human race in your list of suspects. You had to
narrow things down a bit.

'What about that Graziella Montenegro?'

'Terrifying woman. Eats iron bars as an *hors d'oeuvre*, along
with a litre of whisky – or so I've been told on the most reliable
authority.'

'What does she do?'

'She's a journalist. A critic, too. Works for some arty Italian magazine. As far as I can tell, she's in love with Amy. Or was, of course.'

I looked at the view from a fine floor-to-ceiling window of a
bare-branched lime tree and the backs of houses, and then more
closely at the book-crowded shelving which took up two sides of
the room. There were at least a dozen books I would love to own.
Did I dare ask for one?

Helena would have done.

I was about to open my mouth when Lewis's phone rang. 'Good
morning,' he said courteously. 'Oh, it's you, Miranda. The who?
. . . What do they want? . . . Oh, I suppose it was to be expected.
Send them up.'

Replacing the receiver, he said, 'I'm afraid you'll have to leave.
That was my assistant, informing me that the police are on their
way here to question me with regard to Amy, though I don't know
how I can be of help to them.'

'You've certainly been of help to me.' I said, getting out of my
chair.

He rose too. 'Good luck with the search for your collaborator.
And of course, if I hear anything that might be germane, I'll pass
it on.'

'Thank you.'

As I reached the door, he called, 'I agree with you . . . I cannot
see Doctor Drummond as a murderer, however provoked she might
have been.'

I trod cautiously down the slippery brown-linoleumed stairs, passing open offices where people were variously staring dispiritedly at computer screens, drinking coffee, or talking on the phone. At one of the open doors, a woman waited. A strangely glamorous lady, in spiky heels and a figure-hugging dress of navy jersey, with a brilliant scarf tied loosely round the shoulders. She seemed somewhat out of place in this benignly seedy location.

'Hi,' she said. 'I'm Miranda Railton, Don's assistant. Any luck in your quest?'

'Depends how you define luck.' I wondered what she thought I was trying to find. And why she was interested in the result. 'But not much, unfortunately.'

'We were all very shocked to hear about Amy,' she said. 'You wouldn't wish something like that on your worst enemy, would you?' Her brilliant smile was completely at odds with her words.

'Not really.'

'I expect Don told you about Amy's recent husbands, didn't he?'

'Recent?'

'He doesn't always mention the first one. A rich old American she came on to at age seventeen or so, who took her off to New York. She was with him for quite a long time. Until he died, actually. Now it's her turn. So sad, isn't it?' She smiled at me again. 'You were the one who discovered her, weren't you?'

'Unfortunately, yes.'

She switched off the smile. 'I wish it had been me,' she said.

Not a lot I could say to that.

Armed with the address, Amy's house had not been difficult to find. I came up out of the Underground at Highbury & Islington tube station, consulting my A–Z as I went, fetching up eventually in front of a handsome little terraced house. The woodwork had all been freshly painted white. The navy-blue front door was decorated with shiny brass door furniture. An ornamental bay tree stood to one side of the entrance in a square lead pot and the small front garden held a smartly trimmed design of low box hedges. But there were signs of recent neglect. The curtains in the front window had been carelessly pulled half-open, dead leaves clogged the roots of the box hedges, and were lined up along the path. If the latest husband stood to inherit this, he was sitting pretty.

And it went without saying that he had a fine motive for eliminating his wife.

Standing under a small trellised porch, which in the spring would have a clematis (now badly in need of cutting back) covering it, I could see into the front room. On a sofa covered in old-rose linen piped in white, a man was sitting with his head buried in his hands. Was this Mark, the current husband? Or a candidate for a future one? I rat-tat-tatted at the door.

The man who opened it was in need of a shave and probably had been for several days. His eyes were red-rimmed, and although his sweater was cashmere, it was stained with what looked like HP sauce. He was barefoot and had a can of beer in his hand. 'Yeah?' he said. He was obviously drunk but it was clear that he was undeniably a bit of a hunk.

'I'm sorry for your loss,' I said formally.

'Fuck my loss. What are you, someone from the church round the corner?' He burped slightly. 'Sorry but we don't attend, don't believe in all that crap about God. You've come to the wrong place, lady, and I—'

'If you'd let me explain,' I said.

'Explain what?'

'Your wife – your former wife, that is – was killed in my friend's house, and they think she did it.'

'And did she?' He swayed slightly, clutching at the edge of the door.

'No. And I'm trying to prove it.'

'So you've come round here to try and pin it on me, right?' He sounded so aggressive that I took a step backwards. Yet he spoke with an educated upper-class accent that was strangely at odds with his appearance and behaviour.

'Not in the least.' It seemed a bit pointless to carry on this conversation. Nonetheless, I continued. 'I was hoping you could give me some clue as to who might have been responsible, that's all.'

'Other than your friend, you mean?'

'That's right.'

'Are you from the fuzz?'

I had a nano-second to decide whether to lie or not. I opted for the truth, but only because I figured he would be more receptive. 'If you mean the police, the answer's no.' Close to, I could see that he was nearer thirty than twenty. But still at least ten years younger than his deceased spouse.

He stayed irresolute at the open door, then stood aside. 'You'd better come in.'

I walked into a shiny hall painted a very pale pink. There were Victorian tiles on the floor and many gold-framed mirrors on the walls. An elaborate florist's arrangement of half-dead pink roses and white carnations stood on a gilded shelf. The house smelled of some expensive air freshener and stale beer.

'I'm Mark Sheridan, by the way,' he threw over his shoulder. 'Or the late Mr Amy Morrison, if you prefer.' He sounded like the stuff he was drinking: bitter.

I wanted to say that I thought he was a brave man, to have married Amy, but decided this was not the ideal moment. I followed him into a sitting room with more pink paper on the walls, and facing each other on either side of a fireplace, two of the linen-covered, white-piped sofas, one of which I'd seen from outside. A wall had at some time been knocked down since the room stretched from the front of the house to the back. French windows gave onto a walled garden full of shrubs and flowerbeds, all in winter mode. A silver birch hung gracefully over a white-painted garden bench set against the far wall, and a small fountain featuring a nymph of some kind stood nearby.

It was an attractive and charming room, rather let down by the beer cans stacked on the coffee table, the pizza boxes in the empty fireplace, the newspapers strewn over the expensive oriental rugs, and the pervasive stench of feet. An antique side table held a collection of small boxes: hand-painted Russian *palekhs*, elaborately carved wooden stamp-boxes, enamel snuff-boxes, silver ones, from elaborately chased to a plain modern square. An antique Delft plate was hanging on the wall. Books were stacked in the bookshelves built into the alcoves on either side of the fireplace. Some of them were leather-bound . . . I recognized one as being an edition of Amy's Masaccio book, produced by a firm which specialized in presentation copies. An identically bound book sat on my own shelves.

'You must be devastated,' I said, sitting down and watching while he got himself another beer and opened it, having waved it at me in a do-you-want-one gesture.

'What about?'

'Well . . . losing your wife.'

'Woman was a complete fucking bitch,' hc said. He raised the beer can. 'Three cheers for whoever did the dirty on her, saved me the trouble, because I sure as hell would have done her in myself, sooner or later.'

'The word on the street is that you'd left her some weeks ago.'

He stared at me. 'Where'd you hear that from?'

I shrugged. 'Here and there.'

'Yes, well, I came back, didn't I?'

In time to claim your inheritance? I wondered. 'Why was that?'

'It was here or my parents'. Didn't fancy the latter, the constant nagging on about getting a proper job and all that baloney. General Sheridan does not take kindly to a wastrel son, no siree.' He was trying to feign insouciance and not doing a very good job of it.

I was getting a strong message, whether it was intended or not, about Mark's background, and it wasn't the usual one for casual labour, apart from the holiday jobbers and the work experience brigade. 'I'm assuming you have an alibi for the time of your wife's murder,' I said.

He laughed, showing well-tended middle-class teeth. 'And if you're not the cops, what right do you have to be questioning me?'

'Good point.'

I had no right whatsoever. Not for the first time, I devoutly wished that I hadn't turned in my badge when I 'retired' from the police force. I now spent my life looking at pictures, examining their artistic integrity, teasing out the innuendoes they presented to their audiences and then weaving text about them. I was good at it. But I had been equally good at my job as a detective. And in many ways, the two of them were similar, needing persistence, expertise and, above all, an eye for detail. 'And if my friend hadn't gone missing, I wouldn't be here at all.'

'Do you realize I don't even know who you are?'

'Quick,' I said. 'Alex Quick.'

His face changed. 'And your friend's name?'

'Doctor Helena Drummond.'

'Oh my God! *Baby, Baby,*' he said. For a confused moment I thought he was coming on to me, until he continued: '*Watch This Space.*' He swept a hand around at the untidy room. 'If I'd known

I was going to be so honoured, I'd have made a bit of an effort to tidy up.'

'How do you know about my books?'

'Doesn't everybody?'

'I thought you stacked shelves in the supermarket. Though,' I added hastily, not wanting to be accused of elitism, 'there's no reason why shelf-stackers shouldn't look at arty books, is there?'

'Yeah, well . . . a person has his pride. I'm not into being a kept man, but an art history degree doesn't really qualify you for much.'

Which explained how he had recognized my name. Mystery solved. At least, a tiny portion of it, though by no means the whole. 'So, Mr Mark Sheridan, can you think of any reason why anyone would brutally attack your wife?'

'Scores of reasons spring to mind. There can't be anyone who ever met her who liked her, but—'

'You married her,' I couldn't help pointing out.

'Yeah, well, that's another story. But I was going to say I cannot imagine anyone actually picking up a weapon and smashing in her skull. Not anyone I know, that is.'

'Have you ever attacked her?'

He stared at me incredulously. '*Me*? Hit a *woman*?' The General would have been proud.

'So that's a no.'

'Of course it is.'

'Maybe it all comes down to motive.'

'Ah well: motive. Of course the police are going to see me as a prime suspect, since I stand to inherit all this.' His hand swept around the room. 'Or so Amy led me to believe. But that might have been just another of her lies. And quite frankly, I don't really want to live here. It's not my scene. Snooty neighbours, always whingeing on about something or other, trying to get you to sign some poncey petition or join one of their do-gooding charities or run a fucking marathon for Jesus. It's as bad as living back at bloody Broadlands.'

'Broadlands?'

'Oh . . .' He seemed embarrassed. 'My parents' place.' Any signs that he had drunk too much had completely evaporated.

I'd seen it before, a public-school-type trying to give himself a bit of street cred by pretending that he came from some inner-city sink estate. I gave myself a mental shake. 'We're getting off the subject,' I said.

'The subject being . . .?'

'Do you have an alibi for the night your wife was murdered?'

'Last Monday, right?'

'Right.'

'I absolutely cannot see what concern it is of yours, but yes, I do. Actually.' There was a pause.

I said, 'Are you going to tell me?'

Another pause.

'Look,' I said. 'My only concern is to establish the innocence of Doctor Drummond. I don't really care if you were shagging half the sheep in Scotland or robbing the Bank of England. I'm not concerned about motive here. All I need to know is who *did* kill Amy Morrison, since it sure as hell wasn't Doctor Drummond, and if it wasn't you either, then I can cross you off my list.'

He held up his hands, palms towards me. 'Okay, okay.' Looking thoroughly miserable at having to admit to taking part in such a middle-class activity, he said, 'I was skiing with my parents and sister. At Val d'Isère. We go every year, rent a chalet, have a ball.'

'Leaving your wife behind?'

'Obviously. Or she wouldn't have been getting herself murdered near Canterbury, would she? No, Amy didn't go in for outdoor sports.'

'And she was happy to let you go without her?'

'Completely. Apart from anything else, it meant she wouldn't have to flirt with my father.'

'So that lets you off the hook.' I stood up. 'Just as a matter of interest, how did you come to team up with Amy? You don't seem to be kindred spirits.'

'I'm not absolutely sure, to tell the truth. One moment I was stuffing packets of Pampers on to shelves at the supermarket, the next I was in bed with this customer, enjoying the best shag of my life.'

A dagger of pure physical jealousy stabbed me. Why couldn't I be more predatory, less choosy? Was I old enough, at nearly thirty-four, to be labelled a cougar, and if so, should I be acting accordingly? I told myself I had too much self-respect . . . but there was no question that I sometimes wished I didn't. The Maiden Aunt, that was me. Almost the Virgin Aunt.

'And getting married? Seems a bit of a leap from one to the other.'

'My father, the General, always calls me a wimp, and I guess he's right. I was swept off my feet, to be honest. Carried away by the sheer strength of Amy's determination.'

I raised my eyebrows.

'I'm not proud of myself, believe me. And let me say, here and now and forcefully, I'm really sorry about what's happened. I didn't love Amy but I wouldn't have wished such a death on her. On anyone.'

'I believe she might have been in Doctor Drummond's house with another man.'

'I'm not surprised. She wasn't looking for love, poor woman. She was looking to *be* loved. And I'm afraid that for a number of reasons, she wasn't very loveable.' He swallowed. 'Poor Amy.'

'Do you know anything about her background?'

'Nothing at all. I know she had been married two or three times before, but I don't know who to. She never spoke about her previous husbands. Though I wouldn't have put it past her to be seeing one – or all – on the sly.'

'So none of this cleaving only to him sort of stuff,' I said.

'Fidelity wasn't in her vocabulary,' Mark said. 'It was sex she was after. The rougher the better. And because that's not my scene, I'm afraid I was already scheduled for the chop.' He drew his hand across his neck in a throat-cutting gesture.

'How do you mean?' Was a possible motive rearing its ugly head? On the other hand, if he was skiing with his family, it would have been practically impossible for him to be Amy's killer.

'I'm not into the kind of depraved stuff she enjoyed. I don't mind admitting I'm not a super-stud. I know I didn't satisfy her. *Couldn't.* So every time we got it together, I could hear the sound of the tumbrils, the rustle of divorce papers. It was only a matter of time.'

'You might have got a substantial pay-off.'

'Indeed I might. And had I done so, I can tell you it would all have gone to help abandoned children in Guatemala. There is so much poverty and corruption out there, successive governments totally uninterested in the social difficulties. Thousands of kids live in slums where there's no running water, no medical help, no education.' He drew a deep breath in through his nose. 'I'm planning to go out there in the next three or four weeks. Try to tackle some of the problems. Even the slightest help must be better than no help at all, right?'

'Right.' I got up. Stepped between the beer cans and over the strewn newspapers. 'Would you allow me to have a quick glance round your wife's office?'

'Go ahead, be my guest.' He waved at the hall. 'Up the stairs and turn left, last door you come to.'

'I assume the police have already been here.'

'Yes. They took away her computer, but otherwise, it's more or less as she left it.'

I went upstairs. All five doors leading off the small square landing were open. I could see into what was evidently a guest room, with a rumpled single bed and a pile of clothes lying in a heap on the floor. I deduced that this was where the bereaved husband was now sleeping, especially as the next room contained what must have been the former marital bed, neatly made and untouched. I poked my head in, walked quietly across to a series of built-in wardrobes. Good clothes, carefully arranged. Shelves containing shoes, expensive leather handbags, hats, folded silk scarves, cashmere cardigans and sweaters. I stepped back into the passage. A bathroom came next, then a separate WC, and at the end, Amy's office.

A complete contrast to my own, Amy's was meticulously ordered. Art books on the shelves, precisely aligned, instead of being randomly returned after consultation of their contents. A printer swathed in a plastic cover with a neatly lidded box of paper beside it. A bright red filing cabinet, all the drawers closed, unlike mine where the drawers were often only half pushed in. With the absence of her computer, the room conveyed the impression that this was not a workspace at all but a Hollywood mock-up of what an office ought to look like. I could see nothing that might direct me either to her killer or to the whereabouts of Helena. I quietly opened a drawer or two but the contents were in apple-pie order, almost as if she did her real work somewhere else and this was just a showroom.

I returned to the hallway. Mark Sheridan was still sitting on the pink sofa. 'Thank you for your time, Mr Sheridan,' I called. 'And good luck with your enterprises.'

He got up, a trifle unsteadily. He smiled at me, and I knew that if I passed him in the supermarket with his cartons of crunchy peanut butter or boxes of vegetables, I too might have been tempted to drag him home with me, along with the groceries.

At the front door, I turned. 'Which gym did Amy go to?'

'Bodyshapers. I think it's somewhere in the Essex Road.'

NINE

Bodyshapers was a ten-minute walk from Amy Morrison's house. It advertised itself with a flashing set of neon stick-people doing press-ups. From the outside, it looked very upmarket, despite the tattoo parlour next door and the Burger King two doors down. Three or four yummy mummies in pink tights and pink-and-white trainers, wet hair pulled back into pink scrunchies, were coming out when I appeared, talking volubly in little-girl voices. They didn't hold the door for me.

'Thank you, ladies,' I said, as I pushed open the heavy glass doors and was met by the same old smell I was so familiar with from the gym I no longer attended: elderly coconut matting, rubber shoes, sweat and testosterone.

An ant-like creature in a pink workout suit with *bodyshapers* embroidered above her heart sat behind a desk, painting her nails a sparkly shade of green. Christmas was coming, but the glitter in it added very little to the imminent festivities. She looked up, displaying a complexion so perfect that I wanted to tear it off her and slap it onto my own face. 'Can I help?' she asked. The planes of her insectoid features moved gently as she spoke.

'I'm looking for Jason,' I said.

'Which one? We have three working here.'

'Did one of them recently . . . was one of them married to a woman who's . . . uh . . . just been murdered?' The question was a bit direct, but I couldn't figure out how else to put it.

It didn't seem to faze her. 'That would be Jason P,' she said, adopting an Oh-poor-poor-Jason expression. If she had possessed antennae, at this point they would have waved in a commiserating manner.

'And where would I find Jason P?'

'He'll be in the judoka.' Keeping an anxious eye on the fresh nail polish, she pointed greenly to a swing door from behind which came muted voices mingled with sudden cries and muffled grunts. I pushed open this second set of doors and the gym scent intensified. Someone raised interrogative eyebrows at me and I asked for the judo room. I was offered another pointed finger, and found myself passing a bunch of sweaty guys groaning as they raised huge metal circles set on iron bars, or lay on plastic-covered benches pushing weights above their heads with grotesquely muscled arms. The stench of effort was almost overpowering.

A man-tub rolled in my direction. He was shorter than me, but probably twice as wide. Solid muscle, including his shaven head, parcelled in coffee-coloured skin. He wore a judoga loosely tied round the middle with a black belt, displaying his massive barrel chest. 'Hello there, little lady,' he said winningly, showing a lot of perfect teeth. He sounded American.

He was never going to win me, or any right-minded woman, with that chest buffed with baby oil and on plentiful display, but hey, you have to keep on trying, don't you?

'Hello, there, little man,' I said. He must have been carrying several hundredweight of steel in the form of body piercings, most of it on his face. I wondered if I was still skilful enough to throw him.

He stopped smiling. 'And what can I do for you?'

Lose the soul patch and the lost-tribe-of-Africa plug set into the left earlobe, for starters, I thought. 'Are you Jason P?' I asked.

'Yep.'

'I wanted to ask you about Amy Morrison.'

'And you are what?'

There were a number of answers I could give. I settled for a lie. 'I'm investigating her death,' I said, hoping he would leave it at that.

'I don't see how I can help,' he said.

'You were married to her, weren't you?'

'Back in the day, yeah. But that was like, years ago. Four, at least.'

'Did you like her?'

'I married her, didn't I?' He gave a snorting kind of laugh which set veins crawling on his arms like demented worms. 'Mind you, both of us were stoned out of our skulls at the time. But to answer your question, no, I didn't like her much. Reason being, she wasn't very likeable. But there were no hard feelings on either side, far as I could tell. I mean, c'mon, life's a narrative, a series of encounters, isn't it? You stop for a while, you move on, you continue the journey, am I right?'

'Absolutely. You from California?'

'No, New York. Why?'

The pseudo New Age jargon had alerted me. Wrongly, as it turned out. 'Just wondered. Look, can you think of anyone who disliked her enough to want to kill her?'

He pressed his mouth into a downward-turning grimace, hiding his over-white teeth, for which I was grateful since I'd been contemplating retrieving my sunglasses from my bag. 'Pretty extreme, huh? I mean, murder? Just because she wasn't very nice? No, I don't think so. You need a lot more than that. Murder? Eeugh!' A thought seemed to strike him. 'Hey, I hope to God you're not looking at me for it.' The veins writhed again. 'If so, look away. You came to the wrong place, lady. Me kill someone? I can't bear the sight of blood. As for Amy, from what I read about her death in the papers, I'd say she just got unlucky with her latest stud.'

'You think?'

'The woman is – *was* insatiable. I mean, on a good day I'm quite a swordsman, not bad in the sack, know what I mean? But whoa, no way could I keep up with Amy. No *way*. Never thought I'd find myself saying this, but like, there's more to life than a good fuck, am I right?'

'Probably.' It was a long time since I'd had a good fuck, or even a bad one. 'She did manage to hold down some kind of a day job, *and* to write a scholarly treatise on a lesser-known eighteenth-century painter,' I said.

He tapped the side of his nose. 'So she did,' he said. 'So she did. In any case, I've remarried, got a little boy and another kid on the way. No reason to waste time on Ms Morrison. Let alone whack her.'

'Any idea what inspired her to choose Masaccio?'

'What the hell's that? Some kind of hair product?'

'He's the painter I just mentioned. So did she talk to you about him at all? Show you pictures? Did the two of you travel to Italy together?'

'Look, lady, like I said, at the end of a working day, we'd tumble into bed and start on a working night. If you take my meaning?' He winked lasciviously. Ran a pink tongue across his upper lip. I wanted to slap him.

'Hey Jason . . . what gives?' Some straining youth in a sweat-stained vest was trying to turn his head in Jason's direction without dropping a bar and crushing his chest.

'Gotta go.' Jason stuck out his hand and I automatically took it, immediately afterwards wishing I hadn't since it was slippery with sweat. I was waiting for the inevitable I'm-stronger-than-you-are tough-guy grip but it didn't arrive. He was never going to float my boat, but I decided I'd been too hasty in my estimate of Jason P. Despite the soul patch, he seemed a pleasant guy, who'd probably deserved better than Amy Morrison.

'One last question – and please don't think I'm being insulting – but did you, you know, gain anything from the divorce?'

'Not a dime.'

'Was that because she wouldn't pay out?'

'Sorry, lady, you got it wrong. It was because *I* wouldn't. Didn't want her cash. Didn't want nothing more to do with her. If ever anyone needed help . . .' Shaking his head he turned and strutted over to the guy working on his bench-presses, pausing to murmur encouragement to a guy doing crunches and perspiring heavily. Watching Jason's retreating back, I realized the strut was due to the gross over-development of his quads.

Just Amy's type, I figured.

With one more husband to go, I stopped at a tacky pub and ordered a half-pint of shandy. Questioning suspects was thirsty work. Besides, I needed time to mull over the information I had acquired so far. Assess what I knew now that I hadn't known before. Which was minimal. At least I had a preliminary list of suspects, which included just about anyone who had ever come across her. Because the main theme of what I'd learned was Amy's unpleasant character. On the other hand, as Jason P had just pointed out, you'd have to be pretty riled up to kill someone just because they were not hugely . . . well, I was always steered away from the word at school, but . . . *nice*.

So what next? Motive, I guessed. Find the motive, they taught me on my fast-track course, and you find the man. Or woman. In my head, I ran through what are generally accepted as the main motivations for murder: fear, jealousy, gain, revenge and protection of someone you love. Of the five, I could imagine all but the last being relevant in the Morrison case. The last? By all accounts, the only person Amy had loved was Amy.

I still wanted to visit Husband Number One – or possibly Number Two, if Miranda at Amy's publisher was right – but I could already tell that expecting him to give me any clues that would help me find Helena was a pretty forlorn hope. Looking down at the bubbles in my half-pint glass, I thought about my missing friend. I fully accepted that I'd been wrong about Jason P. Maybe I was also wrong about her. Maybe she really was responsible for killing Amy.

I pictured the scene. She comes home after the night out with friends, tired, ready to hit the hay, probably after a glass or two more than advisable, finds Amy there, not just *there*, but actually in her bed, getting it on with yet another of the guys she seemed to favour. I could easily envisage the main components: Helena shouting *What the bloody hell do you think you're doing?*, Amy trying to cover herself, the bloke sitting up in bed saying nothing, Helena picking up a weapon and— And what? I couldn't see any further.

Which reminded me. I took out my mobile and pressed in the numbers for Fliss Fairlight. At the station, they told me she wasn't available. I rang her home number, and this time got her.

'Yes?'

'It's me.'

'Oh.' A cautious pause. 'Which *me* exactly?'

'Quick. Look, Fliss, regarding the Amy Morrison murder, I haven't seen or heard anything about a weapon.'

'That's mostly because we haven't found one.'

'So what's the preliminary supposition?'

'The ME is thinking something flat-headed. A big hammer, some kind of mallet, along those lines.'

'Are we assuming the perp brought the weapon with him?'

'We're looking at the possibility, yes.'

'Kind of awkward to carry around with him. Lots of questions there. Amy might have wondered if he'd started following her into Helena's house carrying a croquet mallet.'

'I never said it was a croquet mallet, you dweeb. There are dozens of different kinds of flat-headed implements which could have been used to kill her.'

'And Inspector Garside and his team haven't found anything?'

'Not yet.'

'Questions, questions. Are we supposing the killer wasn't her boyfriend? And if not, who would have known that Amy would be at Doctor Drummond's house that evening? And was it Amy they were after, or Helena? And since Helena was out all evening, how the heck did Amy get into the house in the first place?'

'They haven't worked any of that out yet.'

'Perhaps the killer had been stalking her.'

'Or stalking Doctor Drummond. And in the circumstances, would even Amy seriously have slept with this notional pick-up? There were no signs of forcible sex.'

'Okay. Another theory bites the dust.'

'But there *were* signs of consensual sex.'

'Aha. So it looks either as though she knew the killer, or arrived with the killer, or fancied the killer even though she didn't know him.'

'Doesn't it just?'

'And why do the police think Helena was responsible? What do they consider her motive to be?'

'They haven't got that far yet either, far as I can tell.'

'Thanks, Fliss.'

'My pleasure, Quick.'

Switching off, it occurred to me that Amy might have found it exciting to have sex with a complete stranger. That the thrill would far outweigh the possible danger – though it was unlikely that she would have anticipated being bashed to death after a bit of fooling around. Which led me to wonder whether male spiders are aware that they'll be eaten by their mates after copulation. Is the knowledge typed into their genes, and if so, is the sex urge strong enough to overcome it? In a reversion of roles, is that what happened to Amy?

I forced myself to concentrate. Was I wasting my time, talking to people who knew Amy in the hope of finding someone who wasn't Helena but might possibly have killed her? Maybe so, but it was better than sitting doing nothing, since I had no idea where Helena might have gone. Or what would have induced her to flee. If she had.

So rethink the scenario. Helena arrives home, finds Amy screwing some anonymous male in her bed, gets mad, picks up weapon (lamp, candlestick, croquet mallet – yeah, right, lots of those strewn about her house – chair, knobkerrie, or whatever) and brings it crashing down on Amy's head. Anonymous male grabs his Y-fronts and high-tails it down the stairs and out the door, and vanishes into the night, leaving Helena herself to vanish, none knew whither.

Or she comes home to find Amy already dead on the bed – in which case she'd certainly have called the cops. Or she finds the murder still taking place? Same thing: she'd have called the police. And then me. Which would indicate that there had not been a corpse lying on her bed when she returned to her house the previous night. If she did.

But carrying on the notion of this corpse in her bed, in what situation would she *not* call the police? If she had recognized the killer? And where would she go, in such circumstances? Where *could* she go? Melbourne, where she might find temporary safe harbour as a familiar Visiting Fellow? Scotland? Paris or Rome or Madrid? But the police would be on to her eventually. And she couldn't keep hiding, moving on, setting up new identities, let alone maintaining the old one. I looked bleakly into a professional future which did not include Helena.

But the alternative scenario kept intruding. The one where Helena was being kept somewhere against her will.

If only I had the slightest idea where to start looking for her.

TEN

'**M**y problem is that I'm not ambitious,' Sam Willoughby told me. 'At least, I am, but not in the hierarchical sense of climbing ladders to the top, or beating out the competition, or stepping on the shoulders of others to achieve my aims.'

'You mean that your ambitions are small.' We were sitting at one of the café tables Sam had recently installed in a corner of his bookshop, thick white mugs in front of us. His contained a caffe latte, mine held the nursery comfort of a hot chocolate sprinkled with cinnamon.

'Precisely. I want to keep on selling books, and naturally I want the business to do well, but I don't feel any urge to, for instance, found a whole chain of bookshops across the country. And I like living where I am. After ten years in London, working in an insurance company, taking the Tube in and out from Queen's Park every day, battling the crowds and the traffic and the noise, I favour a quiet life.'

'Mmm . . .' I said encouragingly. To a large extent, I agreed.

'See, I don't even watch TV. I much prefer a good book. Or even a bad one, if it comes to that.'

'I'm with you on that one,' I said. 'Most of the stuff on TV is total bollocks.'

'And call me naïve, but I truly believe that most people would prefer a proper book as opposed to an eBook.' He laughed. 'Sometimes I think I'm a poster-boy for dull.'

'You don't look dull down at the gym,' I said. 'Or didn't, when I used to go.' I remembered his biceps glistening with sweat, and the way his thick blond hair flopped over his forehead when he was on the running machine.

'But I have to face it, selling books is kind of wimpish. I mean, how many macho rugby players or transatlantic oarsmen are booksellers?'

'This may well be true.'

'*On* the other hand, how many booksellers are – like me – crack shots and can (with difficulty) bench-press their own weight for ten reps?'

'Very very few, I should imagine.'

He laughed again. 'And as my old granny used to say, my sweaters are always cashmere, which has to count for something.'

'Can't go wrong with a nice bit of cashm—' I am not the sort of woman who breaks down in tears at the slightest excuse, but to my embarrassment, my throat thickened and my eyes welled up. I'd heard Helena saying the exact same thing only a short while ago.

'Want to talk about it?' Sam said gently, passing me a clean handkerchief. 'But not if you don't want to, of course.'

I did. I explained about finding the body, about Helena's disappearance, about my concerns for her. How little she had given away about herself. I snorted and snuffled into Sam's handkerchief. 'And on top of everything else, the police are after her, too.'

'You're sure she's . . . well, that she's not . . .'

'Dead?' I said, brutal because the thought that she might be was so appalling. 'No, I'm *not* sure. Which is why I'm so worried about her.'

'Tell me what you know about her.'

I did. It took all of forty seconds.

'Melbourne, eh?' Sam said, nodding.

'That's right.'

'And the academic books she's written, of course. Plus the anthologies she's done with you.'

'Yes, but that doesn't tell me a lot about her personal life. I can't imagine how we could have worked so closely together and the only interesting detail I'd gleaned was that she'd been married twice. One of her husband's being Ainslie Gordon!'

'The artist?'

I nodded.

'That's amazing.'

'But I only discovered this in the last couple of days. From a colleague at the uni. She didn't tell me herself, even though I'd said several times how much I liked his work.' How safe and ordered my life had seemed prior to Amy being discovered dead in Helena's bed. Would it ever be again?

'How are you getting on with your search for her?'

I spread my hands. 'I'm not. I'm trying to come at it from the other end . . . find someone who really had a reason to kill Ms Morrison, or even find the person who did kill her, and then Helena will be exonerated and can come out of hiding – if hiding is what she's doing.'

'And how's *that* going?'

'I keep hitting complete dead-ends. Of course, people could be lying – some of them probably are – but so far I haven't found anything. I need to hire a private detective, I think.'

'If there's any way I can help.' He hesitated. Flushed slightly. Tugged at an earlobe.

'What?' I said.

'Well, I do harbour a secret dream, though I've never allowed it to drift any further than the doorway into my brain.'

'Come on, then. Spill the beans.' I hoped he wasn't going to confess to some perverted desire or habit. Something I might feel I should report to the police.

He made an embarrassed face. 'It's too *Boys' Own*. Too unlikely of fulfilment.'

'Go *on*. Tell me.'

'Sam Willoughby, Private Eye. Sam Willoughby, Master Spy. That's what I'd really like to be,' he said in a rush. Then laughed self-consciously, trying to make it sound of no great concern. 'Can you see it?'

As a matter of fact, I almost could. The trench coat, the fedora, the safe houses and the letter-drops, the lean body and the honed mind, eyes flicking hither and yon, picking up the tiniest clues, constantly on the alert for threat and menace, taking out assassins, shaking off villainous pursuit, chosen for the most hazardous missions:'*We need you, Willoughby – your* country *needs you.*'

'Yes,' I said. 'I almo— I *can*.'

'Honestly?'

'Yes.'

'Never happen, I know that. Which doesn't stop me working out at the gym, lifting weights, pumping iron, cycling three times the equivalent of the Tour de France on the stationary bike. I've even joined a rifle club and become a crack shot.'

'This gun's for hire, sort of thing?'

'Precisely! I am *ready*!' He threw back his head and laughed again. 'Just another of my unfulfillable dreams.'

I looked at him. And smiled. Kindly. With his floppy blond hair, his specs, his diffident smile and nice face? Nah. Hard to imagine a more unlikely Sam Spade. Though on the other hand, diffidence could hide a ruthless heart, an iron will. It might be the perfect disguise. *Might* being the operative word.

'Tell me another dream.'

'Well, there's the country and western singer one.'

Lose the specs, Buddy Holly notwithstanding, and again I could just about see Sam in a tasselled sequinned shirt, Cuban-heeled cowboy boots and a suede ten-gallon hat, two back-up singers swaying and crooning behind him into a shared mike, lost loves and wayward women, crowds calling out for more.

'Can you play the guitar?' I said.

'I know a few chords.'

'Sing?'

He shook his head. 'Unfortunately I can't carry a tune.'

'So another dream bites the dust.'

''Fraid so.'

'But there's nothing to stop the private detective dream coming true.' I liked his self-deprecating manner. But steely-eyed or not, I'd never heard of a self-deprecating PI.

'Nothing at all.'

We smiled at each other. 'Anyway,' I said. 'I have to get going.'

Outside the shop, I turned left, towards the older part of town. The outlet next door to Sam's was a small wine shop, owned by the appropriately named Edward Vine, who was standing at the window, gazing out at the almost-empty High Street. I waved to him as I passed and saw his pleasant face light up as he waved back.

Back in my flat, I called Amy's publisher and asked to speak to Donald Lewis.

Put through to him, his voice resonated down the line, fruity as a Christmas cake. I could almost smell the brandy. 'Lewis here.'

'It's Alex Quick,' I said. 'I came to see you the other day.'

'Ah yes. In connection with the death of Amy Morrison, if I'm not mistaken.'

'That's right. At that time, you mentioned that she had had three husbands.' Four actually, but I didn't want to muddy the marital waters.

'Indeed.'

'I've spoken to two of them . . .' Both of them proving more congenial than I would have expected. '. . . but the third – Seamus, wasn't it? – I don't where to start looking for him.'

'Just a mo, I'll ask Miranda.' He put a hand over the receiver. I could hear a foggy sort of colloquy taking place. Then Lewis came back. 'Apparently he works on the cruise ships, which is where Amy met him.'

'Ships?' I said.

'Well, Miranda, who knows more about such things than I do, says that the staff on these ships are only contracted for a season at a time so they move around. If they're not taken on by one ship, they probably will be by another. She says he was on one called *L'Oriana* for a couple of seasons and then she lost touch. We're going back about seven or eight years here . . . he could be anywhere by now.'

I thought it interesting that the assistant, with her first-class degree from Oxford, knew so much about an author's husbands, but it was none of my business. 'Seamus what?' I asked.

More hand-covered mumblings. Then he returned. 'O'Donahue. That's the best we can come up with.'

'Thank you,' I said. 'You – and, of course, your assistant – have been most helpful.'

Seamus O'Donahue: he sounded like a good ol' Irish boy. I got onto my computer and Googled the name. There were dozens of them. I narrowed the search to London. There were still a lot of them. I tried P&O, but could see no way to access their personnel, though no doubt someone more tech-savvie than I was wouldn't have had a problem.

Where would you want to live if you worked on the ships? Dover? Southampton? Portsmouth? Since many of the P&O cruises departed from Southampton, I Googled the white pages. There were four O'Donahues. One was T. One was C. Two were S. I dialled the first one: no answer. I dialled the second. After some time, a woman with a thick Dublin accent answered. I could hear the screams of a baby in the background, the moronic sound of a TV, the shouts of two kids who sounded as if they were jumping over the furniture.

'I'm looking for Mr O'Donahue,' I said.

'And who would yez be?' she asked.

'It's in connection with the death of his former wife,' I said.

'There's been no former wife, not in this house there hasn't. Anyways, you'll no' be able to speak to Sean, him bein' away with the ships to Spain an' Italy an' such-like.'

'Sean? I was looking for Seamus.'

'Seamus? That'd likely be Sean's brother.' She coughed wetly. 'But he's long gone from here. Went away to London, must be more than five years now.'

'I thought he worked on the cruise ships?'

'Aye, he did so. Kevin, stop that now or I'll feckin' skin yez alive,' she shrieked, straight into my ear. 'But he decided to look for work elsewhere. Which was good for us, since he handed over his job to Sean.'

'And you don't know where he lives now?'

'I do so. Jus' let me think.' There was a longish pause while she thought. Then she said, 'Would it be some place called Bricksin?'

'Very possibly.' Did she mean Brixton?

'Or, no, tell a lie, it's Ruskin. Near a park, I'm thinking, somewhere there.'

Behind her, a child started to scream, and was immediately joined by its sibling. Before she could put down the phone, I asked swiftly, 'Where is Seamus working now?'

'That would be in the supermarket. Morrisons.' She started laughing. 'Same as that feckin' bitch the poor soul married all those years ago.' More screaming. Something fell and broke. She took a deep breath, preparatory to emitting a super-loud screech towards the culprit.

'Thank you so much,' I said, and quickly cut the call.

A search on the internet led me to a branch of Morrisons near somewhere I'd never heard of called Ruskin Park. I climbed into my car and set off for south-east London, knowing that at least there would be plenty of parking when I got there.

I found pretty much the usual supermarket layout, even though this was supposed to be a step up from your more down-market retail outlets. Fresh bread smells wafting from the bakery department. Ground coffee over by the beverages. A central pen holding a mound of melons. Christmas carols streamed gently over the intercom, interrupted now and again by staff announcements or reminders of what a bargain customers would find if they went to the ready-meal shelves.

I accosted a young guy dragging a trolley of squashed-down cardboard cartons which had once held bottles of window-cleaning fluid. 'Excuse me,' I said, stopping in his path. 'Where can I find Seamus O'Donahue?'

He looked around, though owing to the way the shelves were placed, he can't have seen much beyond where he was standing. 'Dunno. Haven't seen him in ages.'

'Does he live far from here?' I had deliberately chosen one of the more imbecilic-looking personnel, knowing I'd have more chance of squeezing an address out of him than from one of the savvier people. Funny that out of the three, two of Amy Morrison's husbands worked in a supermarket. Should I make anything out of that or had she simply found it a fruitful cruising ground?

'Just roun' the corner, downa road,' the moron said. 'There's some modern-type town houses somewhere 'long there.'

'And he lives in one?'

Perhaps belatedly remembering he shouldn't be giving out personal details of the staff to any Tom, Quick or Harry who came asking, he shrugged but didn't speak. Which I took to mean 'yes'.

Just roun' the corner and downa road proved to be a slog across the park, round several corners and up a slight hill. But there indeed was a row of flat-faced houses with miniature railed spaces in front of them. Some contained a bush, one had a tiny windmill, three dwarfs frolicked in a third.

How to find Seamus O'Donahue? Trial and error seemed the best way. I stepped up to a door at random and rang the bell. Nobody came. I pressed again. I went down the very short path to the pavement and approached the house next door. As I raised my hand to knock, the door opened and an elderly lady came out and stood on the step.

'Can I help you?' She had a middle-European accent and hair that had recently been given a blue rinse. A little less blue and a bit more rinse would have been a good idea. Through her front window I could see three other women sitting at a table, each holding a fan of cards in their hands.

'I'm sorry to be interrupting your bridge game,' I said, indicating her three friends. 'I was looking for Seamus O'Donahue.'

'Ach, Seamus,' she said, lips curving upwards. 'Soch a sveetheart.'

'Really?' From what Donald Lewis had said, or at least implied, he was a wife-beater and a drunk.

'So kind to old ladies like me,' she went on, her accent growing stronger. '*So* kind.'

I began to wonder if she had been hitting the sherry bottle. Or I'd got the wrong Seamus. 'Where would I find him?'

'He is at nomber 154,' she said. 'Alvays these ladies are coming to wisit him. Many ladies.'

'What sort of ladies?'

'Alvays vith this yellow hair, alvays the bright colours, alvays these lovely velvet caps – berets – like in history, Good King Venceslas and so on.'

Before I could properly process the unexpected insertion into the conversation of the Saint with the heated footprints, inside the house someone called plaintively, 'Irina!', giving the word a wonderfully guttural Russian inflection.

'Does he ever talk about his ex-wife?' I asked swiftly.

'This hell-cat vooman? Often he talks of her. And now someone has kilt her, I believe. He vas very unhappy with this news.'

'Still carrying a torch, eh?'

'A torch? I do not know from torches.' She raised a hand to her forehead and to my horror I saw a faint line of blue numbers tattooed on the inside of her wrist. There was another cry of 'Irina!'

'I'm sorry to have interrupted you,' I said again, and stepped back and then down to the pavement as she closed the door. By now, her friends had left their seats and were peering at me out of the window. I gave them a big smile and a wave and they nodded back at me. I wondered if all of them were, like their hostess, survivors of the Nazi death-camps. And what horror stories they could tell. I knew that many of those who had endured Auschwitz and Buchenwald had never spoken of their time behind the high fences.

Walking slowly down to number 154, I considered what Irina had just told me. Yellow hair, bright colours, velvet caps – it sounded as though Amy Morrison was still visiting her former husband, despite their divorce. Not to mention her two subsequent husbands. And as I reached number 154, I realized with a sense of shock that the description I had been given – yellow hair, bright colours, velvet beret – might equally apply to Dr Helena Drummond. Not that I'd ever seen Helena in a velvet beret. Nor could I imagine Good King Wenceslas in one.

Was there some kind of connection between my collaborator, her former student, and that student's ex-husband? I stepped up the path and pushed the bell-stop set beside the door. Then looked up at a brass ship's bell hanging from a chain above it. Should I have rung that instead? It might be some kind of fire alarm, alerting the entire street, bringing agitated householders out of their houses, sniffing for smoke or—

The door opened. One of the best-looking men I'd ever seen stood eyeballing me. Black hair, deep blue eyes, a complexion to die for, barbered eyebrows. I hate really handsome men because they are almost always deeply aware of their assets, don't mind sharing them with you, and are convinced that you agree with them that they are God's gift to the sisterhood. Like, sure.

I didn't bother with a preamble. Men like Seamus O'Donahue usually dived straight in so why shouldn't I? 'I'm sorry for your loss,' I said briskly.

'Loss? Oh, you mean Amy.'

'Yes.'

He stepped out of the door and looked up and down, surveying the street. What for? 'You'd best come in,' he said. Which I did.

He led me to the back of the house and into a kitchen so clean I was almost afraid to set foot on the gleaming floor tiles for fear of sullying them. I made a mental note never to invite him into my own kitchen, in case he fainted dead away from the shock. There was a dim aroma of bleach, overlaid by the scent of proper coffee. 'Sit down and tell me what this is all about,' he said. 'Coffee?' He sounded considerably more educated than his sister-in-law; any Irish accent had been reduced to a lilt that I'm sure worked on the ladies like a charm.

I was glad I had put on a sensible navy suit and a good white shirt. He had obviously taken me for a police officer.

He placed a bone china cup and saucer in front of me and sat down himself. 'You're obviously not a police officer,' he said.

Drat! And here I thought I could pass. 'I used to be.'

'And what are you now?'

'An art historian,' I said.

'And as a colleague of my former wife, you've come to pay your respects, is that it?'

'More or less.' If this guy worked in a supermarket, I was Queen Marie of Romania. Unless he ran the place. Or even owned it. Not that I have anything at all against supermarket staff, friendly and courteous to a man – or woman – it was just that Seamus's manner was that of one used to being in control, not one who was controlled.

'So why are you here?'

'Quite simply, because my close friend and colleague is being fingered for Amy's death, and I need to clear her name by finding the real culprit.'

'And who is she?'

'Another art historian. Doctor Helena Drummond.'

His face changed. 'Is that so?' He sounded as smooth as face cream. Which I was prepared to bet he used liberally on his own face. But it was obvious that in one way or another, and however tenuously, he was connected with Helena. Or had been once.

'Do you know her?'

'What makes you think that?'

'I understand she used to come and visit you here,' I said, taking a punt.

He smiled, leaned away from the table and hooked one arm over the back of his chair. 'Do you indeed? Whatever gave you that idea?'

This interview was getting away from me. 'I have my sources.'

'And would one of them be Mrs Koszklovsky down the road, by any chance?'

'It doesn't really matter, does it?' I didn't want to get the old lady into trouble – though she had called him a 'sveetheart'.

'For your information, I do not know Doctor Helena Drummond. Nor have I ever met her. But I do know the name because at one point, she tutored my wife. Former wife. Amy.'

'Who, from what I've heard, was not the world's most popular woman. All I want to know is whether you're aware of anyone in particular who had it in for her.'

'Like me, for instance, do you mean?'

'I didn't say that.'

'You didn't need to, darlin'.' He reached across the table and lightly touched the back of my hand. I hated the way I couldn't suppress a tingle from walking down my backbone. 'But for the record, I was visiting my parents in Kilkenny – it was their golden wedding anniversary – at the time Amy died, according to the newspapers, that is, and there's a score of witnesses will back me up.'

'So if not you, then who?'

'There *was* someone who sent anonymous letters threatening her. That was while we were still together, years ago. And before you ask, no, I didn't keep them, and I have no idea whether she did.'

'Where did they come from?'

'The only one I saw was sent from Boston. The one in the United States.'

'Did she have any idea who might have sent them?'

'If she did, she didn't tell me.'

'Not even whether it was a man or a woman?'

'Sorry.'

'What did they threaten her with?'

'Death, possibly.' He shrugged. 'I've no idea.'

'So basically, you can't help me.'

'I'd like to but . . .' He wrinkled his smooth brow. 'I seem to remember her talking about some disgruntled ex-boyfriend, though I'd be willing to take a guess that most of them were disgruntled by the time she'd finished with them. But that was a while ago, maybe ten years, and it may not have had anything to do with the letters. If it's him, he's certainly been biding his time.'

'Maybe the opportunity wasn't ripe until now.' I lifted my coffee cup. I could see the shape of my fingers through the delicate porcelain. 'So where did you meet Ms Morrison?'

'On a cruise to the Mediterranean. She was there with some rich old codger and his two daughters.' He looked at me with a wry expression. 'I only discovered he was her husband some years after we tied the knot. Which made me Number Two – and believe me, darlin', that's one of the very few times I've taken second place. He must have been forty years older than her and she sure didn't spend much time with him, or those girls. I was their restaurant steward, and at first I had no idea they were a family, just assumed they'd been allocated to the same table. Actually, at the time, I just thought she was his older daughter, maybe by an earlier marriage. God help me, she took one look at me and that was my goose cooked. The old boy died a few years later and she was back on the ship, stalking me day and night, until I ended up married to a woman I hardly knew, and after the first week or so, didn't even like. She was an extreme predator, could have taught your average wolf a thing or two.'

'And after you handed your job on the ships to your brother, what did you do then?'

'I really can't see that it has anything to do with you, if you don't mind me saying. But in fact I studied for a teacher's diploma, specializing in history and maths.'

'So now you teach?'

'I do.'

'And don't work at the local supermarket?'

'I did that very briefly, in between semesters.'

'They still seem to know you, where you live and so on.'

'Yeah, well, I shop there, don't I?'

I drank some more of his excellent coffee, resisting the urge to lift my little finger. 'Do you know anything about Amy's family? Siblings? Parents?'

'No. None of them came to our wedding. I rather gathered, from what she told me, that they were too hoity-toity, didn't approve of me, though since they'd never met me, I'm not quite sure why.'

'Maybe she was ashamed of them.'

'Or of me.'

I tried another long shot. 'Have you ever met her publishers?'

'Her publishers? Why would I? She didn't write her first book until well after she'd moved on from me to Jason the Body-Builder.'

'So you don't know Donald Lewis?'

'Nope.'

'Nor his lovely assistant, Miranda?'

'Not at all,' he said. 'Never met the woman.'

'Never?'

'That's what I said, isn't it?'

'It's certainly what you *said*.' I stood up. 'Damn fine coffee, thank you. If you think of anything, blah, blah, blah, you know the routine, here's my card.'

'Except if I did think of something, why would I relay it to you rather than the police?'

I nodded. 'Good question.'

Walking away from his house towards the supermarket car park, I reflected that unpleasant though Amy herself had been, her husbands seemed to be likeable in their different ways. Even if they were prone to telling lies. And that of the three of them, Seamus was the one who had raised the most question marks in my mind. Not because I suspected him of being implicated in Amy's death, but because it seemed that he might have been more involved in her current existence than he was trying to pretend. I went back and banged again at his door. When he answered, I said, 'No names, no pack drill, no repercussions, but you do know Miranda from Amy's publishers, don't you?'

He gave me a considering look. Stared beyond me at the street. Lifted his shoulders and dropped them again. Said, 'That would be a yes.'

'Thank you.' I walked away once more. So there was no connection between him and Helena, which was all I was trying to establish. And so far, I had to admit, I was no further on in finding the slightest clue to Amy's killer – and thus possibly to Helena's whereabouts – than I had been when I first started looking.

Except this anonymous letter-writer. Who might that have been? Could it have been one of the rich old codger's girls, now grown? Who lived in Boston? And resented the upstart wife? Was there any suggestion that Amy had been involved in his death? It was something to check.

Back in my own kitchen, waiting for the coffee to brew, I forced myself to relive the scene of Amy Morrison's demise. Had I missed some telling detail, something that might lead me down one or another of the two avenues of investigation I was trying to pursue. I could think of nothing. Since I prided myself on my powers of observation, I tried not to feel like a failure. Perhaps there simply wasn't anything to observe. Okay, so once I had been a reasonably high-ranking police officer – that didn't mean I was some kind of modern-day Sherlock Holmes, deerstalker on head and magnifying glass in hand, the way Sam Willoughby wanted to be.

I wondered how soon I could get back into Helena's house. See if something would ring bells, trigger recall. Although I had not told Inspector Garside this, once I had contacted the police to report a suspicious death, I had opened some of her drawers, using a piece of tissue to conceal any fingerprints, then stood at the door of the bedroom and covered it fairly comprehensively by sight, noting and collating the information as far as I could. Was there anything at all I could focus on? I had no idea whether Helena had even been at the scene.

Where was her computer: had that gone from the house? Trekking carefully through the house, as familiar to me as my own flat, I hadn't noticed one. But she might well have had it with her when she set off to meet me. If she ever had.

Even as the question occurred to me, my phone rang. Garside. 'Mrs— sorry, *Doctor* Drummond. Your colleague,' he said. 'Did she have a computer?'

So, my question answered. 'Yes.'

'Thank you.' He rang off.

'Thank you too,' I said into the dialling tone.

Again the phone rang. Paul Sandbrook of the antique shop. 'I've remembered,' he said.

'That's good.'

'That Peter person that Helena was flirting with? I mentioned him last time we spoke.'

'You did.'

'His name is Peter Preston. He works for some fancy car dealership on the edge of the city. Can't remember the name of it.'

'Thank you, Mr Sandbrook. That's very useful.' And might help me discover what Helena did after she and her friends had finished eating at the restaurant. I got out the Yellow Pages, looked up car dealerships, found two on the edge of town. The first one was engaged both times I tried it. A courteous voice answered the second. 'Peter Preston.' Sauve. Young. Efficient.

'Oh, Mr Preston,' I said. 'My name's Quick. Alex Quick.'

'Yes?'

'I was given your name by Paul Sandbrook.'

'Yes?'

'It's about the evening you went out with him and some other friends on Monday, after a concert in the cathedral. I understand that Doctor Drummond went home with you after you'd had dinner at Prego's.'

'She did.'

'May I ask if she stayed the night with you?'

'May I ask what business it is of yours?'

'I'm her collaborator, and I'm wondering where she is since she seems to have vanished. Temporarily, I hope. You're the last person known to have been with her and I'm hoping you can help.'

There was a pause. Then he said, 'Hang on, while I transfer to another phone.'

'Fine,' I said.

After some seconds of dead sound, he spoke again. 'Sorry about that. This line is a bit more private. Now, Helena . . . yes, she did stay the night at my place. We're very old friends.'

'Of course,' I murmured.

'She got up about seven thirty the next morning, moaning about having to get back to her house and car, got dressed, refused my offer to call a cab. Said she'd take a bus, since they stopped right outside her door, and the bus station is only a few minutes' walk from me.'

'What then?'

'Obviously I was a bit concerned, since it was only just getting light. I watched out of the window, saw her start off down the street, and then this bloke appeared on a motorbike. He stopped, started talking to her, obviously offering her a ride on the back of his bike. Which she equally obviously accepted, since he gave her a helmet and she climbed up behind him and off they went.'

'What did he look like?'

'Darth Vader, to be honest. Black helmet with dark visor, black gauntlets, scarf tied round the bottom half of his face against the cold, leathers. The whole bikey thing. I assumed it was one of her students who happened to appear by some lucky chance.'

'I wonder who it was.'

'Can't help you there. Look, I'm supposed to be on duty in the showroom, if you don't mind.'

'No,' I said. 'And thank you.'

I wondered how fortuitous it was that the bike rider should have shown up just as Helena needed a ride. Not very, I suspected. And I doubted he was one of her students.

ELEVEN

I couldn't sleep. Although violent crime scenes were nothing new to me, the horrific sight I had walked in on at Helena's house was constantly at the back of my mind, lurking like an alligator, waiting to emerge from the muddy shallows when I least expected it. And the more it did so, the more I felt that there had been something in that bedroom which jagged a nerve, but I simply could not remember what it was. Obsessively I went over the details again. And yet again.

Nor could I work out what Amy Morrison had been doing in Helena's house in the first place. I clearly recalled Amy's launch party and Helena telling me that she hadn't been in contact with Amy since she left college, twenty years before. Adding that Amy probably wanted to show off how far she'd come since then, which was why Helena had been invited.

By now, the papers were full of Amy's murder. There were hints of the mutilations, though no specific details were printed. Glamour shots of her had appeared in the tabloids. The *Mail* interviewed the neighbours on either side of Helena's house and tried to work something up, but neither of the two households, nor anyone else in the street, had seen or heard anything useful. 'A motorbike was revving around nine thirty,' one of them, a thin older woman, very erect of carriage, had told me. 'It got on my nerves a bit, quite honestly, especially as I was trying to listen to *The World Tonight*. But no, apart from that, there was nothing out of the ordinary that day.'

The plain fact of the matter was that most of the people nearby had been lounging about on their sofas, glued to the television, or lying in a bath or listening to music, completely unaware that someone was being butchered nearby. One woman had said that there was a constant stream of visitors coming to the house – male, of course. Which while it had little to do with Amy Morrison, nonetheless translated immediately into Helena being completely promiscuous. Which she was not. The idea that her students might occasionally show up for an off-the-cuff tutorial didn't seem to strike her.

Interestingly, so far nobody had been able to dig up any information about Amy's past. No former school friends, no teachers. It was surprising that none of her fellow students from her art-school days had had anything to say about her, though one of Helena's colleagues had made a statement about her being very reclusive and not often seen at lectures, concluding with the information that she had not been granted her degree.

Eventually, I got up, made coffee and went into the second bedroom, which served as my office. I reviewed all I knew so far about both Helena and Amy Morrison, which proved to be remarkably little. Both of them seemed to keep their private lives quite separate from their public faces. Where they came from, what their background was . . . not that there was any reason why they shouldn't have done so. It was their right, after all. Yet it seemed odd that although Amy featured, with her recent accomplishments and a few personal details, on Wikipedia, there was nothing about where she was born, who her parents were, where she grew up, whether she had siblings, or even children.

Some of her history was common knowledge, of course. Hence the fact that I had been able to talk to three of Amy's four husbands. But even then, as far as my researches into the three men were concerned, I felt I had hit a blank wall. Nice guys but, in my opinion, completely harmless – though I was far too seasoned in the ways of murderers to believe that nice guys were incapable of vicious killing. Even Mark, the present incumbent and the one with most to gain from her death, had a rock-solid alibi. The others seemed almost irrelevant. I wished now that I had thought to ask them if they had learned any personal details about her past during the days of their marriages to her.

Nonetheless, someone had hated Amy Morrison enough to kill her. I had to keep that constantly in mind.

I reflected on Helena's husbands, of whom she so rarely spoke. Here again I had received very little information. Once again, I checked her out on the internet, but there was nothing of any use. When the working day started, I would try to contact someone in the university personnel department – or Human Resources, as they called it these days. I tried hard not to worry about Helena, pushing away from me the police mantra about mispers: if in doubt, think murder . . .

Focus, Alex, focus. Think of the crime scene. Think of that lamp-lit room, the shades of red and orange, the crumpled bed, the rolled-up pages of manuscript shoved inside the victim, the vicious tearing apart. That took strength and anger, as did the damage perpetrated on the eyes.

Eyes. Vagina. Why had the murderer concentrated on these two particular areas? The eyes might have something to do with Amy's profession, which like mine involved a constant looking at pictures and paintings. Was someone trying to deny or negate her link to the world of art? The attempt at mutilation of her genitals could point to sexual jealousy, or frustration, or even anger. And what significance was there in the papers, almost certainly taken from the typescript of Amy's book?

I glanced at the clock. It was still far too early to telephone anyone. I took my mug of coffee back to bed.

It was after nine thirty when I woke again, having drifted off to sleep. Beneath my pillow, my mobile was buzzing. I reached under and hoicked it out.

'Quick? How's it going?' It was DI Felicity Fairlight.

'If you mean my painstaking search for Amy Morrison's killer, in a fruitless attempt to prove that Helena is not guilty: badly,' I said.

'No reason why it should be anything else. A lone woman, with nothing going for her but brains and ingenuity, pitted against the mighty resources of the force? It's a no-brainer.'

'Thank you very much,' I said. 'What about your lot? How are they doing?'

'Same as you, I believe. Focussing on Doctor Drummond instead of the Morrison woman. Which means they're not getting anywhere – though you didn't hear it from me. It's like your friend has just vanished off the face of the earth. Are you sure you don't know where she is or where she might have gone?'

'Would I lie to you?' I said. 'Seriously, I have no idea what's happened to her. Anyway, why are the cops so sure Helena did it? Apart from the fact that the murder took place in her house.'

'Partly because she's known to have had a deep-rooted dislike of Amy Morrison.'

'As does everyone who's ever come into contact with the woman. Including me.'

'And partly because she had both the means and the opportunity. And partly because she seems to have fled the scene, which as you know is a sure sign of guilt.'

'And partly because they don't know who else to point the finger at.'

'That too.'

'I was going to call you, except you got in first. It's about those pages which were pushed up inside Amy Morrison's . . . ahem . . . twat.'

'What about them?'

'Has any analysis of them been done?'

'I'm not certain. Not in any detail, I'm sure. Not yet, anyway. But didn't you say you thought they were from the woman's book?'

'I did. But not from the final version which she would have presented to her publisher, they looked like proof pages.'

'She probably had various versions before the final one.'

'Not fully printed out, I wouldn't have thought. When we do one of our anthologies, Helena and I might print out odd paragraphs along the way, while we're still putting it all together. But the one at the scene of crime, as far as I could see, seemed like a completed typescript, with pictures and everything. The real question, Fliss, is where would the murderer have found the manuscript pages? It's hardly credible that Amy would be carrying them around with her. Or if she was, where are the rest of the pages?'

'I'll see what I can find out and get back to you.'

Something struck me. Maybe this was in response to the niggle in my head. Morrison must have worked on her book for years, because the paper thrust inside her was clearly not in mint condition. It had that faintly yellowish edge to it, and the letters were infinitesimally blurred, as though produced on an older printer.

As soon as I had disconnected, my phone buzzed again. When I picked up, a man with the deepest voice I had ever heard, said, 'Is this Alex Quick?' He sounded as if he had just stepped off the boat from Sydney and wasn't too thrilled about it.

'Yes, it is.'

'This is Liam Hadfield. Professor Hadfield. I'm calling from Oxford.'

There was a pause, as though he were waiting for me to react with cries of unbridled joy.

'And you're what, going to award me an honorary doctorate?' I said.

He gave a half-amused grunt. 'That might come later. For the moment, I'm wondering whether you have any idea where my wife might be.'

Why the hell would I know where his wife was? 'Do I sound like Lost Property?' I asked. Then realizing I was being a little discourteous, I went on: 'I'm awfully sorry, I'm not quite sure . . . do I know your wife?'

'Doctor Drummond,' he said, crisp as a poppadom. 'Helena is my wife.' Emphasizing the final word, in case I thought she was his local butcher or his manicurist.

'You're Helena's . . .' She had told me she was divorced and single, and had nothing to do with either of her former husbands. 'But I thought . . .'

'I know what you thought. But it's not true.' He was even crisper. 'I've been trying to contact her, to tell her I have to give a lecture at the University of Kent at the end of the week, and I'd be happy to take her out for dinner afterwards, in return for a bed for the night. I've telephoned, but I'm getting no reply. It occurred to me that you might know where she's gone.'

'I wish I did.'

'I'd just arrived from Australia, when one of my colleagues informed me that she's all over the papers, under suspicion of murdering one of her former students. Amy Morrison. That can't be right.'

'Unfortunately it is. At least, it's right that the police *think* Helena did it, not that she *did* it.'

'Well, what can be done about it?' A man used to finding solutions, I could tell.

'Believe me, Professor Hadfield, I've been racking my brains, trying to think of something.'

'She can't hide forever.'

'You think she's hiding?'

'She must be.'

'She's hoping to avoid the police, I should imagine, since they're convinced she's a killer.'

'Helena? A killer?' He laughed deeply. 'Come *on*.'

'Which is why I've been working from the other end, looking for someone with a reason to kill Ms Morrison, in order to take the heat off Helena.'

'Doing the cops' job for them? Very commendable.'

Though the more I thought about it, the more random it all seemed. How could the killer have known Amy would be at Helena's house, for a start? Unless, as I had already conjectured, Helena was the intended target. The two women were just about similar enough to be confused, in a poor light, and from a distance. But even so . . . I tried to envisage a different scenario but failed to come up with anything that was both plausible and fitted the facts.

'If she gets in touch by Thursday evening, please let me know immediately.' His deep voice rasped at the base of my spine as he gave me his phone number. A graphic illustration of the phrase *shiver me timbers*.

I remembered something. 'Perhaps she's staying with your daughter,' I said.

'I don't *have* a daughter,' he said impatiently. 'Nor, for your information, a son.'

'I understood she had a daughter?' Though in fact Perry Nutley had amended his statement and decided he was mixing Helena up with another colleague. Still, it was worth checking out.

'Not with me she hasn't. And I think I would have heard if the old boy in France had fathered one with her.'

Was he referring to Ainslie Gordon? 'Would it be a good idea for us to meet up?' I asked.

'Why?'

Is there a difference between brusque and plain bloody rude? Probably, but right then I wasn't certain what it was. 'If you're coming down this way anyway,' I said, my tone permafrost cold.

'I can't see much point. Cheers.' He rang off before I could say anything more.

Leaving me with a puzzle. Was Helena still married to Hadfield, or wasn't she? He seemed to think so, while she had been quite firm on the subject, the one time we had discussed it. 'I'm free of them both, the bastards,' she said. 'Free and clear.'

I hadn't questioned it. Why would I? Now I felt that this new information might be significant. If Helena had lied about her relationship with Liam Hadfield, she might have lied about other things as well. Or was it simply that the man was Catholic and despite the legality of the process, didn't believe in divorce?

The phone shrilled yet again in my hand. I was so startled that I nearly dropped it. 'It's Mark Sheridan here,' said a cultured young voice. No beer round the edges now.

Sheridan the Shelf-stacker. 'Yes?' I said.

'When you were here the other day, did you . . . uh . . . *take* anything?'

'You mean steal something?'

'Well, yes, I suppose I do.'

'Of course I didn't. Why do you ask?'

'Because I think someone has been in the house. You may have noticed that I was a bit the worse for wear when you were last here. Drinking too much, that sort of thing. I'm not normally like that. It was the shock of hearing about Amy being murdered.'

'The General would not have been happy.'

'Tell me about it. The thing is, I've straightened myself out now. But it's more than possible that during that time, I could have left the front door open, or unlocked, and someone got in.'

'So what's missing?'

'I'm not quite sure.'

'Anything valuable?'

'Not that I would recognize.'

'Have you called the police about it?'

'Uh, not yet. Mostly because maybe I'm just imagining it.'

'What are you imagining might have gone?'

'The odd item here and there.'

'Which you wouldn't recognize?'

'Yeah. Or no.'

'And that's all?'

'Uh . . . yes.'

I sensed a reluctance on his part to discuss it over the phone. 'Want me to come up and take a look round?'

'Would you? You're the only person who's been in the house since the police searched it, shortly after Amy was . . . discovered. And seeing as you're a trained observer and all . . .'

It would give me an opportunity to nose around a bit more. Or even a lot more. 'Okay,' I said. 'I'll come. Should get there just after lunch.'

Since my last visit, the little front garden of Amy's house had been swept clean of dead leaves, the straggly box-hedges had been trimmed. The curtains at the front were open and now hung demurely straight on either side of the windows.

Inside, the sitting room had been cleared of takeaway debris, there was a scent of lavender furniture polish in the air, and some fresh flowers sat on a side table in a cut-glass vase. Mark Sheridan looked very different from our last meeting: hair brushed, cheeks shaved, in a clean shirt under a smart navy-blue sweater. On a coffee table was a brochure about flights to South America.

'Coffee?'

'Please.'

He brought me a mug on a small oblong dish, with what looked like a home-made chocolate-chip cookie set to one side. He sat down opposite me.

I sipped my coffee, broke off a piece of cookie, chewed it, and said: 'So tell me about this possible home-invasion.'

He looked around the room. 'It's difficult to pinpoint exactly what I mean.'

'And you don't really know what's missing?'

'If anything. As I said on the phone, I'm not really sure. I don't take much notice of *things*. I just have this general feel that things are gone.'

I carefully scanned the room, taking my time. 'I'd say some of the books are gone,' I said eventually, waving at the bookcases along one wall. I could see gaps, books leaning slant-wise against other books, which I was sure had been filled on my previous visit. 'Any idea what kind of books she kept on the shelves?' I asked, continuing to survey the room as I spoke.

'Art books, I think. She had a lot of those. I remember some of them because they were texts I'd used at university. And when I wrote my thesis for my PhD.'

I nodded. So he had a doctorate, as well as a General for a father. Very interesting. Very un-Amy. 'What was your thesis on?'

'*The Correspondences between Art and Music during the*

Renaissance.' He sounded proud – and so he should be: it was a big subject.

'Right,' I said. One thing I did notice was the space in the display of expensive little enamelled snuff-boxes. The plain silver box, no more than three centimetres square, which had been there on my last visit, was gone. I pointed its absence out to Mark. 'Odd,' I added. 'It was modern, and therefore would be worth considerably less than some of the others.'

'You're right.'

'And there was a leather-covered volume on the shelves last time I was here,' I said. 'Looked like a presentation copy.'

'Yeah, I know. Her publishers gave her that after the Masaccio book came out. She was really chuffed. Said she was on her way at last.'

Sadly, she had been on her way to nothing more than a violent and early death. 'Well, it's gone now. Should I look at her office, while I'm here?'

'That would be great.'

'Though I may not be of much use.'

'You'll be better than I would.' He gave another of his vague waves, this time towards the door of the room. 'Help yourself.'

I climbed the stairs to the landing. I hesitated. Then, with a cautious backward glance down the stairs, to make sure Mark wasn't keeping an eye on me, I walked softly into the bigger bedroom which Mark had shared with Amy. Like her office, it was almost a parody, the sort of woman's bedroom that might have featured in a 1950s Doris Day or Bette Davis movie. Scent-bottles, silver-backed hairbrush with matching hand-mirror, jewellery casket of mother-of-pearl inlaid wood, an ivory-and-leather box containing – I flipped up the lid to check – various make-up brushes and eyebrow pencils.

Quietly I opened the jewellery box. There wasn't anything of great value inside, and most of it was silver. No diamond rings or ruby earrings, no cabochon emerald bracelets or expensive amethyst necklaces. I knew Amy had possessed real sparklers because I remembered her fingers flashing as she girlishly clasped her hands together at her launch party, but they weren't here. Such as she had she obviously kept somewhere else, unless the notional intruder had taken them.

I conducted a quick trawl of the drawers and wardrobe, checked under the bed and in the bedside tables, found nothing that seemed significant. Left the room.

Further down the short passage was the office I had checked out last time I was here. The only thing to have changed since then was the thickness of the dust layer which lay over everything. I stood at Amy's desk and could see nothing which looked as though it had been moved since then. Except . . . hang about!

I tapped into my inner Inspector Morse. There was a quite definite line in the dust, where the box of printer paper had obviously been moved and then carefully, but not carefully enough, been returned to its original position. Why would someone want to do that, especially if they were hoping to avoid suspicion? Unless they wanted to print something out. But even from my position in the middle of the room, I could see from the dust layers that the neat plastic cover over the printer could not have been removed in the recent past. It made me wonder just how much Amy had used it: this amount of dust could surely not have been distributed in the ten days or so since her death.

I walked across the room and lifted the box, placed it on the table where Amy presumably had worked. I lifted the lid and saw, as before, the stack of virgin paper. I riffled through it. And riffled again, taking a larger wedge the second time. This time, I saw that there were printed sheets underneath the clean paper. Lots of them. There was no title page, but it was clearly the manuscript of Amy's book. I did some more riffling and it became clear that at least half a chapter was missing. I lifted the whole lot out of the box and lightly fanned it across the table.

Pages 69 to 87 – a whole chapter and some extra pages – were no longer there. Again, the printing had the same quality of not-quite-sharpness which the pages found in her body had possessed. The only reason I could come up with as to why Amy would have stored the typescript of her book at the bottom of a box of paper was in order to keep it hidden. Perhaps she was afraid of a rival art historian breaking in to steal the fruits of her hard work and research. I replaced the papers, hesitated, lifted them out again and took page 88 (what difference would one more make?), folded it into my wallet, and after doing some further cursory searching and finding nothing more, went back downstairs, carrying the box.

Mark was in the smart little kitchen, making himself another coffee. When I came in he turned. 'I remembered something which seems to have gone missing,' he said. 'I was looking for the spare car key, which Amy kept in that jewellery box on her dressing table. There's a golden chain thing she quite often wore which is definitely no longer there.'

'Was it valuable?'

'She always said it only had sentimental value, but I think it was worth a lot more than she let on. There was a really old French coin set in gold hanging from it. There were matching earrings, too, little gold coins. I've always assumed that Number Two or Number Three gave them to her.'

I guessed he was referring to Judo Jason or Super Seamus. If the hand-beaten gold link I had lifted at the scene of Amy's murder came from the necklace he was referring to, it seemed very unlikely that either of them would have bought it for her, since antique gold francs didn't come cheap. 'What about Number One?'

'He'd be the one, wouldn't he? He was super-rich. Even though she didn't end up with all his loot, thanks to his children by earlier marriages, she got a sizeable settlement. Perhaps she bought it for herself.'

'Was she wearing it when she left here last week?'

'Could be . . .' He moved his head up and down. 'Yeah, she was. That's probably where it went. She must have taken it off and forgotten about it.'

My turn to nod. 'Probably.' I didn't like to say that it hadn't been round her neck when I found her body. 'What about this?' I showed him the box of typing paper. Opened it. Delved under the blank sheets. 'This looks like the manuscript of her Masaccio book,' I said, holding out the typescript.

He nodded yet again. 'Yes, it does.'

'But there are some pages missing.' I wasn't sure that the police had told him details such as the papers pushed into his dead wife's intimate crevices, so said nothing.

'Strange.' He sounded indifferent, so much so that I wondered if it was an act. 'Does it matter?'

'Probably not.' I gave him my dead-eye stare. Was he the one who had removed the pages from the box? 'But I wonder why anyone would go to the trouble of breaking in to your house, stealing a small silver box, a book and some pages of a not-yet-published typescript.'

He shrugged. I guessed his thoughts were mainly in Guatemala rather than north London.

'You said that you might have left the door unlocked, or even open. If you didn't, how else might anyone have got into the house?'

Again he shrugged. 'The side entrance, maybe. There's a narrow little alley up the side of the house, though Amy and I never used it.'

'I'll go and inspect it.'

Outside, I turned to the right. Yes, a gate led to the back of the house, which I hadn't noticed before. It was a tall gate, maybe six and a half feet high, and offered no glimpse of what lay behind it. It had an old-fashioned latch and a shiny-looking Yale lock. Mark was behind me and put a key into the lock, while I flipped up the latch. Together we pushed, but it wouldn't budge. We pushed again, harder this time. Examining it more closely, I said, 'This isn't stuck, Mark. It's actually painted shut. When was the house last done up?'

'Must have been back in September,' he said. 'I knew Amy was a bit paranoid about security, but I hadn't realized you couldn't actually open it. I always come in through the front door.'

I peered more closely at the clean white paint job. 'There are no marks on here,' I said. 'If someone had climbed over, there'd have been scuff marks.' I turned to him as he peered over my shoulder. 'Let's have a look at the front door.'

But again, there were no signs of a break-in. The same with the windows. Besides, given the cheek-by-jowl nature of the terraced street, if someone had attempted to climb into the house via the windows, they stood a strong chance of being noticed.

'Amy would have been carrying a set of house keys, wouldn't she?' I asked.

'Yes, of course. In that big Must-Have handbag she was so proud of.' He gave a well-bred sort of snort. 'Made of Italian leather – cost enough to feed a village for a month. Bloody obscene, in my opinion. She was always buying them – some of them cost *thousands*.'

'That might be the explanation. Her murderer must have taken the bag, because there certainly wasn't one around when I found her,' I said, hoping it hadn't been one of the bags produced by my brother-in-law Leonardo. 'That must be the answer. The person who killed her was also the person who entered this house and stole stuff.'

There was only one problem: the break-in took place *after* Amy was killed, when her bag had been stolen, so where did the manu-script pages appear from? And how had the murderer obtained them?

TWELVE

Back home, I poured myself a glass of red and looked through the mail I had brought in from my postbox in the lobby. It was the usual mixture of junk and bills, plus a few letters and cards from friends. I checked out an envelope of the very best quality hand-made stationery, so heavy I could hardly lift it off the mat. It was addressed to Mesdames Drummond & Quick in a fine finishing-school hand, using a fountain pen filled with royal-blue ink. Unusual in these days of email, tweeting and texting.

I slit it open carefully with a paper knife, in order to preserve the integrity of the envelope. Inside was a thick invitation card, written on cream-coloured paper, with a complicated embossment in blue of various capital letters which included both L and M. The sort of monogrammed stationery that privileged Americans tend to use. Possibly the English do too, but I obviously don't know the right sort of people. Mrs Lamont was asking Helena and me to attend a private function at the Eaton Square address of Robert and Mercy Lamont. 7:00pm. Black tie. Wow! Professionally, this could only be good news. Personally, it would be a lot less fun if Helena were not there to share it with me.

I put the thought behind me, and picked up the piece of paper which had gotten itself half-stuck to the underside of one of the bills. A page torn from a small lined notebook, one of those with a spiral of wire down the side. In lower-case letters, the message ran *imok*. What the hell did that mean? *imok*. Some obscure West African artist? A reminder of something I was supposed to do? A character in *Star Wars: Return of the Jedi*? But who did I know who would write in such an illiterate way? Was it worth Googling? I studied it again. Not *imok*, but IMOK? I was none the wiser.

And then, making coffee in the kitchen and staring out at the turbulent sea, I got it. *I am OK*. What else could it mean? And who else could have written it but Helena? My spirits rose like bubbles in a glass of champagne. It had to be Helena. And she was all right. Somewhere hiding out of sight, but all right! And maybe even in the vicinity, if she was able to hand-deliver a message. I thought of Sherlock Holmes' crew of raggedy barefoot urchins, always ready to run errands for him, but these days there weren't all that many barefoot urchins around, especially in winter. Helena must have delivered it herself, but since I had been away most of the day, she was unlikely to still be hanging around outside.

A burden of doubt and depression lifted from my shoulders. If she was all right, then I could get on with some work. Sign and send back the contracts which had arrived from Cliff Nichols, forging Helena's signature, if necessary. Pictures and images to research for the first of the three books he had commissioned, the fruit and flowers one, *Ripe For the Picking*.

And then the phone rang and I forgot everything. It was Fliss Fairfield. 'They're issuing a warrant for Doctor Drummond's arrest,' she said.

'You're kidding me.'

'I'm afraid not.'

'Has Garside lost his mind?'

'Which mind would that be?'

'And what evidence does he have?' I felt as though I was going to choke. 'You know she didn't do it, Fliss! You *know* that!'

'*I* may – though it's only based on your assurances – but the rest of the force doesn't know her, and as I said last week, it's looking extremely bad for her.'

'This is ridiculous.'

'Maybe. But as far as they can tell, she had the means and the opportunity – and it wouldn't be hard to come up with a motive. Garside is looking jubilant.'

'I can't see how he can make charges stick. Any evidence he's got must be purely circumstantial.'

'That's a different matter.'

'And I know Helena doesn't have the money to hire a top-class defence barrister.'

'Maybe the CPS will advise them that they haven't got a case.'

'Hmmm . . .' I said. 'So we're back to square one.' The news of the warrant was absurd, based on such a flimsy premise that I refused to let it bug me. Meanwhile, I had to get on with my professional life, until Helena showed up again and we could continue our partnership.

'Looks like it.'
'Crap.'

There was a big article on the arts pages the following morning. The fabulously wealthy Lamonts had just purchased another painting, for a whole heap of money. A Léopold Survage, this time. As an ex-copper, I wondered how wise it was to be proclaiming to the world the fact that all these prime canvasses were hanging on the walls of their Eaton Square place. I knew for a fact that there were specialized art thieves who not only targeted victims like the Lamonts, but also stole to order, people who made it their business to study the papers in order to read about the latest news from salesrooms and auction houses. They would be well aware that a private home would be much easier to break into than a gallery or museum, however good the security systems in place. The same people were equally assiduous in reading the gossip columns, checking out who would be on vacation or attending a wedding or funeral, making their homes that much more vulnerable.

I was prepared to bet that the Lamonts would have the very latest state-of-the-art thief-repellent devices, but even so, a determined burglar would probably crack them eventually, especially as required reading for would-be intruders these days included manuals which showed how to bypass or unlock most systems. I looked forward to seeing the two new paintings, and sent off my acceptance of the invitation. I wasn't quite sure what 'Black Tie' meant these days for women: short or long? Not that I had much choice. I went to my wardrobe and hoicked out the cocktail dress I had bought for Meghan's reception in Italy, after her marriage to Leonardo. I noticed a dribble of Leo's expensive wine on the skirt, sniffed it and smelled traces of sweat under the arm. It would need cleaning. New tights would have to be bought. Hairdresser's appointments made. Soon I would have to turn from private individual to public persona, from comfy to chic, something I hated.

The room I was shown into was not a living room by any stretch of the imagination. It was not even a drawing room. A *salon* was the only word for it, a huge space in which to display a collection of museum-quality furniture, from seventeenth-century antiques in rosewood or walnut to Duncan Phyfe sofas and tables and a collection of his chairs which quite literally made me drool. In one quick survey, I clocked two four-foot-high urns of Sevres porcelain, the glazed display cabinet holding a set of rare Flora Danica plates and bowls, a collection of little boxes made of enamel, silver, ivory, porcelain, and the gorgeous paintings hanging on the walls.

The guests were nearly all in dinner jackets, except for a few consciously arty types in unstructured black linen suits and open-necked white silk shirts. *Très* classy, I had to admit. *Très* hunky. There to be seen as much as to see. Especially the curly-haired one talking animatedly to a corpulent man with white hair who often fronted arts programmes on the TV. Most of the women were in long gowns, though a few of the younger ones wore cocktail dresses of various kinds, like mine. All glammed up, I smoothed down my French navy satin skirts, feeling that while I couldn't begin to compete, at least I had struck the right note. Since there was a buzzing crowd around my host and hostess, I decided I would greet them later, and instead made my way across the room to gaze at the latest Lamont acquisitions.

Ten minutes later, I was still staring when Mrs Lamont came up to stand beside me. 'Yes, we're absolutely delighted to have been able to buy two such paintings in such a short time,' she said. She held out her hand and when I offered mine, took it in both of hers. 'Alexandra! We're both so glad you could come tonight.'

She stood erect as a dowager princess, in a long jacket over a matching skirt, both made of coffee-coloured silk. There was a gorgeous choker of golden pearls around her neck, with more of them hanging from her ears. She glanced up at her new paintings. 'They hardly ever come up for sale, so we feel immensely fortunate.'

'They're both so beautiful,' I said. I wanted to stand in front of them for the rest of the evening, absorbing the juxtaposition of the flat planes, the blocks of pale colour. 'It looks as though we have the same tastes.' Though obviously not the same income.

She smiled at me. 'Last time we met, I mentioned the possibility of setting up a small publishing concern, and my husband and I should very much like to talk to you further about it.' Her gaze wandered towards her other guests and returned to me.

'I look forward to it.'

'As I said in my invitation, we would be delighted to put you up at a hotel tonight, and send a car for you in the morning, at eleven o'clock, if you would like.'

She had indeed made such an offer, but I had refused it. I don't like being beholden. Or steam-rollered, for that matter.

'It's very kind of you, but I'm staying in Chelsea with my brother,' I said.

She put her elegant head on one side. 'On the contrary, it's you who are kind, to join us.'

Oh, so gracious. And behind the careful hair, the discreet make-up, the gorgeous but understated jewellery, oh so desperately sad. I dredged up what my mind had retained about the Lamonts, but could not recall any personal tragedy.

'Your brother is Hereward Quick, isn't he?' she said.

How in the world would she know that? 'That's right.'

'We run into him from time to time. He's obviously very proud of you.'

'Oh, is he?' I coughed, not wanting to sound as if I didn't believe her. I couldn't imagine my brother discussing me with anyone. Or being complimentary. 'Um . . . would it be ill-mannered of me to wander round and gaze at your paintings?' I asked, knowing full well that it would be.

Another gracious smile. 'Of course not,' she said in her low-pitched voice. Her golden-brown eyes were almost the exact shade as her pearls. 'It's nice to have someone who seems to appreciate them as much as we do. Now, please make yourself known to our other guests, won't you?' She greeted a couple who had walked over to the two of us and were now standing patiently waiting to talk to her, then moved away to talk to a group who had just come in, among whom I noticed a well-known art critic, a TV guru and a famous author.

I thought of the gold link, wrapped in tissue, which lay at the bottom of my sequin-encrusted evening bag. Was it possible that there was more than one of these necklaces? I thought it extremely unlikely. Should I mention the link to Mercy Lamont? Definitely not, at least not until I'd worked out her connection – if any – to Amy. And to Helena.

Which reminded me of the crude little message which I had received. *imok . . . I am OK*. Thank God for that! I raised my glass in a silent toast to my absent friend, then took another glass of wine from the black-jacketed servitor who appeared, one white-gloved hand behind his back, the other hand balancing a tray of glasses, both full and empty. I wondered if it was a requirement for serving at posh parties like this one.

One of the arty lot came over. The curly-headed one. 'Hi,' he said. 'I'm Lev Goldsmith.'

He paused in that way that implies that of course you've heard of whoever it is. And although I hated to admit it, of course I had. I nodded. Non-committal. But I knew perfectly well, since it's my business to know such things, that he was the editor of an upscale arts magazine. I'd never met him before, but I had written three articles for his publication.

'You're Alex Quick,' he stated eventually, when I failed to respond in the awestruck manner he'd clearly expected.

'This is true.' He was after something, I could tell by the bright look in his eyes. I hoped it was another piece from me.

He produced another statement. 'You're the one who found Amy Morrison.'

He seemed to deal in declarations rather than questions. Or even conversations. 'This is also true.' I waited for the usual rejoinder about Amy but it didn't come.

He sighed. 'Poor Amy.'

'Poor? Not many people use that word about her.'

'That's because they didn't go to school with her.'

He didn't elaborate. 'And you did,' I eventually prompted.

'Sir Francis Jefferson Primary,' he said. 'Catholic, of course.'

'And why did you call her "poor Amy"?'

'Anyone with Big Pete and Fatty Fee for parents was bound to be overwhelmingly disadvantaged in the great Race of Life.'

I digested this. Fatty Fee . . . I could almost see her, tits slung bra-less into an over-sized cotton jumper pilled with too many washings, roll of stomach over the waistband of her sagging jeans, missing teeth. A million miles from the fastidious Amy I had met at her book launch, several aeons ago, or so it felt.

'Not to mention her charming brothers, Vince and Terry. Shaven-headed bruisers, tats on every available surface, I'm sure you know the type. Bullies at school, chanting racist slogans at football matches, glassing innocent members of the public in the pub, beating up girlfriends. Progressing to drugs as they grew older.'

'Sounds like a nice family.'

'Oh, believe me, it was. The brothers had ASBOs more or less as soon as they were old enough to reach double figures, if not before. Big Pete was in and out of the nick, Fatty Fee wasn't above turning a trick or three for beer money and a fag. And then of course there was Mel, the sister, a right little slag she was, boyfriend killed her in a drunken rage.'

Despite myself, I began to feel almost sorry for Ms Morrison. 'And how did Amy escape all this?'

'She was clever,' Lev said. 'She could see that the only way out was to reinvent herself. So once we went on to secondary school, while all her contemporaries were getting themselves knocked up and applying for benefits and housing and so forth, Amy – not that that's her real name – was working hard at school, taking Saturday jobs, sucking up to everyone worth sucking up to. Especially rich old gentlemen . . .' He winked at me. 'If you take my meaning.'

I rather thought I did. I rather wished I didn't. I remembered an old song my parents had liked. 'Where do you go to, my lovely?' I said.

He obviously knew it too. He tapped the side of his nose. 'Nail on head.'

'If it's not a rude question, how did you . . . erm . . . move on yourself?'

'Got into art college. Looked around, liked what I saw, went for it. And anyway, I didn't have quite so much dust to shake off my feet as she did. My family was perfectly respectable. Poor but honest.'

'So what was Amy called, back in the day?'

He grinned, showing small white teeth. Eyes shining, he said, 'I hardly like to say . . .'

'Oh, go on. You know you want to.'

'Noreen.'

'You're joking!'

He shook his head.

'No wonder she changed it.'

'Exactly.'

'Presumably Morrison wasn't her real name either.'

'She was born Noreen Briggs. Morrison was the name of the extremely wealthy American guy she seduced and then married. He swept her out of art school and off to sunny New York and there she remained until he had a heart attack about eight years ago, leaving her very comfortably off, thank you.'

'What about the rest of the family? Were they aware that little Noreen had metamorphosed in Amy?'

'I doubt it. Big Pete's dead – fell down a lift-shaft when pissed – and Fatty Fee's got alcohol-induced dementia and is in a home.'

'What about the brothers?'

'Vince took after his father. Inside more often than he's out. And Tel? No one's seen hide nor hair for years. I think he may have joined the Army but I'm not sure.'

'So you're still in communication with friends from the old days, are you?'

'To a large extent, yes. But then, unlike Amy – or should I say Noreen – I don't mind going back to visit.'

The party was beginning to thin out now. People were thanking their hosts, starting to leave. The servitors could be seen in the hall, holding coats and wraps.

'Look here,' Lev said. 'Why don't we continue this somewhere else? There's a pretty reasonable wine bar about five minutes' walk from here.'

'I'm not going into a wine bar – or anywhere else – dressed like this,' I said. I looked down at my satin dress, my sparkly high-heels.

'Point taken. Lunch tomorrow?'

'That would be good.' I had a number of further questions I wanted to ask him about Amy.

He mentioned a restaurant I knew. Said, 'Better exchange numbers, in case something happens to either of us.' Smiled his small-toothed smile again. 'Looking forward to it.'

'Me too.'

We swapped cards. I deliberately didn't look at his, just put it into my sequinned (God help me!) bag.

He took hold of my hand and raised it to his lips. It was a gesture I loved: nothing made me feel more special. If I'd been able to dimple, I would have done. 'See you tomorrow.'

Walking over to Mercy Lamont, I smiled at her. 'Thank you for a lovely party,' I said.

'I do hope you enjoyed yourself.'

'Very much. There were some really interesting people.'

'Good. Now, when can you come and examine our paintings at a more leisurely pace?'

'When would suit you?'

'Sooner rather than later. I'll contact you. My husband and I have to return to New York very shortly and I've no idea when we'll be back.'

'I look forward to hearing from you,' I said.

THIRTEEN

The restaurant was small and pretty, decorated with tablecloths in sweet-pea pastels, and different walls painted to match. I'd been there before with friends, and knew that it had won all the accolades going from the food critics for its innovative cuisine. Nonetheless, it had managed to stay unpretentious, a place where you went to eat, rather than to be seen.

From the seriously gastronomic menu, I chose tiny lamb chops with a lemon and rosemary sauce, braised red cabbage, and chanterelle mushrooms sautéed in butter.

'So,' I said, as we waited for our food to arrive, 'do you have any theories about who might have murdered Amy Morrison?' That was the main reason I had agreed to this lunch: I hoped Lev wasn't working to a different agenda. Me, in other words.

As he had yesterday, Lev sighed. 'Trouble with Amy was, she was so determined to remove herself from her background that she didn't allow anyone to get close.'

'Despite all the husbands?'

'Apart from poor old Dexter Morrison, or whatever he was called, she married for emotional security and, of course, for sex. Don't forget that she was raised within the Catholic Church, and sleeping with someone outside the holy bonds of matrimony is a sin.'

It was more or less what Donald Lewis had said. 'So no ideas as to whom her killer might be?'

He looked pained. 'Must we, over lunch?'

As our food was placed on the table, I explained my need to get the police off Helena's back.

'I can see your point. And if someone told me that it was someone from her past, I'd be completely ready to believe it,' he said. 'Thing is, I don't really know to what extent she still kept up with anyone from those days. She and I lost touch for years until she swam into everyone's ken with this brilliant Masaccio book.'

'And there's nobody from the old days that she got seriously across?'

'Plenty, I should think. And I heard a rumour that there was at least one guy who committed suicide because of her, although I never heard the details.'

'Goodness.'

'Or badness . . .' He snorted slightly. 'To put it bluntly, she was a bit of a prick-tease.'

'I can imagine.' I sipped at a glass of the chilled white wine he had ordered for us. 'So you can't give me any leads at all as to the possible identity of Amy's killer?'

'They would be purely speculative if I did.'

'That's okay by me.'

He considered the point, stroking his chin. 'Well, if I were a detective, I think I would almost certainly check out those brothers of hers. At least,' he amended quickly, 'I'd check out Vince. Terry seems lost to us, and for all I know he's reinvented himself, just like his big sister, and lives a life of impeccable propriety.' More chin-stroking. 'Though I must say I can't see Tel as a solicitor or architect, or even schoolteacher.'

'Maybe he followed his sister into the world of art.'

'It's a possibility. He's younger than me, so I didn't really keep up with him. One doesn't really, does one?'

'Any idea what he *was* good at?'

He shook his head. 'None at all. I only knew he was one of the bad boys at school. Just like his brother – when Vince bothered to attend, that is.' Leaning towards me, he reached out and touched the back of my hand. 'Look, I hate to sound prurient, but could you give me more details – how you found Amy, what the poor girl looked like, and so on? They never print these things in the papers . . .'

I moved my hand from the table to my lap. 'With good reason.' I couldn't decide which I disliked most: the tiny rodent teeth, or the perverted interest in Amy's death. I wasn't going to say anything negative to his face – you never knew when he might not commission another article from me – so I gave him a very watered-down description of what I had found in Helena's bedroom. Even if you believe that no man is an island, I couldn't really blame him for his *schadenfreude*. Hearing of the death of another is one sure way to reassure ourselves of our own invulnerability, even while the world around us tumbles into mayhem and anarchy.

'Poor poor woman. What a way to go,' he said. Okay, so I didn't care for the teeth, but he was the only person I'd met who hadn't been one hundred per cent negative about Amy Morrison – whom I would never *ever* manage to think of as Noreen Briggs. He dug at his pheasant. 'And you don't think Doctor Drummond was responsible.'

'Even if I could come up with a motive, I still wouldn't see her as the perpetrator.'

'So where do you think she is?'

I shrugged. 'Anybody's guess.'

'But . . . uh . . . still with us?'

'I very much hope so.'

It was late when I pulled into my allocated parking spot outside the flats. It was a freezing black night. Somewhere in the darkness, the sea was rough, pounding away at the shingle, alternately sucking and roaring, waves crashing onto the beach. The wind was fiercely cold.

Head bent, shoulders hunched against the gathering storm, I hurried in through the entrance doors and into the communal lobby. I took the stairs, too cold to wait for the lift to descend from the top floor, and let myself in to my flat. As soon as I shut the door behind me, I was instantly alert. Someone was, or had recently been, in my flat. I listened but could hear nothing. It was the smell which warned me; not a smell exactly, more a suggestion of one. Faintly acrid. Alien, and yet familiar in some way, though I couldn't have pinpointed how.

Unhooking the antique policeman's truncheon – a wedding present from our colleagues when Jack and I got married – from among the coats by the front door, I walked through the flat, switching on lights as I went.

There was no one there. Not under the beds, nor in the closets. Not behind the sofas, nor squeezed into the tiny linen cupboard. There were none of the big ventilator shafts or heating ducts into which fugitives scramble when on the run in thriller movies. I even climbed up into the small roof-space and flashed a torch around. Inched around the water tank. No one was there, nor anywhere else. There was literally no hiding place. I checked that doors and windows were shut and locked.

Had the place been bugged? I'd bought a bug finder about three years ago, after suspecting that my computer had been hacked into. I got it out of my desk drawer now, and ran it swiftly over as much of the flat as I could, but found nothing. Eventually, I pretended to go about my normal bedtime routine, for the benefit of anyone keeping track of me – though I couldn't imagine where they'd be hidden. I stripped down to my underwear and ran the shower, without stepping under the spray. I put on a black sweater and black jeans, stuffed a couple of cushions between the duvet and the bottom sheet in my bedroom, added a thick dark fleece rolled into a ball and tucked it among the pillows. It would fool an intruder for maybe forty seconds. Then I pulled an armchair across the room and set it behind the door. Took a spare duvet from the blanket-box at the end of my bed. Made myself comfortable, along with my truncheon and a torch, a lidless plastic bowl of table salt and a police whistle.

If there was some hiding place I had missed, and there was someone still in the flat, or about to break back into it, I would be more than ready to attack. In fact, I almost wished I'd left a door unlocked, to make it easier. Now, I waited. I had spent many days on stakeouts during my time in uniform. I knew how to wait. I recalled one of the oft-repeated mantras from my accelerated-course tutors: *You will be expected to tackle danger head on while members of the public turn away.* Right. I was ready to rock. Bring on the danger and let me tackle it.

I had no reason to believe that anyone *would* break in again, but now that I was back and in residence, lights on and car returned to its parking space, it was logical to assume that the intruder would try again. I don't know why, but I felt certain he would be back again that evening. Whatever. Like Sam Willoughby, I was ready.

It must have been three hours later that I was woken from the lightest of dozes by stealthy sounds coming from the kitchen. The faintest of chinks. The brush of a jacket against the back of a chair. The crunch as the intruder trod in the sugar I had deliberately scattered on the floor.

I couldn't understand how anyone could have got into the flat in the first place, let alone now, after I had checked doors and windows. Nor did I have the slightest idea what he/she/it was after. This couldn't be a random break-in, especially since it was a repeat of something earlier in the day. And because of that, it seemed logical that I, not my possessions, was the target. Or something that I kept with me. This had to be connected in some way with either Helena or Amy Morrison – or both. Or did it? Maybe this intruder had nothing to do with them, was a legacy from my days on the force. Most villains are bloody stupid, with no brains and long memories. It could be someone I'd been instrumental in putting away, who'd only just got out and was now intent on punishing me for my temerity in building a case against him. Or even one of Jack's cases. He'd busted a couple of local criminal gangs, one of which turned out to have international links. Perhaps this was payback time. It was a continuous threat, a hazard of being a police officer, one we all had to live with.

I waited. There was no sound at all, apart from the occasional shifting noises that all houses make, even the ones like mine, which have been heavily modernized, their function changed.

I listened for the creak of a floorboard, as the intruder mounted the stairs towards the upper floor. There was nothing. Hidden as I was behind the door, I couldn't see a thing, though through the crack I could make out just the very faintest beam of light from a torch pen or something similar. It reached the landing, turned towards my bedroom. I gripped my salt and my truncheon. Salt is a most effective weapon, as indeed is pepper. A couple of handfuls thrown into the face of an attacker usually renders him temporarily helpless, especially if it lands in the eyes or the open mouth, with the added bonus that it doesn't require a licence. There's something extremely satisfying about watching some expletive-yelling yob receive a gobful of salt. Shuts them up pretty damn quick. Not that I should advertise the fact. Given the right (or wrong?) circumstances, it's more than possible for salt to be classed as an offensive weapon.

I waited. Outside the open door, the tiny beam of light halted. Then moved with infinite deliberation towards the bed. Did I dare risk a small snore? Probably not. The intruder stepped carefully into the room. As soon as he was within striking distance, I was on him, blowing the police whistle, smashing the truncheon into the side of his head hard enough to make him stumble to one knee. I launched a handful of salt at his face and lifted the truncheon again, but he seized my wrist and bent it painfully back, so brutally that I was afraid it would snap. All the time I was blowing my whistle. He had turned his head away, so that most of the salt went over his shoulder. As he staggered to his feet, I lurched backwards, trying to release my arm from his grip. He aimed a kick at my thigh, so hard that it immediately went numb. Once more I threw salt at him, and this time got him. 'Bitch!' he choked. 'Goddamn bitch.' He let go of me and raised both hands to his face.

His torch had long since dropped to the floor and lay against the skirting board like a glow-worm, so I was pretty sure he couldn't tell exactly where I was. I bent swiftly and picked it up, flashed it at him, saw only an indistinct figure, dressed in black leathers which creaked slightly as he moved. A balaclava. A black baseball cap.

The tiny torch-beam was lost in the shadows of the room and the impenetrability of his clothing. And then, as I raised my truncheon again, he turned and ran into the darkness of the hall and down the stairs towards my front door. I ran after him, grabbed him round the waist, brought him to the floor. He writhed in my grasp like a snake, this way and that, rammed a fist into my face, caught me painfully by my arms and pulled me as close as a lover, then twisted our entwined bodies this way and that until he was on top of me. I could dimly see his raised fist, ready to smash into my face again. I reached for his balls, always a good way to disable a man, if only temporarily. But the leather was slick and my fingers skidded across it, making it impossible to grab hold of him.

By now, the neighbours had been alerted by the sound of the whistle, and fists were pounding on the door, people were shouting.

'Are you all right, Alex?' someone called. I heard the front door open (how? I'd have to check that. Could I possibly have left it unlocked?) and someone else said, 'Where's the light switch?' And then my would-be intruder-cum-burglar was on his feet, limber as a gymnast, grinding and shoving his way head down through the small crowd like a piston, running away down the passage, leaping down the two flights of communal stairs, and out through the entrance doors.

I recognized the first speaker as Miles Thomas, an architect with the County Council.

Another person followed him, the woman from across the passage, with mad hair the colour of a digestive biscuit. 'What was all that whistle-blowing?' she asked.

I got unsteadily to my feet and limped over to the window overlooking the parking area in front of the building. I saw someone racing out of the entrance doors and across the tarmac, throwing a leg over a powerful motorbike – a Harley-Davidson, as far as I could make out – revving up and roaring noisily down the short drive and off along the road beside the sea, the sound of the engine gradually dying away into the distance.

'Are you all right, dear?' Mrs Galloping Major from the floor below put an arm round my shoulders.

'I think I hurt him more than he hurt me,' I said shakily.

'Here . . .' It was the Galloping Major himself, in a magnificent crimson dressing gown. 'Have a swig, m'dear.' He held out a silver hip flask. 'Learned years ago to carry a reviving tincture about my person at all times. Never know when it'll come in useful.' I took a gulp. And another.

'Very useful indeed.' I handed the flask back. 'Thank you.'

I surveyed them standing there, nice, decent people, and wished I had taken the trouble to get to know them better. 'What I can't understand is how he got in,' I said. 'I always lock up before I leave, and when I came back, I checked everything again, windows *and* doors.'

'I just bet it's the door from the kitchen onto the fire escape.' That was Dave, our resident artist, a young American who'd moved in just after Jack moved out.

'But I *checked* it.'

'It's got a faulty lock,' Dave said. 'The agent who sold you the place should have told you.'

A chorus arose. 'Quite right.' 'Disgraceful.' 'Very careless.' 'Estate agents are scum, in my opinion.' This last from a red-faced guy in striped pyjamas and a grey dressing gown with tartan facings. 'Lower than tabloid journalists, and that's saying something.' In happier days, Jack and I had labelled him the Tabloid Journalist; I did a hasty mental revision.

'I've lived here for several years,' I said. 'I've never noticed anything wrong.'

'You obviously haven't realized that the lock doesn't catch properly,' Miles said. 'It's a design fault. The bolt isn't quite long enough to fit into its groove so it's easy to push the door open from the outside, if you want to.'

More nodding from Mrs Digestive. 'Most of us have had our locks replaced.'

'Point is,' said Dante, 'you should get that fixed, pronto.'

'And be sure to make the agency pay for it,' said the Galloping Major.

'I'm surprised your husband didn't notice when he was still living here,' said Mrs Digestive. 'Supposed to be a policeman, wasn't he?'

'The *police*! Can't trust them to see what's right in front of their noses . . .' was the general consensus. They began to regale each other with stories of police incompetence until Miles said he didn't know about anyone else, but he needed to get back to bed.

'Well, thank you all for your help,' I said.

'Will you be okay on your own?' asked Dave.

'Thank you, yes. I'll go and block up that kitchen door before I go to bed.'

One by one they drifted away, back to their own flats.

The following day I sat staring at a beautiful reproduction of Carolus-Duran's gorgeous portrait of his wife – *The Lady With The Gloves* – and wishing that I could paint. Though where would artists be without people like me to admire and envy their work? And, most importantly, buy it? But my mind wasn't really on the picture. What had my intruder wanted last night? Wanted so badly that he had risked coming back a second time? Did he want to kill me? As an ex-copper, I don't like questions to which I don't know the answers.

From the kitchen came the sound of an electric drill as an estate agent-hired carpenter replaced the faulty lock on the outside door.

The phone rang. It was Mary Quick. 'Hi, Ma,' I said. 'How're things?'

'Very good. I'm calling to tell you that your father and I are off to Paris tomorrow for a few days. Just to save you driving over and finding we aren't here.'

'Very thoughtful of you. And who's feeding Stanley?'

'Mrs Thing next door has promised to come and check on him.'

'Good.'

'So as I say, no need to come down. I'll telephone when we get back.'

'Any special reason for the trip?'

'There are a couple of exhibitions that we want to see. And as so often, we want to have a wander round the Musée d'Orsay.'

'Lucky you.'

'One of the joys of being retired. You can take off at a moment's notice. Are you well?'

'Pretty much.'

'Good.'

'Apart,' I said, 'from the fact that—' But never one to waste time on niceties, she'd already hung up.

Leaving me to wonder just what was going on. I could safely say that my mother considered she had done her parental duty by raising and educating us. She did not then feel that our lives intersected after that. If she and my father wanted to go away – as they often did – they would do so, without reference to their children. So why was she so uncharacteristically informing me of their up-coming trip across the Channel? It sounded suspiciously as though she were warning me not to go to their house, even were I so minded. The thought had never crossed my mind – until she telephoned. Now I decided that as soon as I was back from France myself (only the previous day, I had booked a flight to Bergerac), I would drive on over to their place and see what was up. If anything.

FOURTEEN

I t wasn't hard to find the address I wanted, thanks to a swift visit to the gallery in New Bond Street which handled Ainslie Gordon's work, coupled with my navy-blue skirt and jacket and the semi-official manner I was beginning to perfect.

After a short flight from Stansted Airport, I picked up my pre-booked hire car from the airport at Bergerac and, using the satnav provided, set off on the hour-long drive to *La Tuilerie*, Gordon's place. In England, it was cold, wet and miserable, but although it was the middle of winter here in France, the sun shone, the sky was cloudlessly blue, and a balmy mildness hovered above the pantiled roofs of villages and farms. Through the open window I could smell warming earth and the promise of spring. All should have been right with the world – but wasn't. The only personal comfort I had was that the police still had not discovered Helena's whereabouts. Any more than I myself had. But thanks to her cryptic *imok* message, at least I felt fairly certain that she wasn't shackled in some pervert's soundproofed cellar.

On either side of the road the landscape of faded winter green rolled gently down wooded or pastured slopes to rise again to more hills. Glossy cows moved languidly through winter-depleted meadows of grass, and although I was there on a mission, I felt the same sense of letting go as I always did when I was in *la France profonde*, the silence gently pushing away the bombardment of noise which usually surrounded me: traffic, people, blaring horns, gunning engines, shouts and screams, music blasting from windows, shops, mobile phones, planes overhead. Not to mention raucous seagulls. Here there was nothing but birdsong, leaf-rustle, grass-whisper.

I drove along a main highway, then turned off onto a rutted chalk-strewn road which led between fallow vineyards and groves of bare-branched walnut trees, past stone farmhouses and restored barns. I had not forewarned Ainslie Gordon of my arrival. Fliss Fairlight had told me that Inspector Garside had contacted the French police, who had then arrived at Gordon's place with sirens wailing and blue lights flashing. Plenty of notice for a fugitive such as Helena to hide herself, if she was there.

Reaching the hamlet, I drove very slowly past a low stone wall marking the boundary of a garden which would be charming when spring arrived. Stone steps led up and down to different levels of grass, flanked by lavender and rosemary and other small bushy shrubs whose name I didn't know. Even in winter, they gave off a flowery scent. Along one side I could see a series of low buildings, most of them semi-derelict, lacking walls or floors. One was being used to house a battered old car and several bicycles; in another I could make out a shiny motorbike with a ruby-red thorax half-covered by a drab canvas wrapping. In front of a long L-shaped stone house, a wooden loggia sat beneath a leafless tree. In summer it would be covered in clematis and roses, but now it was occupied mainly – at first glance – by moss and spiders plus a marble carving of a voluptuous fertility goddess.

All the doors of the house stood open to the gentle heat of the day. Inside, I could see a huge table and on one end of it, a plaster reproduction of Jacob Epstein's *Deidre* with a bowler hat perched on top of her flowing chalky hair.

Not wanting to attract the attention of the occupants, I continued on past the house and parked out of sight behind a church around the corner. I pulled a summer hat over my hair and put on a pair of sunglasses in an attempt to partly disguise myself, in case anyone should be watching from a window as I returned to the opening in the stone wall and walked across stone flags towards the front door. Nearer the house, I could hear raised voices, both male, something like an enamel basin being hurled, clattering, to the ground before subsiding amid circles of metallic sound, a sudden tattoo of what might have been drumbeats, a voice shouting, 'Fuck, fuck, fuck and damnation!' Then a man came bursting out of a side door at full tilt, before coming to a sudden halt when he caught sight of me.

'Who the hell are you?' he asked, then suddenly yelled the word 'Strangers!' over his shoulder. Somewhere in the back regions of the house, I heard the slam of a door. Then there was quiet.

'I come in peace,' I said. 'I just want to know that she's all right.'

He adopted a ridiculously over-the-top expression of bewilderment. 'What the fuck are you talking about?' he demanded. He spoke in short energetic bursts, the words exploding from his mouth as though shot from a cannon. He was wearing an artist's smock of faded navy canvas, dirty beige combat trousers and espadrilles which might once have been yellow but now were just an indeterminate dirt colour. Looking at him dispassionately, I was absolutely certain I did not want to see his toenails. His head was liberally covered in Dylan Thomas-ish black curls turning grey, which flopped down and up again in time with the rapid gestures of his hands. Grubby but charismatic, I concluded. Definitely not a restful man.

'Are you Ainslie Gordon?' I said.

'Who wants to know?'

'I do. I am your number one fan.' Sounding more like Kathy Bates in *Misery* than I wanted. I had learned over many years that there is nothing more mollifying than kind words and admiring comments. Besides, it's difficult to maintain belligerence in the face of compliments.

'As it happens . . .' He smiled rather awkwardly, showing terrible teeth.

'Your Unicorn series is absolutely brilliant,' I said. 'The deceptively simple juxtaposition of silver-white purity with the dark creatures so obviously based on the monsters from *Where The Wild Things Are,* says something profound, speaking as they do of lost innocence and corrupted virtue . . . wonderful!' Oh, I can produce artistic bollocks-speak with the best of them, when required.

For a moment he stared at me as though I had suddenly gone insane or had stripped off in front of him, his expression a mixture of scepticism and complete agreement with my fulsome appraisal. Any minute now he was going to ask me if I was taking the mickey. 'Are you taking the mickey?' he asked.

'I meant every word.'

'And who did you say you were?'

'I didn't.' I held out my hand. 'I'm Alexandra Quick.'

'Quick . . .' It was immediately obvious that he recognized the name. It was equally clear that he did not want to admit it. Was this because it would imply that he was still in touch with his former wife? Or because he feared he might show up on the radar as having killed or abducted her? Or simply because he was a curmudgeonly old sod?

He took my hand in his huge mottled ones and shook it rather too hard to be enjoyable. He glanced over his shoulder at the open doors into the house, then back at me. 'And what's *your* . . .' He coughed. '. . . uh . . . area of expertise, Alexandra Quick?'

'Come now.' I smiled at him. There were fields beyond the house, bordered by thin woods, and I could see a black figure crossing one of them at a fast trot, obviously aiming to disappear among the trees. I thought I recognized Helena by the flow of blonde twists which hung down the figure's back, but I couldn't be quite sure. 'I'm looking for Helena, on the off-chance she's found refuge with you.'

'Why would she do that? We haven't been in touch for years.'

'Whatever . . .' I said. 'As long as she's not been kidnapped by some insane psychopath . . . that's all I wanted to ensure. The police in England are after her, but I expect you know that. If you're in touch, tell her that *Ripe for the Picking* is coming along splendidly, and there is a three-book contract sitting on my desk.'

With that, I turned to walk slowly away from him, picking a sprig from a flourishing rosemary bush which grew beside one of the flights of mossy steps and crushing it in my hand while I waited for him – as I knew he would – to call me back.

'Just a damned minute,' came his voice behind me. Scottish, educated, and, yes, slightly sinister. A swift glance around showed me there were no other houses within window-sight of his pretty house and garden. Was I safe here?

'What?' I said, without turning to face him.

He seemed wrong-footed, a state I guessed he didn't often find himself in. Again he glanced over his shoulder. 'Um . . . who do you think is . . . um . . . here?'

'Isn't it obvious I mean your former wife?' I said. 'Doctor Helena Drummond.'

'You're not representing any current husbands?'

'No.'

'You're not connected with that bastard, Hawkes, are you?'

'Nope.' I wondered why he asked and who the bastard Hawkes was. A creditor? A wronged spouse? Which raised the possibility that the figure hurrying towards the concealing woods was not Helena after all, but someone else's wife. I had often considered the sexual allure of painters. Not just their allure, but their rampant sexuality, the women they bedded, their affairs and complicated love-tangles, such as those within the Danish group known as the Skagen painters, the French Impressionists, or more modern painters such as Lucian Freud or Augustus John. Why did women fall so heavily and so easily for them? What was it about them? Looking at the irascible man in front of me, with his clenched fists, deep frown and jutting jaw, I could concede that while I might not necessarily want him at my dinner table, there was an undeniable energy about him which, at the risk of using a cliché, I could only call animal magnetism. Didn't work for me, but I could easily see why it might enthral others.

He scowled. 'Just as well for you. And how did you get here?'

'By Ryanair from Stansted, then by—'

'No, I mean what led you here to my studio?'

I was tempted to tap the side of my nose and reply, 'Aha!' Instead I said, 'I recently discovered that my missing friend Doctor Helena Drummond was once married to you. A total surprise, I may say. And since I'm trying to find her, coming to see you seemed a logical move. And you, of course, being so famous and all, were easy to track down.'

'I see.'

'I'm not sure if you're aware, but Doctor Drummond is a major suspect in the murder of Amy Morrison.'

His cheeks suddenly changed colour from sunburn-red to tomato-scarlet. 'That little bitch!' he said.

Interesting. He'd obviously had dealings with the woman. 'So . . .?' I looked at him expectantly.

'I taught for a year in New York,' he said. 'The slag tried to seduce me and then when I . . . succumbed . . . she wanted me to change her grades. Upwards, of course. And then . . .' He choked on what seemed like righteous indignation. '. . . when I resisted her, she reported me to the authorities, said I'd harassed her from day one. Utter bollocks, of course, but I had the devil's own job getting out of that.'

'Putting that aside, have you seen Helena? Or has she been in touch with you?'

'What's it to do with you if she has?' Strangely, I felt that aggressive though his behaviour was, he was frightened of something.

'She's my colleague,' I said. 'My *friend*. The police think she's a cold-blooded killer, and she's *not*.' I felt close to tears. 'And now she's vanished.'

After a silent pause, once again I turned as if to go.

He glanced at his watch. 'Instead of racing off, come in and have a glass of wine. There's a good St Emilion, if you're interested.' I could hear the effort he was making to sound emollient.

'That would be nice. And perhaps I could also look at some of your current work while I'm here . . .'

'Of course.' He gave me his under-used, gap-toothed, tobacco-stained smile again. He might have thought he'd got off lightly, but I planned to renew my interrogation once we were seated together with a bottle between us. It would be much harder then for him to wriggle out of my questions.

I followed him into a wide single room, which it didn't take much detective work to see was his studio. Wooden stairs led to an upper storey. The walls were made of rough rocks plastered together, what the French call *pierre apparente*. The big work table I'd seen from the road was covered in a clutter of tins of paint, jars of coloured pencils, pens, pairs of scissors, old clay pots with honey-glazed rims full of paintbrushes, the kind of tools a sculptor would need. Rolls of paper stood in corners, five or six unused canvasses leaned against a wall, pages torn from a large sketching block had been stuck untidily to the walls with strips of masking tape. There was a slight but pervasive smell of turps.

From Gordon's remarks, it seemed fairly obvious that he had been in touch with Helena recently, and also that she hadn't given him all the details surrounding Amy's Morrison's murder. The question I was most anxious to discover an answer to was why Amy had been in Helena's house in the first place. And there was another point I wanted to raise. But he indicated a bench running along one side of the table. 'Sit down,' he said, and started pulling the cork out of a bottle which was already open. He showed me the label.

'Looks good.'

'I buy it directly from the vineyard,' he said. 'It's only about an hour and a half from here. Well worth the drive.' He filled a large goblet for me.

I held it to the light, sniffed, swirled, swallowed. 'Mmm, lovely.' I put my elbows on the table and leaned confidentially towards him. 'I also learned recently that Helena had a child. A girl. Are you the father?'

Again he did the complexional colour change, this time from

scarlet to sunset-purple. He shook his head, but so unconvincingly that I thought he must be lying. If so, her surname was likely to be Gordon, unless she was one of those principled people who didn't like to ride on the coat-tails of a famous parent. I wondered what line of work she might be in. Even if she existed, it was unlikely that he would tell me. Or that I would ask. I looked round the studio, trying to find a clue of some kind which might lead to Helena, which is when I noticed a lighter patch of colour on the grimy tiles underfoot, which had obviously not seen a broom or a mop for some months. Yet this area had clearly been scrubbed, and fairly recently, since the grouting between the squares of terracotta was still damp, and a darker colour than in other parts of the room. Perhaps I was being over-fanciful, but it seemed to me that violence had been done here not long ago. I was suddenly watchful, alert to any movement on the part of my host. On no account did I intend to turn my back on him: there were far too many weapons of destruction scattered about the room, from a rusty samurai sword to a couple of knobkerries with viciously heavy heads, to various sharp knives and several pointed things.

There was a sudden tattoo of steps on the wooden floor above our heads, producing the drum-like noise I'd heard earlier. Moments later, someone appeared at the top of the stairs leading to the ground floor where we were sitting and clattered down them, Halfway down, seeing me, he stopped. A slender, wiry young man in close-fitting jeans, with a clean striped dress-shirt tucked into them, an elaborate leather belt, and a close-cropped head, stood there. He came further down the stairs, found a glass, filled it with wine and drank some, while eyeing me. 'For God's sake, Ainslie,' he said disdainfully. 'Two sluts in one day? Isn't that overdoing it a bit?' Good accent, bad manners.

Ainslie held up a hand, as though to stop him. 'Moderate your language, boy. It's not what you think.'

'It never is.' The guy looked across at me. 'So what's *your* name?' His voice was heavy with contempt.

I took an instant dislike to him. Arrogance is one of the least endearing of human traits. 'I can't see that it's any business of yours,' I said.

He was taken aback by my response. 'Uh . . .' He stared at me hard, willing me to look away, which I didn't do. 'Only asking,' he said eventually, carefully avoiding my gaze as he slid onto the bench beside Gordon.

'Never mind Laurence,' Gordon said. 'Laurence, meet Alexandra Quick. He's my current pupil. Learning the trade and acting as my general factotum.'

'So a wannabe painter?' I asked. *Laurence, Laurence*? The name rang bells, and not the happy kind.

'I'd like to think I was a bit more than just a wannabe,' Laurence said sulkily, picking at the table with a red-handled Stanley knife which had been lying there. He rubbed the top of his short-haired skull as though surprised and uneasy to find it so near to nakedness.

'You are, dear, you are,' soothed Ainslie. 'But there's still a ways to go.'

'And if you want a hint for future success, I would suggest you learn some manners before you try to advance any further,' I said. Rude? Very. But not as rude as he had been.

He raised his head and gave me a flat-eyed stare, full of menace. I wanted to say that nobody did the fish-eye as well as I did, but feeling that I might have met my master here, refrained, while Gordon rolled his eyes behind the little bastard and held the bottle over my glass.

I shook my head. 'I have to catch a plane back to England this afternoon, which means driving to the airport,' I said. 'So better not.'

'As you wish,' said Gordon, generously refilling his own glass.

I gestured at the clean patch of floor tile. I smiled innocently. 'Goodness! Looks like there was an accident of some kind here. Even a murder! What did you do, drop a tin of green paint on the floor or something?'

Both of the men looked at me. Laurence with alarm, Gordon with anger. 'What?'

I shrugged. 'Not that it's any of my business,' I said rapidly. My heart beat faster than usual. Even separately, these two men exuded threat. Together, they could definitely be lethal. For the first time I began to fear for Helena's well-being, though I couldn't think of any reason why either of them might want to harm her.

Was she the woman I'd seen running away across the fields? Ever since entering the studio, I had been looking around for any sign

that she had ever been there. Now I suddenly saw one. On a seduc-
tion couch set against the far end of the room, hidden beneath a
pile of cushions of dusty velvet and fraying gold thread, shabby
linen, shredding silk, I saw the corner of something I thought I
recognized. One of Helena's gaudy patchwork shawls, hastily shoved
out of sight. I could think of no way I could retrieve it without them
seeing me. Even if I could get my hands on it, it would be too bulky
to hide satisfactorily in my bag. And maybe I was being over-
imaginative. Maybe Ainslie – painter of fleshy nudes in lurid colours
– used it as a prop to drape over the *chaise longues* and couches
upon which he arranged his models. Those naked women were
tourist pieces, I often thought, without any of the merit or class of
his more reflective, muted landscapes.

The petulant Laurence drained the contents of his glass and slid
away from the table. 'Work to do,' he muttered, still not catching
my eye.

And as he did so, that sneering pout triggered some memory in
my brain. 'Laurence what?' I asked. 'Just so I recognize your name
when you're famous.'

He looked over at Gordon, who gave him a tiny nod. 'Turnbull,'
he said unwillingly.

Laurence Turnbull. Of *course*. I might even have recognized him
if he hadn't shaved off most of his hair. It had been a sensational
case about two years ago. High on cocaine and brandy, he had
driven at speed down a suburban 30mph street, veered onto the
pavement outside a school where kids were waiting for parents or
school buses, killed two young girls, badly injured three others,
driven off without stopping. There'd been enough witnesses for him
to get no more than a mile away from the scene before he was
apprehended. His lawyers had pleaded mitigating factors such as
his abandonment by his natural parents when he was born, the
trauma of being adopted, the abuse he had suffered on a systematic
basis at the boarding school where his affluent adoptive parents had
sent him, until he absconded and lived off the streets, earning enough
as a rent-boy and dealer to get by, until a social worker had taken
pity on him, brought him into her own home and tried to redeem
him. She had finally got him accepted at an art college in London,
where he had shown considerable promise until he got in with the
wrong crowd and began on the drugs again.

What had been particularly appalling about the case was the fact that owing to a technical error, the judge was forced to let him off the charge of culpable manslaughter with nothing more than a slap on the wrist, a suspended two-year sentence and a three-year driving ban. 'Despicable,' the judge had called it. 'An act of the most depraved and contemptible irresponsibility.' After that, Turnbull had disappeared and, despite the best efforts of the tabloids, had not been located since. Just as well. The internet had been toxic with death threats. And now here he was, standing opposite me, clearly unsure of whether I was familiar with his name. I wondered what he would have looked like if he'd actually been sent down. Pale, puffy, the cockiness kicked out of him, I guessed.

So yes, I remembered Laurence Turnbull all right. And the frustration on the part of my colleagues at his lenient treatment. 'Turnbull,' I said. 'I'll try to remember that.' I endeavoured to give the impression I'd never heard of him.

'He's going to be good.' Gordon patted Laurence on the arm. 'Just needs to apply himself.'

'Of course.' I wondered what Laurence's dreams were made of, whether he ever flash-backed to those girls being hurled into the air, the sound their heads made as they struck the pavement or fell beneath his front wheels, tumbling through the air in a rain of blood and broken bones.

I also wondered what his connection to Ainslie Gordon was – and if it had anything at all to do with either Amy Morrison or Helena Drummond.

'So how well did you know Amy Morrison?' I said to Ainslie.

He did the swelling-tomato thing again. 'Too well,' he growled.

'And how did that come about?'

'Like I just said, she took one of my classes when I was a visiting professor in New York. She couldn't paint, couldn't write, couldn't appreciate the artistic gems I offered the kids. On the whole, I'd say she was the most irritating, no-talent, selfish, ball-busting woman I have ever met. And—'

'Believe him, he's met a lot,' put in Turnbull. He sniggered unattractively.

'Ball-busting?'

'She liked to find some talented but needy guy and then – if you'll excuse the expression – suck him dry. She broke quite a few hearts – male *and* female.' He gave a theatrical shudder. 'God, what a bitch.'

'She sounds like a monster.'

'She was.'

'But nobody committed suicide because of her?'

'Not on my watch, they didn't. Though I did hear a rumour somewhere or other . . .' He gazed at me, his hot blue eyes flaming in his face. 'I shouldn't say this, but not only am I glad she's dead, I also hope she died painfully. She caused enough damage in her lifetime.' He seemed to be echoing Sadie Johns' sentiments precisely.

'Any names of broken-hearted students that I should know about? Any death threats made?'

He shook his head.

'None that you ever heard of,' Laurence added in his sulky way.

'This is very true. But they were a pretty open bunch of kids. Extroverts almost to a man. And woman, of course.'

'Did you know her, Laurence?' I asked.

'I think I might have met her,' he said. 'Can't quite remember where or why.'

The conversation wasn't going anywhere. I did a faux double-take. 'Golly,' I trilled. 'Is that a piece of patchwork under the cushion over there?' I was up and walking across the room as I spoke. 'I'm *so* into patchwork . . .'

But when I pulled it out from under the cushions, it turned out to be nothing more significant than an empty cushion-cover, and nothing to do with my missing friend.

FIFTEEN

'*It was good to see you at our little gathering last week. My husband and I would love you to come for drinks next Tuesday, so you can have a closer look at the gallery. And we can also have a business discussion,*' the note read. '*Very informal. Bring a friend if you wish.*'

Bring a friend . . . Well, now . . . Did she know that Helena wasn't around? It sounded as though she did. Those Yankee bluebloods were sticklers for protocol; if she hadn't known, she would have written '*Dr Drummond*' rather than '*a friend*'.

I walked down to Willoughby's book shop. It was crowded this morning, people buying Christmas presents, I guessed. Both Sam and Alison, his part-time assistant, were working flat-out and I could see he was far too busy to stop for a chat with me. I idled by the till, pretending to scrutinize the flyers for various events taking place in the town, until he had put through his next transaction, then I said quickly: 'I want to ask you a favour . . . come round to my place this evening and I'll open a bottle of wine.'

'Absolutely love to,' he said abstractedly. 'What time?'

'Any time after you've closed.'

'Today's late-night closing.'

'That's okay.'

He rang my doorbell at 8:32, handed me a bottle of red ('*from Vine's wine shop next door to me*') and collapsed onto the big squashy sofa in front of where the fireplace would be if it hadn't been ripped out by the company which had renovated my building.

'I'm tired,' he said. 'So forgive me if I'm not my usual ebullient self.' He smiled self-deprecatingly, knowing full well that 'ebullient' and 'Sam' did not usually inhabit the same sentence.

'Have a glass of wine,' I said. 'Also from Vine's. Or would you prefer something stronger . . . whisky, brandy?'

He opted for a glass of Armagnac, after which he perked up a bit. 'The Christmas rush is always exhausting,' he said. 'Not that I

would be without it. The four weeks leading up to Christmas Eve
generate more than a third of our total annual sales.'

'At least books are still being bought. Considering the size of
the town, it's amazing that you manage to stay in business.'

'But for how long? The competition from eBooks and self-
publishing is fierce.' He sighed. 'Luckily there are three private
schools in the area plus several state schools, plus that big EFL
institution out in the country, which caters to the rich sons of foreign
dictators and politicians, so I don't do too badly. Obviously I make
sure I stock all the necessary textbooks or I take care to obtain
contracts to supply them to the different teaching establishments. I
carry cribs and collections of sample exam questions. And I have
a thriving second-hand section – though there again I'm in competition with the charity shops. Not that anyone could realistically expect
to make a living out of flogging pre-loved books – as the phrase is
– for £1.99 a pop. Or even less. Especially in the age of electronic
readers and the like.'

'And here I thought you were a dozy kind of dreamy individual,
nose stuck in a book all the time.'

'Oh, I'm that all right.'

'As well as a hard-headed businessman?'

'These days, you have to be. In fact, I took a six-month business
course when I first came down here from London to help out Annie
Marston.'

'Annie Marston . . .' The name rang bells.

'Who used to own the shop? Until she retired,' he continued. 'I've
recently branched out into stationery plus cards for every possible
occasion, wrapping paper and ribbons, magazines, computer acces-
sories, that sort of thing, so that brings in the punters.' He pushed
back the flopping blond hair – in need of a cut, I couldn't help
noticing, realizing that he probably didn't have time to get to the
barber at the moment – and produced another of his wry little laughs.

'And you've also squeezed in those four café tables and the coffee
machine.'

'Squeeze is the word. I really need to expand. But it's heck of a
risk to take when book sales are dropping.' He took another luxurious mouthful of brandy. 'Oh, I feel so much better.' He hoisted
his glass at me. 'Thank you.' Looked expectant. 'So . . .'

'The reason I asked you to drop in this evening was because this morning you were too busy to stop, and I wanted to ask if you would like to join me . . .' I handed him the card from Mercy Lamont.

'It sounds good,' he said. 'Nice address. Yes, please, I'd love to. Alison can hold the fort. And I could certainly do with a break.' He smiled at me. 'Yes, lovely. What's the gallery?'

'The Lamonts are big art collectors, and they have this amazing corridor – they've amalgamated two flats, in Eaton Square no less, so as you can imagine, they must be rolling in it, and turned a connecting passage into a kind of arcade of family portraits, dating back two or three centuries.'

'Sounds interesting.' He took another sip from his glass. 'And you still haven't located Doctor Drummond?'

'Not yet. But at least I'm assuming she's all right.' For a moment I debated not telling him about the four-character note I'd received, but could see no reason not to. I explained how I knew.

'Interesting.' He looked thoughtful. 'You sure it was her who shoved it through the door? Not someone else, trying to trick you into thinking it came from her?'

'Don't *say* that!' I couldn't bear to contemplate the possibility. Blame and guilt rained down me. 'I feel responsible for what's happened.'

'Why?'

I looked at him miserably. 'I'm not entirely sure. I just do.'

'Doctor Drummond is an adult, responsible for herself. As indeed was Amy Morrison. But if something terrible *has* happened to her,' Sam said, his voice pushing harshly into my self-recrimination, 'it has nothing to do with you, Alex. Nothing whatsoever.' He took me by the shoulders and gave me a little shake. 'It's *not* your fault.' He let go of me, took my hand and held it tightly between his own. He repeated, 'Not. Your. Fault.'

'Yes,' I said awkwardly. 'Or no . . .' I wasn't sure quite when we had become this close.

'It's so easy to think that things might have been different if you had been with her.' He rubbed my cold fingers with his own warm ones. 'But it wouldn't, you know. Even if you'd been there, you couldn't have changed a thing.'

'Thank you,' I said. 'Thank you, Sam.'

On Tuesday, we travelled up to London together by train. Much simpler than trying to find parking in the city. When we arrived at the Eaton Square flat, we were met by a housekeeperish young woman in a white-collared black dress and shown into a sitting room, somewhat smaller than the grand salon of last time, but nonetheless decorated with almost as much luxurious magnificence.

Mercy and the mostly silent Bob were on hand to greet us. Bob gestured at an enormous silver tray set on a sideboard holding a sparkling array of expensive glasses and offered us almost anything we could imagine to drink: Sam had a gin and tonic while I opted for a glass of red wine.

We chatted about this and that. Sam's eyes were round as he absorbed the paintings which hung on the walls. After a while, Bob suggested we move to his office, where he began to speak more seriously, while his wife verbally hung back.

'I believe Mercy has already spoken to you of the possibility of us setting up a small publishing house,' he said. 'Concentrating on exactly the kind of popular art books that are Drummond & Quick's speciality.'

'It sounds like a really good idea.' I thought of Clifford Nichols and his three-book offer. I had not yet signed the contracts and returned them to him, as I had been waiting for Helena to return. Meanwhile, my gaze travelled over the two walls that weren't covered in books. The people they knew! There were the Lamonts with Obama and Michelle, with François Hollande, with Oprah and Clint Eastwood. There was Mercy with her hair shrouded in a black lace shawl, shaking hands with the Pope. There was Bob with Condoleezza. The two of them with Bill and Hillary.

'It's not just a good idea,' Bob said severely. 'As we see it, this would be a prestige concept. High-end. Premium books for premium people.'

'What you've produced so far is good,' said Mercy. '*Very* good. But it could be even better.'

'Must-have books for the luxury crowd,' Bob continued. 'And priced accordingly. No one with any pretensions to culture will be able to afford to be without at least one copy.'

'If they can afford to buy it in the first place!' Sam said. It was exactly what I was thinking.

Bob shot him an inimical look. 'The product could really take off – and the marketing would be a piece of cake.'

I could easily see how his dynamic approach must have turned his father's fortune into millions more. 'I'm not too keen on my work being seen as "product",' I said.

'It's an advertising term. I have absolutely no intention of belittling or demeaning your projects.'

'It's definitely something I must look at very carefully,' I said. 'Actually, we've just been offered a three-book deal with a publisher specializing in art books.'

Bob's face flushed. 'I hope you're not trying to up the ante,' he said.

'Of course I'm not!' I wasn't best pleased with his insinuations. 'I don't play games.' Already I was wondering whether I wanted to be associated with someone quite so ready to take offence.

'I'll double their offer,' he said.

'Meanwhile . . .' said Mercy. She laid a soothing hand on her husband's arm. 'Let's not forget the gallery. That's what they came for.'

She pointed at one of the tall panelled doors set into one of the long side walls. 'As I told you on your last visit, behind the middle door there's a passage we've turned into our own private portrait gallery. A mixture of pictures from our collection, family portraits, paintings by members of our families or friends – you know the kind of thing.'

'You should know,' Bob said, 'that we don't let everyone in. In fact most people don't even know it's there.'

'Exactly. I should feel almost . . .' Mercy paused, searching for a word. '. . . defiled if someone went in uninvited.'

'We're flattered.' I nodded and smiled. Defiled . . . strong word. It sounded a little melodramatic, a bit Ayn Rand, but I suppose the owners of expensive artworks develop a powerful possessiveness about them.

Bob refilled our glasses. 'Feel free to take these with you.'

Sam and I moved towards the door Mercy had indicated, slipped through, closed the door behind us, raised our eyebrows at each other in a silent 'Phew!'

'Oh, wow!' I said. 'And double wow!'

We found ourselves in a long, glass-roofed hallway, the walls on both sides lined with portraits, rather like the Vasarian Corridor at the Uffizi Gallery in Florence. I walked down the right-hand side, enjoying the diverse mix of eighteenth- and nineteenth-century paintings and contemporary art. The Lamonts had been eclectic in their choice of subjects: mothers with children at their knee, sportsmen leaning nonchalantly against trees, family groups, horses standing on the cobbles of their stableyards or trotting over velvety greenswards, pug dogs, cats, fish, even a Dürer-like detailed drawing of a toad.

I recognized several of the paintings. At the end of the long corridor, I turned and walked slowly back up the opposite side. There was more of the same, but as I approached the door leading back into the salon, Sam said suddenly: 'Alex, come and look at this.'

'What?'

He was gazing at a husband and wife, mounted in an elaborate gilt-plaster frame entitled 'Pierre and Marie Lamont', and a date of over 150 years ago. There was another similar canvas, with another couple of the same vintage, both of them looking deeply apprehensive. This time the couple was called Jaime Arturo and Caritas Parnassi. Then came a woman whose likeness to Mercy was unmistakable, with three children – two girls and a boy – lounging against the skirt of her plain black velvet gown, neckline plunging, shoulders a little bit *Dallas* but not too much, as though the sitter was aware that it was a style which would never be classic. And yet another painting, done in conscious imitation of the old masters: a woman, two little boys, a husband leaning against a tree with a gun across his shoulder. The dress was off-the-shoulder, the hair and make-up very Eighties. So were the kids. Obviously the present-day Lamonts.

Round Mercy's neck and swinging between her boobs was a gold necklace with earrings to match. It was the same necklace that the woman in black velvet was wearing, now I came to look more closely, as indeed was Caritas Parnassi. A family heirloom, then. A one-off, personally commissioned maybe a century earlier by one side of the Lamont family or the other.

It was unmistakably the necklace from which the link I'd found beside Amy's body came.

Little hammers started knocking at each other inside my brain. *Knock* . . . how did Amy get hold of it? *Knock* . . . if Amy had been wearing it when she was killed, where was it now? She'd had a rich husband, of course. Perhaps he had been a friend of the Lamonts. Perhaps he had seen the gold chain at a dinner-party *chez* Lamont, noticed how his wife had admired it, had commissioned a copy from some prestigious upmarket jewellers.

'I'm certain I've seen that very necklace somewhere before,' Sam said, keeping his voice low. I knew he was wondering whether microphones were placed strategically here and there.

Sam and I went back into the elegant salon, where Bob was pouring himself a second G&T. Or possibly even a third. 'So what did you think?' Mercy asked, while Bob handed me another glass of wine.

'Exhilarating.' I gave her a short critique of some of the paintings. Specified several. Mentioned the Vasarian Corridor in Florence. Her face lit up. 'That's exactly what we modelled it on! There was that passageway between our two apartments, which didn't seem to have any real function except to connect them, and my husband suggested roofing it with glass and turning it into a gallery. As you saw.'

'I would love to produce a . . . not a *catalogue raisoné*,' I said, 'but an anthology of your paintings. Or some of them. Alongside a discussion of the people featured, their history, their *story*. Each of them must have a narrative which might be of interest not only to social historians, but also to art-lovers.'

'That's a fascinating idea.' Mercy's face shone as she turned to her husband. 'Don't you agree, darling?'

'It's certainly an attractive proposition.' Bob nodded. I could almost hear the cogs and wheels whirring inside his head, calculating costs and returns and what's-in-it-for-mes?

'It could be a really intriguing project,' Sam said.

'In fact . . .' Bob looked at Mercy. Mercy looked at Bob. 'This,' said Bob, 'is exactly what we've been discussing for the past eighteen months or so.' He gestured behind him to the door of the gallery. 'Not just the family portraits, but all those wonderful paintings we should be sharing with the world.'

'When your second anthology appeared,' Mercy said, 'we were fairly sure we'd found the very person to do justice to our wonderful pictures.' She beamed at me, the desolation at the back of her eyes temporarily eclipsed by fervour.

'Obviously we would give you all the support you would need. A salary, expenses and so on. A generous *per diem*.'

'I'd have to talk it over with my colleague, Doctor Drummond,' I said cautiously.

'Of course you would. But to give you some indication of how

highly we value the Drummond & Quick mark – and these are, of
course, only ballpark figures – we would be prepared to offer . . .'
And he mentioned terms so hugely favourable that it was a toss-up
whether I stared at him with my mouth hanging open, drooling
slightly, or ran out into the austere and elegant spaces of Eaton
Square and screamed in disbelief.

Again Mercy put a hand on her husband's arm. 'I think we should
let Alexandra think it over. Perhaps we could draw up a draft contract
and messenger it down to her.'

'Sounds like a plan.' Bob crinkled his eyes at me. 'We'll look
forward to your response.'

'We'll be in touch in the next couple of days,' Mercy added.

'I was intrigued,' Sam said boldly, 'by a necklace which appeared
in several of the paintings. Gold, with sort of hand-beaten links,
and a pendant antique coin.'

Mercy's eyes darkened, and again I was aware of a profound
sadness until, almost by force of will (or so it seemed), they cleared
once more. 'I know the one you mean. It's most unusual, isn't it?
My great-grandfather had it made for his wife to celebrate the birth
of their first child.'

Just before we left, Mercy came up to me and asked quietly if
everything was all right between Helena and myself. 'We were
surprised that you brought your young man,' she said.

'He's not my y—'

'So Doctor Drummond is fine?'

'As far as I know. She's away at the moment,' I added hastily,
then looked at my watch. 'Sam, we need to hurry if we're going to
catch that train.'

'Let me get our driver . . .' she began.

'Thanks, but the Tube is so much quicker.'

Back in my flat, Sam once again collapsed into the sofa. He took off
his glasses and rubbed his eyes with his balled fists. 'God, I'm tired.'

'Whisky?'

'Some more of that Armagnac I had the other night would be
good.' He sipped for a while. His eyes closed and stayed shut for
so long that I thought he had fallen asleep. Then he roused himself,
sat up straight, said, 'I feel like a new man.'

'I rather liked the old one,' I said.

He smiled. 'So what did you make of today?'

'What did *you*?'

'I . . .' He looked up at the ceiling. 'I don't want to rain on your parade, but I got the distinct feeling that it was all just a little bit too good to be true.'

I nodded. I had felt the same. 'Go on.'

'I also felt that there was an agenda there, though I have absolutely no idea what it might be.'

'So you think they might not be on the level?' .

'They probably are. But it's a different level from the one we're standing on.'

'A more expensive one?'

He shook his head. 'I'm not sure it has anything to do with money. And that necklace bothers me. I am absolutely certain I've seen it somewhere before.'

'I haven't. But I've seen part of it.'

'How do you mean?'

'Do you swear not to tell anyone?'

'Of course.'

I got up and went to my desk. Right at the back of the right-hand drawer in the top was a box of drawing pins. I brought it over and spilled the contents on to the coffee table in front of us. The gold circle I had taken from the carpet of Helena's bedroom shone dully in the light from the table lamps.

Sam looked at it, then at me. 'Is this what they call withholding evidence?'

'I'm very much afraid that it is. I really don't know what came over me, but when I saw this lying there on the carpet, soaked in blood, my first thought was whether it would implicate Helena in Amy's death.'

'Do you think it does?'

'I might have once, but now I'm absolutely certain it does not.'

'And how are you going to get it back to the authorities?'

'Good question. A bridge to be crossed in due course.'

'So if Doctor Drummond is innocent, who is guilty?' asked Sam. 'Got a pen and some paper?'

I found a pad of lined paper and a felt tip and handed them over.

'We need to do a bit of detective work. Or at least produce a précis of what we know already,' Sam said.

At the top of the page, he wrote: *Did Amy know her killer?* The answer was almost certainly yes, since the house had shown no indication of a break-in, which would imply that he came with her, or she let him in. 'And at the risk of being labelled sexist, I'm going to refer to the killer as "he".'

'But the real question is how did Amy get in to Doctor Drummond's house?'

'And why go there in the first place? She must have been aware that, like everyone else, Helena couldn't stand her. I imagine she didn't have a key. Is it possible that Doctor Drummond let her in?'

'I suppose so. Or had arranged to leave the front door unlocked, though given the animosity between them, it seems highly unlikely. Or maybe she just carelessly left it unlocked, as she so often did.'

'What about the next question: *did the killer bring the murder weapon with him, and take it away again when he left?*'

'Not the thing stuck in her eye, since he left that at the scene,' I said, trying desperately not to bring Helena's bedroom back into my mind – the blood, the smell, the stains – 'but maybe the one responsible for the blunt trauma.'

'Seems likely.'

'I know the police took away a couple of objects capable of caving in Amy's skull but have since returned them as being blameless. Or so my source tells me.'

'Which implies that the murderer had come prepared.'

'Or else used something in the house which he took away when he left. Helena's house is so full of stuff, it's almost impossible to say if anything's missing.'

'Moving rapidly on—'

I held up my hand. 'He also seems to have gone off with Amy's expensive handbag, which according to her husband, Mark, she took everywhere, and which was not visible at the scene of crime.'

'Fine.' Sam scribbled on his bit of paper. 'Moving on to the next point – and feeling like utter failures since so far we have no answers – *what, if any, was the connection between Amy and her killer?*'

'That's anybody's guess,' I said. 'There didn't even have to be any particular connection.'

'I doubt that. She obviously went to bed with the guy, so she must have known him. I mean, even Amy, promiscuous as she seems to have been, wouldn't jump into bed with a complete stranger. Or

would she? And who was this person anyway? Did the two of them
have a rendezvous at Helena's place, thinking that she was away
for the night?'

'That seems a bit far-fetched. I realize that with her husband in
the house, Amy wouldn't have been able to meet him in Islington,
but couldn't they have gone to a hotel or something, if they were
that randy?'

'Who knows? Did they arrive together?'

'Basically, we simply don't know,' I said. 'Neither, as far as I
can gather, do the police. My source says that they've questioned
the neighbours but nobody saw or heard anything. A motorbike
revving the following morning's about the best we've come up with.'

Sam looked at his sheet of paper again. 'Right, next question: *why
was Amy killed?* What was the purpose behind the murder, because
there has to be one? Did she have something that somebody wanted?
Did ghosts from her previous incarnations rise up for revenge?'

'It does seem to have been something more than a simple murder
– if murder is ever simple,' I said. 'Though mind you, you'd have
to say that the wife throttled by a drunken spouse, the stabbing
outside the pub, the act of self-defence against an unprovoked attack,
would surely have to count as simple.'

Sam adopted a knowing expression. 'Find the why, and you find
the who,' he said. 'If you're lucky.'

'It's obviously something to do with Amy's Masaccio book, gotta
be,' I said. 'Those manuscript pages shoved inside her body . . .
what was that all about?' I gulped my whisky, beginning to feel
exhaustion settling on me. 'And then there's the fairly obvious sexual
connotations, and the destruction of the eyes.'

'Thank God I didn't see it,' Sam said. 'But from what you've
said, it's quite clear that whoever is responsible was furiously angry,
just bursting with rage and hatred.'

'I feel I ought to be able to put it together,' I said. 'And I just
can't.' I recapped for him my visits to Amy's three living husbands,
to Helena's former spouse in France, to Helena's colleagues in the
art world and the revelations from Lev Goldsmith. 'And so far, the
finger of suspicion doesn't seem to point to any of them, far as I
can see.'

'So your copper's instincts aren't yet aroused?' He moved slightly
towards me. 'Though I have to say mine are.'

I ignored him. 'Not as far as Amy's killer is concerned, nor where Helena has got to. But they certainly are aroused to the fact that it's now getting late and I need to go to bed.'

'Need any help?'

'No thanks.'

He stood. 'Maybe I'll get lucky one of these days, Alex.'

'Don't count on it, Sam.'

'I won't.'

We faced each other, hemmed in by the coffee table, and unaccountably I leaned forward to kiss his cheek, by now bristly with stubble. He turned his head so that I missed his cheek and got his soft, expectant mouth instead. I pulled back, blushing, and made shooing gestures at him. 'Go, Sam. I'm tired.'

I was finally tucked up in bed, drowsing over *To Kill A Mockingbird* for the twentieth time, when the phone rang. I frowned. 11:50. Kind of late for social calls. Which meant something bad. In the time it took to reach for my phone and press buttons, my mind had flashed through a dozen scenarios, most of them involving my parents and siblings dying hideous deaths on motorways or crushed by falling rocks or dragged off beaches by rogue waves.

It was Sam. He sounded excited. 'Can I come in for a nightcap?'

'You've already had one. And I'm in bed.'

'Doesn't bother me, shweetheart, if it doesn't bother you,' he drawled, in a passable imitation of Humphrey Bogart.

'How long will it take you to get here?'

'I'm standing on your doorstep.'

'I'll come down. But I warn you, I shan't be dressed.'

'Doesn't bother me, shweetheart . . .'

When I opened the door, winter blew in on a blast of arctic air. I could hear the waves crashing against the shingle of the beach, and the rattle of halyards against metal masts from the Yacht Club further along the front. Sam was standing there, clutching a file to his chest.

He came in to my sitting room, looking extremely cold. 'Coffee?' I asked. 'Or more of my brandy?'

'Any or all, please. It's one of those hell's-frozen-over nights.'

'You know where the booze is . . . help yourself.' I went into the kitchen and started the coffee procedure. The satin skirts of the robe my sister had given me last Christmas sighed against my bare legs in an unaccustomed and sexy way.

When I carried the tray in, Sam was hunched over the coffee table, turning the pages of one of those celebrity magazines which feature an exclamation mark in the title. He had a brandy snifter in his hand a third full of the Armagnac I'd bought at the duty-free shop on my return from visiting Ainslie Gordon. There was another, not so full, waiting for me.

He looked up at me. 'Don't bite my head off,' he remarked, 'but you look gorgeous with your hair down like that.'

I gathered it in my hands and pulled it behind my neck. 'Thank you,' I muttered. I've never mastered the art of receiving compliments graciously, except the professional kind, perhaps because I so seldom have any others.

He reached up and pulled my hand away. 'Leave it be,' he said. 'I like it like that.'

I'd never realized before how blue his eyes were. He patted the sofa and handed me the other glass of brandy. 'Sit down here and have a look at this.' He flipped through the pages of the trash-mag in his hands, an old battered copy, dating from several years back. 'I'm sorry to be banging at the door again at this hour, getting you out of bed and all, but I thought you wouldn't want to wait to see this.' He slapped at the magazine. 'Look at that!'

I scanned the spread. Lots of glamorous photographs and faces I half-recognized. At first I thought it was the Oscars, but it was some gala function, women with their hair piled high, gorgeous frocks, fantastic jewellery, men at their sides dressed in immaculate evening clothes. Flunkeys were passing trays of champagne around, there were enormous flower arrangements dripping over golden pillars and columns. 'None of it means a thing to me,' I said.

'Look more closely at that picture on the right, in the centre.'

I did. An elegant woman with elaborate golden hair piled high on her head. A sweeping ballgown of pale blush-pink. A somewhat elderly man, in white tie with opal studs down the front of his stiff shirt. Understated jewellery hanging round the woman's neck with—

'Hang about,' I said. 'That's the Lamont necklace!'

'So it is. And who's that wearing it?'

'*Mr and Mrs Dexter Morrison, attending the Arts Ball at the Lincoln Center,*' I read aloud. 'Dexter Morrison? Who's he?'

'More to the point, who's *she*?' Sam reached out and stroked my hair as reverently as if it were an art object in itself. 'Gorgeous,' he murmured.

'Oh my God!' I stared at the photograph, resisting the desire to duck my head and flick his hand away. 'It's *Amy!*'

'Precisely. See, when we were looking at those portraits at the Lamonts' gallery, I knew I'd seen that necklace before somewhere. And though I know it's a strange interest for a man poised in readiness to serve his country at any time, I love looking at these magazines, the glimpses of lives I shall never lead, the women I shall never have – not that I want them, let me quickly add. I keep some of them for years.'

'And see how very useful it's been,' I said. 'One can never have too much information.'

'True.'

'But my God,' I said again, 'Amy Morrison. And presumably the old guy must be the husband who swept her off to New York all those years ago. So what do we conclude from seeing her wearing what must be Mercy Lamont's necklace?'

'Either that she feels it's hers, in some way, or she didn't think Mercy would ever see her wearing it.'

'The latter is a bit stupid, isn't it? I mean, Mercy is part of the social scene in New York. She'd almost be bound to see that photograph, if she wasn't actually at the event itself.'

'*Or* . . . she thinks she has a right to wear it. And if so, how did she come to that conclusion?'

'Someone gave it to her?'

'Who? Certainly not Mercy Lamont. And she told us it was a one-off, there isn't another like it in the entire world.'

'Could the rich husband have got Aspreys or somewhere similar to make a replica?'

'Even if he had, where would he get the original in the first place? It would be pretty hard to copy it from a painting or photograph, I should think.'

I got up, went into my office and came back with a powerful magnifying glass, which I used all the time in my work. Together we minutely studied the magazine photo. Finally Sam said: 'It looks exactly like the one Mercy was wearing the other day.'

'I agree. I particularly remember that slight dent in the god's face, almost under his left eye.'

'So what do we conclude?'

I tucked my bare feet up under my robe; they were getting cold. 'Do we think that somehow Amy stole it, and Mercy stole it back?'

'Killing her in the process?'

'Not by accident, that's for sure.'

'Unless you go for the red mist scenario – a sudden rage at Amy's *chutzpah*, the seizing of the weapon and bashing in of the head, the sticking of that bradawl thing into both of her eyes – which I find hard to believe since Mercy seems such a controlled woman. She's much more likely to have forced Amy to hand it over.'

'Using what kind of leverage?'

Sam picked up the bottle of brandy. 'May I?'

I held out my glass. 'I'll have a drop more too. So what kind of pressure could Mrs Lamont use against Amy?'

'Exposure?'

'What kind of exposure?'

Sam shrugged. 'I have no idea.'

'Could she have been responsible for the demise of old Mr Morrison, who was a friend of the Lamont's, and Mercy threatened to tell?'

'In that scenario, more likely that Amy would try to kill Mercy than vice versa.'

'Seriously,' I said. 'Is it feasible that Mercy Lamont is responsible for Amy's death?'

'Apart from the necklace, what on earth would be her motive? That was quite a savage murder and she seems eminently civilized. Would you really kill someone because somehow they had stolen a necklace which belonged to you, even if it was a family heirloom?'

I shook my head in frustration. 'And Helena, where is *she*?'

SIXTEEN

found out the following day.

The phone rang at six thirty-five, waking me from a deep sleep. After Sam had reluctantly gone home last night, I had swallowed a homeopathic sleeping pill, dived under the duvet and gone out like a light. I still wasn't firing on all cylinders.

'Quick?'

'Think so . . .' Wake *up*, I ordered myself. People don't ring at this hour for an idle chat.

'It's Fliss.'

'Mmm . . .' Open your eyes, Alex. Wake *UP*!

'Are you asleep?'

'Yes.'

'Then wake up. Now.'

'Just what I'm telling myself to do.'

'I have some news, Quick.' She paused. '*Bad* news.'

That jolted me awake. She sounded sombre, and I knew instantly what she was going to tell me. 'It's Helena, isn't it?' I said, striving to keep my voice calm, though the tension in my chest was building to such an extent that I feared my body might rupture and my entire torso would disintegrate. 'What's happened?'

'They've found a body.'

'And they think it's Helena's?' I seemed to have been transformed into something rigid, a block of stone, a tree trunk. Pain coursed along the pathways of my body, as though my veins had been colonized by biting ants. 'Oh, please, Fliss. *Please* not.'

'I'm afraid so, Alex. She was wearing one of those ethnic bags slung across her coat, the ones that look like they're made of matted felt or horse-blankets or something, with a long woven woollen ropey strap thing.'

Tears came into my eyes. How often I'd seen her prancing along with that bag hanging over her shoulder or across her chest.

'It had all sorts of identity in it,' continued Fliss. 'Wallet, credit cards, library cards, key cards to get through the locks of the university art department. That sort of thing. And of course the paramedics who were first on the scene recognized her from all the flyers we've sent around.'

I beat the cover of my duvet with a clenched fist. Over and over. Trying to stay composed. 'Wh-where did they find the . . . where was she found?'

'A jogger saw her body floating in the river. Thought she was having a swim, at first, but realized that in this weather that was bloody silly.'

'Strange the way the mind tries to persuade itself away from the fact of death.'

'And anyway, she was fully dressed. Winter coat. High boots. We think—'

I interrupted her. 'Where was this?'

'Uh . . . just a minute . . .' I heard a rustle of papers. 'On the edge of a village called Dovebrook. Along the river. Not far from you.'

'Dovebrook is where my parents live,' I said. 'Why would Helena be anywhere near there?'

'We're looking at the possibility of accident or suicide.'

'Suicide? Helena?' I was outraged. 'This was a woman who loved life in all its manifestations. *Nothing* could be more unlikely than Helena committing suicide.' Though as I said this, I remembered how often those suffering from depression manage to hide it even from their closest family and friends.

'That's what people always say after the event,' Fliss reminded me. 'What about the possibility of an accident?'

'The SOCOs will know more about that. How far from the village was she?'

'About a mile along the river bank.'

'A *mile*?' I frowned. 'There's something odd about this, Fliss. Helena was not into country walks. Nor exercise of any kind. Life's too short, she used to say. And on top of that, she was hydrophobic. So why would she be walking along the river path?'

'Don't know.'

'Any idea of *when* she died? Or even how? Just because she's been found in the river doesn't m-mean she d-drowned.' I could feel my composure slipping.

'The ME says she's been dead at least several days. Though as you know, these estimates can't ever be entirely accurate. Especially after immersion in water.'

'How long had she been in the river?'

'Not that long. Obviously whoever killed her eventually dumped her a little higher up and she slowly floated down to where she was found. That river doesn't have much of a flow.'

'I know.'

There was silence between us. Daylight was beginning to filter into my room. I don't think I have ever felt as bleak as I did that early morning. I tried to repress a sob but couldn't.

'Oh Alex,' Fliss said. 'I'm so very sorry, she was a lovely lady. I only met her once, when she was giving a lecture at the uni, but she was so lively, so full of fun – and of course, I know how very close you two were, how—'

'Stop, Fliss, or I shall start bawling my head off, and I don't want to do that. Not yet, anyway, not until I've nailed the bastard who's . . .' My voice tailed off. I swallowed hard. Slammed the duvet cover. Swallowed again.

'Look . . .' Fliss gentled her voice. 'As her closest friend, you may have to come in and identify her if we can't find someone who—'

'Why me? What about her colleagues at the uni?'

'You were closer.'

'Her husband is here, over from Australia. He could do it.' If there was one thing I did not think I could cope with, it was seeing Helena dead who had always been so very much alive.

'And who would the husband be?'

'He's called Professor Liam Hadfield, he's currently in Oxford, and I can give you his telephone number because I have it right here in front of me.'

'Okay, let's have it.' I heard keys tapping. Then, 'But if he won't do it, you'll have to.'

'Oh, crap . . .'

Fliss called me back almost immediately. The bastard wouldn't do it. 'Said he had a series of lectures to deliver, students to tutor and colleagues to liaise with. Besides, he – and I quote – hadn't seen the blasted woman for years, wouldn't know what she looked like now, and would therefore be unable to identify her.'

I decided that were I ever unfortunate enough to meet this guy, I was not going to like him. 'That must be a lie,' I said. 'He rang me only a few days ago hoping to be able to stay with her for a night or two while he delivered a lecture down here at the arts faculty of the University of Kent.'

'Nice voice, though.'

'Like the very best eighty-five per cent chocolate,' I agreed.

'But not nearly as scrumptious. He seemed to lack any compassion at all. I was amazed. None of those conventional little niceties that one expects to hear in these circumstances.'

'I only spoke to him briefly,' I said, 'but I got the clear impression that Professor Hadfield doesn't do conventional. Nor niceties.'

'If you're worried, Alex, she wasn't in the water that long. And it's winter. So there won't be any . . . um . . .'

'Decomposition?'

'Precisely.'

'I'm not going to do it. I *can't*.' But after some pressure from Fliss, and with great reluctance, I finally agreed to go down and identify Helena's body the following morning.

Call ended, I stared up at the ceiling. Got out of bed and looked out of the window. Watched the sea moving, calm and drab this morning. Saw the glint of frost on the shingle. Felt tears on my cheeks.

Then I called Sam Willoughby to ask if he would come with me.

We showed up at the police mortuary the following morning around half-past seven. I hung back at the door. I'd attended many postmortems in my time on the force. I wasn't even particularly bothered by death. But I had never had to look at the dead body of someone I'd known and loved.

Sam held my hand. 'I'm here,' he said. That was reassuring. Part of my mind wondered at the way this unassuming man had begun to play such a considerable role in my life.

We were led to a window, through which we could see a gurney covered in a purple sheet, a grotesquely faux-sacramental colour with which to conceal the militantly atheistic woman lying beneath it. Made of some synthetic fabric, it gleamed faintly in the light from the overhead fixture and I knew how Helena would have shuddered, how much she would have hated the sleazy feel of it in real life. To add extra insult, the front of the material had been embroidered with a gold cross. Non-believing Helena would have been outraged.

An unseen hand folded the material forward so it lay on her chest, and we were able to see Helena's strong, intelligent face supported on some kind of pillow. Her blonde ringlets were spread out around her, matted but at least not bloodied, and her eyes were peacefully closed. Her hands were folded on her chest and I could see the four-leafed clover tattooed at the base of her thumb. She looked as though she were having a quick kip, and I wanted to rap on the glass, shout at her to wake up, we had work to do. There was a large grey-black bruise on the side of her face furthest away from us, and some areas of discolouration on her neck.

'Can you confirm that this is your former colleague?' the attendant standing behind us asked quietly.

I nodded.

'Could you say so, just for the record, please?'

'Yes,' I said firmly, squeezing Sam's fingers tightly. 'Yes, that's Hel— Doctor Drummond.'

'You're certain?'

'Absolutely.' I turned away. If I could just have touched her, rested my cheek against hers, I knew that she would wake up, but I could not. She was cold now, unliving, out of my reach – and from now on, always would be.

Before we left, the police intimated that they would not be releasing the body for burial until they could determine the circumstances of the death. Nor were they prepared to discuss the nature of the injuries at this stage.

'So there *were* injuries?' I said.

They agreed there were.

'Injuries not consistent with someone falling or jumping into the river?'

'We cannot discuss them at this stage.' After that . . . They spread their collective hands in a commiserating gesture.

After that, what? Did I have to organize funerals and flat-clearings? Was it up to me to contact lawyers? The absurd thought struck me that it would have been so much more fun if Helena were there to help me. And then I was gulping back tears, wiping my

gloved hands across my wet cheeks as we crossed the car park to
Sam's car, sobbing as he handed me into the passenger seat, resting
my head against the dashboard, at last forcibly struck by the forever
absence of my dear friend.

'There are no words,' said Sam, his voice gentle.

'I know.' I brushed at my face. Sniffed horribly. Wiped my eyes
with a screwed-up wad of tissue. 'I'll get over it,' I said. 'Eventually.'

I could feel my phone vibrating in my pocket. I fished it out.
'Yeah?' I said.

'Fliss here. Look, Quick, you're not going to like this, but all the
indications are that your friend killed herself. There's all sorts of—'

'No. Not poss—'

It was her turn to interrupt. 'Listen. There were stones in her
pockets. And that bag thing slung over her body was full of them.
There were no signs indicating that she might have lost her footing
and skidded down the bank. The path wasn't muddy. It wasn't cold
enough for slippery frost or ice. Add to that her state of mind . . .
the police are after her for murder, she has nowhere to turn. Maybe,
sad as it is, she felt that suicide was the only option.'

'No,' I said again, louder this time. 'With a huge stretch of the
imagination, I could just about envisage the possibility of her taking
her own life. But I can tell you absolutely categorically that if she
did, it would not be in a river. She was like a cat. She *hated* water.
I don't think I would say she was scared of it, but she certainly
kept well away from it. Didn't even like crossing bridges over water
in case she fell in.'

'That doesn't—'

'So don't try to convince me that she killed herself by jumping
into the river,' I shouted. I slammed the phone shut. Not exactly
polite. I would ring later and apologize, but she was a good enough
friend to understand. By now I was boiling mad, my grief temporarily displaced. 'Sam,' I said, 'would you be kind enough to drive
me over to Dovebrook?'

He made a quick phone call to the bookshop and then we set off.
I didn't trust myself, with my emotions running high, to get behind
a wheel.

I didn't feel like talking, which he seemed to understand. My
head swirled with half-formed ideas. I remembered my mother's
mention of the two of them, Edred and Mary, going away, her

off-hand remark to the effect that I shouldn't bother going to the house since they wouldn't be there, the fact that she had never said anything similar to me in my entire adult life. So what had inspired her to do so now? Why had she stepped so far out of character? Was it possible, or even likely, that Helena had sought refuge with my parents? The more I considered it, the more plausible it seemed. There was no reason for the police to connect them with Helena, at least not initially. Through me, the three of them had developed a close friendship. She might well have chosen them to run to. And they lived close enough to my own place for her (or one of my parents) to sneak in and push that *imok* message into my postbox in the lobby. Why hadn't I considered it before?

When we reached the quiet road where Edred and Mary lived, Sam parked and we both got out of the car. It was obvious that they weren't at home, even if I hadn't known them to be away. As we walked up the garden path, I could see, in among the gobbets of packed snow, patches of snowdrops under the leafless trees, and tight-budded crocuses like golden exclamation marks dotted about the lawn, which had grown unexpectedly early because of the cold weather. Behind the house lay the tidy spread of Mary's vegetable garden, nothing but a stretch of earth, turned over and composted, and frozen hard.

I pulled my keys out of my bag and let us into the house. I breathed in the familiar smell of my childhood home while a thousand half-forgotten memories swept through my brain. I called out, but there was no reply. Nor had I expected there to be.

'What exactly are we looking for?' Sam asked. 'And how do you think I can help?'

'I don't know yet. Perhaps you can't, except as back-up. As support.'

'That's all there for you already, Alex.'

I gave him a watery smile. 'Thank you, Sam. I just thought if we look hard enough, we might find some clue to why Helena died. Because if she was here, if this was the last place she was before she died, she might have left some indication as to why. Which I'm telling you was *not* by her own hand.'

'Trouble is,' Sam said apologetically, 'I don't really know what I'm looking for.'

'Just observe.' I put my hand on the elaborate newel-post at the bottom of the banisters. 'If Helen *was* staying here, she would have used one of the spare bedrooms, so I'll go up and see what I can find.'

My suppositions were correct. It was immediately obvious that Helena had been in residence, and equally obvious that she had not been planning to leave just yet. I tried to imagine her walking along the river bank (almost impossible) and suddenly deciding to jump fully clothed into the water (equally impossible), having first weighted her clothes down with stones (totally impossible). The room was the usual familiar Helena-jumble of glorious colours, rich fabrics, books scattered across surfaces, a spill of talcum powder on the carpet, tangled strings of beads and entwined chains lying on the cushions of a disgraceful old armchair upholstered in tattered red velvet, which for years my mother had been meaning to have recovered as soon as she got round to it. Helena and Mary were two of a kind: it was no wonder that they had gotten along together so well.

Although I had been in Helena's home many times, I had never poked around her private papers and possessions. Now, in my parents' home, I opened bags and drawers, suitcases and boxes. Before leaving her place the night of the concert, Helena had gathered together a few personal documents and, remembering the interview with Clifford Nichols to which she had never arrived, a set of her favourite clothes – which included several pairs of knickers in pastel colours decorated with hearts or kittens, and a satinized bra with tiny roses all over the straps. I would have felt staid and inadequate, recalling the unexciting undies I was currently wearing, if I hadn't reminded myself that during my marriage to Jack I too had possessed stuff like this. Now I had no one to titillate, what was the point of filling drawers with silks and satins in exotic colours and fabrics? Some of the items still had labels attached, which must indicate that they had not yet been worn, but had recently been bought – by whom, my mother? Hard to imagine.

Or had she had some new man in mind? This Peter Preston bloke, for instance?

It struck me then, not for the first time, how alike she and Amy Morrison had been, as far as their choices in men were concerned. Young, lusty, appreciative. Helena had once told me that there was no aphrodisiac as potent as appreciation. 'Even in these days of casual sex,' she'd said, 'and despite their boasts down the pub, most young men aren't getting nearly as much as they would like.'

'Which is where you come in,' I said.

'Exactly.' She had grinned at me. 'But you, now you're much too young for that sort of thing.'

I doubted I would ever be old enough for it, either.

I picked up one of the three books beside the bed. Two of them were paperback thrillers, from my parents' own bookshelves. The third was *The Magic of Illusion*, Amy Morrison's book. I wondered why Helena would have taken that with her for the evening. Flicking through, I saw that several sentences, even paragraphs, had been heavily underlined. Helena (I recognized the writing) had even scrawled '*bitch!!!*' in the margin against a few sentences, though from a quick glance through, I couldn't see why.

The book opened easily at page 104, because Helena had been using a photograph as a bookmark. I examined the picture, which showed two men standing together in a clematis-festooned doorway, an older one with his arm across the shoulders of a younger one. Two men, easily identifiable as Ainslie Gordon and Laurence Turnbull.

Questions, questions. A whole raft of them. Like, where did the photo come from? What significance, if any, did it have? It looked very recent to me: how current was it? Why did Helena have it beside her bed? Why, for heaven's sake, why was she reading Amy's book? Not only reading but taking notes? Had the woman I thought I knew so well been keeping a whole load of crucial facts from me, and how true was the version she had given me of her life and circumstances? I began to wonder if I had concentrated on Amy Morrison at the expense of Helena.

I longed to know, too, why she had been staying with my parents, and why they hadn't informed me, even when I had told them how distressed I was at her disappearance? Perhaps that was what had triggered the *imok* note.

I went downstairs again. 'Look at this.' I handed the photograph to Sam. 'Any comment?'

'I don't know either of them, but I'm assuming they must be father and son.'

'Why?'

'Well, for a start – look how alike they are.'

I snatched the photo back from him and stared at it intently. He was right. Ainslie and Turnbull: the likeness leaped out at me. 'Why didn't I notice that when I was down there?' I asked.

'Could it be that your investigative techniques aren't as finely honed as mine?'

'I would remind you that I was once a police officer.'

'I rest my case.' He dodged out of my way as I aimed a light blow at his bicep.

'But don't you see? If the two are related, that puts a whole new complexion on things.' I sat down at my parents' scrubbed-pine kitchen table. 'Look, what about this scenario? Suppose Ainslie and Helena got divorced and then she found out that she was pregnant, too far gone for a termination. Raising a child on her own was never going to fit in with her lifestyle. Suppose she had the boy, Laurence, and handed him over to the authorities, whoever they would have been thirty years or so ago. Suppose Ainslie, who hadn't known about the pregnancy at the time but found out much later, went looking for his son – or the son went looking for him, of course – and picked him out of the gutter, took him back to France, tried to clean him up, etcetera, etcetera.'

'Good, yes, I can accept that.'

'Suppose Turnbull then nurtures a deep and murderous hatred of the mother who abandoned him until he can contain it no more, comes back to England, breaks into my house since Helena's is still wrapped round with police tape, to see if he can find any clue as to where she might be, returns when I'm back home, possibly intending to use violence to force the truth out of me, but is thwarted.' I recalled the slim figure in black leathers who had wrested himself out of my restraining arm and run downstairs, taking the steps two or three at a time, and out into the forecourt. 'Breaks away,' I added. 'Jumps onto his motorbike and roars off.'

'Extremely plausible. I wonder if that's what happened. But we could probably come up with other scenarios where the lad is innocent and nothing to do with Helena.'

'I know he's got a motorbike, because I saw it in France,' I said. 'Though whether he'd ride it all the way to Calais . . .'

'But if he *is* the one who killed Helena, how do we bring the vicious little sod to justice?'

'If this time round the little sod actually *gets* justice. Or rather, his victims do.' I explained Laurence Turnbull's previous brush with the law, and its unsatisfactory outcome.

'It seems to me that someone needs to go back to Ainslie Gordon and question him in more depth.'

'What would that accomplish?'

'Possible guilt.'

'Or innocence.'

He looked at me hopefully. 'If you decide to go, I'd be more than happy to come with you.'

'What about your bookshop? And the Christmas season rush?'

'It's not going to collapse because I take a few days off here and there. I can always hire in a student or two: some of the PhDs are always looking for casual employment. Besides, coming with you means I'll be flexing my detective muscles, something I've wanted to do since reading Father Brown and John Dickson Carr by the light of a torch under the bedcovers.'

I looked at my watch. 'I think a glass, or even tumbler, of something alcoholic might be drunk in order to celebrate, don't you?'

'We haven't caught our hare yet, Alex.'

'But I genuinely feel that at last we're close enough to put salt on his tail.'

He grinned. 'I didn't realize that was how you caught hares. Was Mrs Beeton aware?' He grew more serious. 'Look, Alex, we don't even know that Doctor Drummond was murdered.'

'Not for sure, we don't. But *I* know. Her acute hydrophobia says it all, far as I'm concerned. Not many people knew about it, which might be the way we track down the person responsible for her death, since he was trying to make it look like suicide—'

'Or even an accident.'

'Either way, drowning is the last method Helena would have chosen. If it's Laurence, the guy we think it is—'

'An absolutely suppositious notion. It's not even circumstantial.'

'—and we can find evidence to prove it, maybe we can solve the case.' I found gin, ice, martini in my parents' fridge. Poured us each a glass, added a slice of lemon, passed one to Sam, swallowed mine quickly and poured another. The alcohol travelled through my system, loosening the knots, both physical and emotional, which bound me. 'Forgive me if I sound frivolous, but away we go!' I nodded my glass to him. 'Here's to homicide.' I wasn't smiling.

SEVENTEEN

S am and I drove slowly past the garden wall of *La Tuilerie*. Nothing much had changed since my previous visit, though a few over-eager crocuses stood half-open in the grass under the bare tangled branches of a plum tree which already showed a few frail pink buds. The sun shone mildly from a blue-white sky. It was hard to believe that in south-east England, people were shivering inside thick coats.

We knew someone must be home, because all the doors of the house were open, as they had been last time I was here. I directed Sam to drive on and park around the corner. 'Gives them less time to prepare,' I explained.

'Or scarper.'

'Indeed. Though I would guess that Ainslie Gordon's scarpering days are long gone. But it's not him we're here to see, it's Laurence Turnbull.'

'If Ainslie really is his father, do you think he knows about Laurence's past? The terrible car accident, and those poor girls he killed?'

'Possibly not. I would imagine the relationship has only recently been renewed.'

'Activated might be more accurate. From sperm to full-grown adult is a bit of a stretch.'

'Either way, it's quite possible he hasn't been informed.'

'Are we going to confront them with our knowledge?'

'I think we go in and act as if we're perfectly aware of the connection, haven't assumed anything else,' I said. 'Without necessarily bringing it up.'

We got out of the car and quietly pushed the doors shut, not wanting to announce our presence before we had to. When I turned, it was to see a gnarled gentleman in a greasy old beret wearing *bleu de travail* standing behind an iron-barred gate, with three surly dogs poised alertly at his side. There was muck and straw behind him, two or three muddy tractors stationed inside wall-less barns, stacks of wood to one side, a hint of hens, trails of red baling twine. He stared at me knowingly, though I had no idea what he thought he knew. Perhaps he imagined I was another of Ainslie Gordon's conquests.

Speaking in French, I told him that we had come to see Monsieur Laurence.

'Laurence? *Ce type?*' He spat phlegmily into the muck round his boots.

'If,' I added, 'he has returned.'

'Returned?' echoed the old boy.

'I understood he went to England a few days ago?' I was all innocence.

He did that shoulder-lifting thing that the French are so good at, far more expressive than a mere shrug. 'It is possible. I don't see him every day, that is for sure. He does not inform me of his movements. And I certainly do not inform him of mine. If I think about it, I definitely did not see this person in the past few days. It has to be said that, yes, when I met Madame Montras at the market on Tuesday, she did tell me that this Monsieur Laurence had gone abroad.'

'Abroad?'

'She did not say where. Anyway, he was away for some time until the other day, when he came roaring back up the lane on that infernal machine of his, waking my poor old mother from her *après-déjeuner* nap, and setting all the dogs whining and barking, not to mention the baby.'

'Baby?' Sam said. The man looked much too old to have a baby. Or a mother, for that matter.

'The child of my daughter,' he explained.

'And which day was it that you heard this motorbike roaring in the lane?'

He paused, lifting his beret to scratch beneath it. 'Must be three, maybe four days ago. I am getting old, I do not remember so well.' He grinned, showing stubby yellow teeth.

'Where would we find this Madame Montras?' Sam asked.

'She sells fish,' he said. 'Every day she moves from market to market with her fish, because here in Aquitaine there is always a market in a different town.'

'Yes, but—'

'Eels, scallops, lobster, halibut, octopus,' he recited, as though from an unseen sales board. 'Anchovies and monkfish, bream and brill. Grenadier, mullet, salmon.'

'Sounds fascinating,' I said.

'Also pilchards.'

'Could somebody turn him off?' I said.

'And oysters, of course.'

'Where will she be tomorrow?' asked Sam.

'At Riberac. Her stall is just along from the dried fruit and spices.'

'This Laurence, he is the son of Monsieur Gordon, *n'est-ce pas?*' Sam asked.

'I do not know. I do not enquire, me. His business is his business, just as mine is mine.'

'Exactly,' I said.

'But I think he may not be,' the farmer said rapidly, as we turned to go, not wanting to lose his audience. 'He may be the son of one of Monsieur Gordon's *petites amies*, of which there are very many.' Again he made with the shrug. 'I do not know, but maybe not also of Monsieur Gordon. He does not call him Papa.'

'If Monsieur Gordon is not his father,' Sam asked, 'why did he come here to France?'

'He is a student, a pupil. He wishes to be an artist, like our famous Monet or Matisse.' The farmer spat brown liquid at one of his dogs.

'Does Monsieur Gordon often have a student living here?' I asked.

'This is the first, I think.'

In English, I said to Sam, 'Do we need any more information?'

'Not really. Especially since we don't know what further questions to ask.'

'You do realize my theory about Laurence only works if Helena is his mother?'

'I'm very well aware of that, *ma chère.*'

'Do you also realize that if we are to catch this Madame Montras and talk to her, we shall have to stop overnight?'

'I hadn't, no. But it sounds like an excellent idea.' Sam lifted rakish eyebrows at me.

Dream on, I thought.

We reverted to French to say thank you and goodbye, while his dogs set up such a racket that I could barely think straight. French backwater dogs are trained with kicks and sticks to make a heck of a noise, so as to repel strangers, but this seemed a little over and beyond, especially given that there were six other houses nearby, all of whom must have been regularly disturbed by the noise.

Any notion of a surprise arrival was by now out of the question. Indeed, when we turned down the lane back to *La Tuilerie*, Ainslie Gordon was standing in the doorway, scowling.

'What the bleeding hell is that infernal racket,' he growled. 'And who the hell are— Oh, it's you. What do you want this time?'

'Hoping to have a quick word with your son,' Sam said, smooth as double cream.

'I haven't got a fucking son.'

I kept to myself the retort about a celibate one which sprang to my lips. I looked up at my companion. 'Mr Willoughby means Laurence – who I believe is *Helena's* son, not yours.'

'Are you out of your mind?' Gordon's purple-red-suffused face darkened. 'Of course he's bloody not. Helena doesn't have a son, any more than I do.'

Was he telling the truth? Did he even know? What difference would it make to him, either way? One thing his remark told me was that he had probably still been in touch, however desultorily, with his former wife.

As for Laurence, I wished I had access to his computer. Or at the very least, his papers: documents, diary, chequebook, whatever. I was guessing he didn't keep much order in whichever room he was occupying. Short of communicating telepathically with Sam to ask him if he would keep Gordon occupied elsewhere, I couldn't see any easy way I could nip upstairs and have a look.

'Is Laurence actually here?' Sam asked, sounding more like a police officer than any police officer I knew.

'As it happens, he's not.' Gordon glanced at the semi-derelict barn which had housed the motorbike on my last visit.

'Does he often disappear for the day?'

'What kind of damned question is that? He's gone to Bordeaux, not disappeared. And if he decides not to come back until tomorrow,

that's his affair. So what the hell does it have to do with you, whoever
the fuck you are?'

'Nothing much,' Sam admitted.

I took a deep breath. 'Except that he could turn out to be the
chief suspect in a murder enquiry.'

Gordon began to splutter. 'In a murder . . . chief suspect . . .
Laurence . . . what fucking bullshit are you . . .' He stopped. 'Who's
dead?' he asked, in a more reasonable voice, which it was clear he
was fighting to keep under control.

'Don't you know?'

'Obviously not, or I wouldn't bloody well be asking, would I?'

'I'm afraid,' I said, as kindly as I could, 'they found your former
wife's body floating in the river at a place called Dovebrook. Three
days ago.'

He stared strongly at me, his eyes glassy. 'You *are* joking, aren't
you?' he said more quietly, though it was quite clear that I wasn't.

I shook my head.

'Dear God.' He had turned a curious greyish peach colour.
'Helena? Dead? I don't – I can't believe it.'

'I'm afraid so.'

'Not Helena . . .' He turned and walked inside the house. 'Not
her. Not . . . *dead.*'

With shaking hands, he found a bottle on one of the counters,
tore out the cork, raised it to his lips and drank deep, his unshaven
neck bobbing up and down as he did so. Brandy . . . it seemed to
do him good because the heart-attack colour returned to his cheeks.
He motioned at the bench alongside the table.

'Sit down. Explain it all to me.'

We did so while very slowly, like an old, old man, he found three
glasses, a bottle of wine, a corkscrew, muttering to himself all the
time. He looked as though he had aged ten years since I had
announced the unpleasant news: it was clear that Helena's death
had been a tremendous blow. His large spatulate hands still trembled,
but not so much. Every now and then, as we told him what had
happened, he snorted derisively, and once a tear quivered in the
bags below his eyes.

'I can tell you here and now that it bloody well wasn't suicide,'
he said eventually, though the sting had temporarily gone out of his
belligerence 'Not by drowning, it wasn't.'

'Hydrophobia.' I nodded knowledgeably.

He pushed the bottle of wine at us. 'So why are you here to see Laurence?'

'They've made a connection between him and Helena,' Sam said.

'What connection? There is no fucking connection.'

'Frankly, Mr Gordon . . .' I leaned confidingly towards him, and put a hand on his arm, knowing there was nothing like accusation to get a reaction. '. . . they think he may have been responsible for Doctor Drummond's death.'

'What bloody bullshit and bollocks!' he roared. His face had now returned to the same deep red colour as his wine. He stood up and banged the table, making the bottle and glasses jump and slopping wine on to the rough wood. He ran his thick artist's fingers through the greying mop of his curls. I was glad Sam was with me: I wouldn't want to feel those big-knuckled hands round my throat. I had a sudden flashback moment to Amy Morrison's neck and that deep line of red which marred it. 'Anyway, when was Helena supposed to have . . .' He sucked in a breath. '. . . died?'

'They're not quite sure. Certainly within the past week. See, what they think happened is that Laurence . . .' I outlined my theory about growing resentment gradually boiling into a murderous rage, the impetuous decision to track down the mother, the sudden fatal blow. The use of the nebulous 'they' lent a bogus authority to what I was saying, and – so far – Gordon didn't seem to have realized just how spurious it was.

'So what exactly is Laurence's connection with Doctor Drummond?' Sam asked.

'Like I said, there isn't one. Not that I know of, anyway. Not in a blood-relative sense at any rate – unless she somehow managed to substitute herself for my sister when Athol was being tupped by one of her many one-night stands.'

That rocked me back on my heels. My theory was crumbling into speculative dust. If Helena wasn't Laurence's mother, he had no obvious motive for killing her. 'So when your sister found she was pregnant, she went on to have the baby but gave him up for adoption?'

'Exactly. And then thirty years or so later, three or four months ago, to be more precise, he turns up here, calling me Uncle Ainslie, saying he was at some poncey art school but got kicked out, did I think he could make it as a painter, would I have a look at his work?'

'Which poncey art school was he talking about?'

Ainslie shrugged. 'I never asked him. They're all poncey, far as I'm concerned. Can't teach art to save their lives.'

'So it could have been somewhere Doctor Drummond taught,' said Sam.

'Very possibly. I wouldn't know.' He was lying.

'How did he know you existed?' I asked.

'He's apparently spent a lot of time and trouble trying to track down his birth mother, in other words my sister, Athol, and then getting in touch with her and her family.'

'Next question,' I said. 'Just before she died, Helena was reading the Masaccio book by Amy Morrison.' I didn't go into the ramifications of it originally being beside her bed in her own home, nor how it ended up in that of my parents'. 'And tucked into it I found a photograph of you and Laurence, standing outside your door. *That* door.' I gestured at it.

'You and he look so similar, like father and son,' Sam put in.

'Not surprising, given that we're uncle and nephew.'

'I just wondered how Helena happened to get hold of the photo,' I continued, 'or did you send it to her?' There must have been some connection between her and Laurence.

He stared at me. 'Um . . .' he said, clearly trying to think up some plausible lie.

'Did they have a flaming row or something?' Sam asked. 'She took off back to England, he vowed to get even, one way or another? Something like that?'

'Mutual friends of hers and mine came to stay this summer,' Ainslie said eventually. 'Helena showed up too, just for a weekend. One of them was taking photos, so he probably gave Helena a copy.' He poured more wine for us all. 'Helena,' he said. Tears stood in his eyes. I guessed that once we had gone, he would put his head down on the table and weep.

'But,' said Sam, 'if Laurence only arrived here a month ago, how could that be?'

'I'm no good on times and dates,' Ainslie said, irritation corrugating his face. 'Maybe it was three or four months ago – the weather here stays summery well into the autumn months, which is one of the reasons I choose to live here. And for your information – or *theirs*, whoever *they* are – Laurence didn't leave the place at all last week, or this. Too busy working on a painting – I had to practically tie him up and force feed him to get him to stop working and eat something.' He wouldn't meet my eyes, an admission in itself.

'So you can alibi him?'

'Certainly I can.'

'We have witnesses who saw him leaving on his bike,' Sam said, extrapolating from the farmer next door plus the so-far indefinite fish lady.

'The boy isn't a prisoner here,' bristled Gordon. 'Perfectly free to go when and where he bloody well pleases.' He gazed at the watch strapped to his hairy arm. 'Now if there's nothing else, I have an exhibition to prepare for.'

'Where's that?'

'London. First week in May. I'll send you a ticket to the *vernissage*, if you like.'

'Thank you.' I fished out one of my business cards and laid it on the table.

'Ever sold to the Lamonts?' Sam asked.

'Bob and Mercy? I should hope I have. Without their imprimatur, you'd have to work twice as hard to get recognized. They more or less guarantee your reputation.'

'This art school which Laurence had been kicked out of,' Sam said. 'Was it Doctor Drummond who was responsible?'

He hesitated, which was all the answer we needed. 'Uh . . . I'm not sure.'

'What was the reason?'

He shrugged. 'Dunno.'

'Drugs, I imagine, from what you told me last time I was here. He'd probably gone back to dealing, or using his body. Something sordid, anyway.'

'You do realize that this gives him a motive for killing her, don't you?' Sam said, before Ainslie could work himself up into another rage.

Ainslie shook his head forcefully. 'No. Absolutely not. The boy is an artist, with the makings of being a damned fine one. No wonder he was mad at being expelled for some footling little reason or other. All he wants is to paint.'

'Yeah,' I said.

Madame Montras was attired in a white boilersuit stained with fish guts, white wellington boots, a white cap on her hair, and an apron that might have been white many fish ago. Disconcertingly, she had only one tooth, which did not match the pervading colour scheme, by being black rather than white. As we approached, she burst into a loud and raucous pitch for the fish spread enticingly across her stall on plastic parsley. A fine example of a fish wife.

As a sweetener, we purchased some prawns prior to introducing the subject of Laurence. Her face wrinkled with disdain on hearing his name, before she launched into a rant that was as salty as her wares. We gathered fairly quickly that she didn't care for the lad. Nor for his womanizing ways. Nor for his *affreux* motorbike. Nor for his attitudes. He is *mal-élevé*, she told us vigorously, several times. Arrogant, indifferent, selfish, boorish and discourteous were just some of the kinder adjectives she used to describe him. I began to wonder if she had a daughter who had fallen for Laurence and been used then discarded. Or maybe she herself had succumbed to the young Englishman's charms, though given her general demeanour and dental challenges, it seemed unlikely.

'He has gone away,' she finished, 'gone back to England and good riddance to bad rubbish, say I.'

'How do you know?' asked Sam.

'He told me.' She slapped a shiny grey fish against her marble counter, laid it back among the plastic greenery which decorated her stall, and picked up a fan of pink skate wing.

'What? He came to your house? Or to the market?' I said. It sounded unlikely that he would have made a special stop to speak to her, given her low opinion of him, of which he must have been aware.

'We bumped into each other the other day.' She sounded as slippery as one of her own pilchards. Evasive as an eel.

Somehow I couldn't see Laurence wandering round the place, greeting the locals. It didn't ring true. 'Just like that?'

'*Oui, madame.* He told me then.'

'A likely story.'

We didn't get anything further from her. When she turned to attend to a customer wanting a dozen scallops, we moved on.

'What do you think?' asked Sam.

'I don't know. There seems to be some kind of agenda there which I couldn't quite follow.'

'*Cherchez la femme* . . .?'

'Or in Laurence's case, *chasez la femme*, do you think?'

'If he was chasing anyone, it certainly wasn't Madame *la poissonière*.'

'There's something else that's bothering me,' I said. 'Several things, actually.'

The previous night we had spent a chaste evening in Riberac, renting two rooms at a choice little hotel we found in the centre of the town, eating in a local café. Now we were in the hire car, heading for the airport at Bergerac.

'Yes?' Sam said.

'That motorbike: surely Laurence wouldn't ride it all the way to Calais, would he?'

'If he's a motorbike enthusiast, I can't see why not.' Sam gestured at the landscape outside the windows. 'Nice views, empty roads, places to stop for a sandwich or whatever.'

'It takes eight hours by car. Imagine being crouched over the handlebars of a bike for that length of time.'

'I don't see it as a problem.'

'I suppose it would be possible to fly over from France and hire a machine in England,' I mused.

'Probably. But you're underestimating the thrill of the open road.' He touched my knee. 'What're the other things?'

'If he wasn't the one who killed Helena in a rage at being abandoned as a baby – and I am aware that it was only a theory, based on little or no facts – or for being kicked out of art school thanks to her, then who was? And what had she done to deserve it?'

'That won't be hard to find out.'

'Also, who broke into my flat and searched it? And what was he, she or it looking for? And was the intruder the same person who killed Helena? And is the same killer responsible for both Helena and Amy?'

'Looks like we'll have to dig deeper. And whether or not he, she or it was the same person who murdered Amy Morrison, my hunch is that one way or another, you've already come across the person responsible.'

'Assuming we rule out passing rapists or mad axe-men, you're probably right. Thing is, I cannot come up with any rational explanation for why Helena would be strolling along a river bank and accidentally fall in. And you have already heard the basis of my objections to the somewhat ludicrous notion that she might have killed herself, despite the discovery of stones in her coat pocket.'

'What *about* those stones?'

'As Ainslie Gordon would say, bullshit. It's all smoke and mirrors, Sam. Somebody is trying to pull the wool over our eyes – and failing – because whoever it is did not have a sufficient knowledge of the victim.'

'You mean this fear of water?'

'Absolutely.' I was aware of a sudden deep weariness. How long was it since Helena had been discovered in the river at Dovebrook? Three days? 'So now we have to work with the knowledge we have and check out all our suspects, see if we can come up with something else.'

I thought of Professor Hadfield. He might be worth cross-examining, though with him, I doubted we'd get away with any attempt to sound official. But he seemed blunt and from-the-shoulder: we might get more from him than he intended to give.

'I don't want to sound picky, but who exactly are our suspects?' asked Sam.

'Good question.'

EIGHTEEN

I t was late in the evening when Sam and I arrived back at my flat. By then, the weather had moved into tempestmode. A bitter sleet-specked wind had got up and was screaming round chimney pots and church spires. The moon came and went as dark clouds surged across it, while waves crashed onto the shingle, flinging up tall plumes of spray which gleamed white against the blue-black sky.

Once we were indoors, with winter locked outside, I went round the place, checking all the windows and doors, including the formerly defective one leading onto the fire escape, but couldn't find anything to indicate that my space had been invaded yet again. I looked at the answering machine but there were no messages – so nothing new on Helena's death. If there had been, DI Felicity Fairlight would certainly have telephoned with a progress report. I had picked up the mail on my way in, and now I started sorting through it, while Sam poured us both a small nightcap. Among the usual drabness of bills and charity begging letters, there was a picture-postcard showing an aerial view of Paris. On the rear side it said: *Back 8th.* No signature. No unnecessary words. From my mother, of course.

Today was the 7th. 'I shall have to drive over to Dovebrook tomorrow,' I said. I wondered if either Edred or Mary was aware that Helena was dead. Like most offspring, I saw my parents as ever-fixed, unchanged by time, immutable and enduring. But of course they were not. Even though these days the sixties were no longer the killer years, Edred would be sixty-four on his next birthday, Mary sixty-three. So they were no spring chickens. I didn't want the shock of Helena's death to overwhelm them. 'I need to be there when my parents get back.'

'Understood. Meanwhile . . .' Sam said, lifting his glass to his face and sniffing the single-malt it contained, a look of near-ecstasy on his face. '. . . pleasant as it was, did we learn anything from our little foreign excursion?'

I made a face. 'Almost nothing. Except that the fishmonger lady needs to see a dentist.'

'What about Laurence? Do you still like him for it?'

'I think he's unpleasant and arrogant enough to kill someone – in fact, as we know, he already has done.' I remembered Helena's description of her stalker: slim, tall, dressed in black leathers. And the sound of a motorbike either coming or going. It could easily have been him. 'But since we've had to discard my theory that she was the mother who gave him up at birth, what would be his motivation?'

'Something to do with his days at art school? Do we know what college he attended, or whether he and Amy ever connected?'

'That's certainly something to check out. But even if we find that any or all of them coincided at any point, it's a long way to come to seek revenge for an essay given a poor grade or a painting criticized.'

'And anyway, why now?'

'It just has to be connected in some way with Amy Morrison and her book.'

'I agree. But *what* way? Laurence is much younger than Ms Morrison, so they can't have been contemporaries.'

'Except we already know she had a bit of a thing for men young enough to have just about started shaving.' I yawned. And again. 'Sorry, Sam, I'm exhausted. I'm going to have to kick you out. You'll get home all right, won't you?' Thinking: of course he will, he only lives a mile or so from here.

'I expect so. Unless you'd like me to stay, do the bodyguard thing.' He looked wistful. 'Or anything else, for that matter.'

'That's sweet of you,' I said firmly. 'But no thanks.'

The following day I was seated at my desk, drinking a cup of coffee and examining a spread of paintings Helena and I had been contemplating for inclusion in *Ripe for the Picking*. Somehow the whole concept had lost its zest without her. I wasn't even sure I wanted to continue putting together these compilations on my own. I pulled towards me an exuberant painting of some quinces on a blue dish, and thought how much they were a metaphor for life. So ripe, so golden, such maternally rounded haunches, such sweet promise. And how tough that yellow skin was, how bitter and inedible the fruit, how disappointing.

There was a ring at my front door. I thought of ignoring it but then it came again. If nothing else, interacting with someone, however briefly, might serve to lift my melancholy mood. Through the spyhole I clocked a man standing outside, half-turned away from me. I knew I had never seen him before and yet there was a teasing familiarity about him. Quietly I shot the knob of the door-chain into its groove then opened the door as far as the chain would allow.

He turned. 'Oh, good morning. You don't know me—'

'I'm well aware of that.'

'—but my name is Terence Briggs.'

I shook my head. 'Sorry, don't know anyone by that name.'

'I'm Noreen's brother.'

'Don't know anyone called Noreen either,' I said.

He sighed lugubriously. 'Amy, then. Amy Morrison.'

For a moment I stared at him through the narrow gap in the door. The hint of recognition was explained. He had his late sister's colouring, her high cheekbones and full mouth. But according to Lev Goldsmith, he had been a wild boy in his youth, violent and uncontrollable, popping up before the Bench more often than a jack-in-the-box, covered in tats, terrorizing the rest of the housing estate along with his brother Vincent. ASBOs. Drugs. In and out of the nick, like his father and brother. Despite the high-grade shirt, the dark suit with ten-button waistcoat, the good-quality overcoat, was he to be trusted? I looked him up and down. Not tall, quite stocky, even overweight, bit of a paunch. Built like a street-fighter. But older than I was by a good ten years. I decided that in any struggle, I could take him.

In any case, he didn't look all that threatening. I pushed the door closed, released the knob, opened it wider. 'You'd better come in.'

I showed him into the living room, offered him coffee, which he accepted, made some and brought it in.

'Thank you.' He was mildly-spoken, mildly-mannered.

He was carrying a pair of yellow pigskin driving gloves, the perforated ones with the back of the hand cut out. Rimless specs, which gave him an air of *gravitas* and reliability. He seemed the last person likely to lunge at me and attack. Apart from anything else, what possible motive could he have? Nonetheless, I remained wary, remembering that he used to be somewhat more than a mere tearaway.

'So what exactly can I do for you?' I asked again.

'I understand you were the person who found her . . . who found Noreen,' he said. 'Please, just fill me in on my sister's death. How you found the poor woman. That sort of thing. I want to know, not from any prurient curiosity, I assure you. We just want what they nowadays call "closure", something we are sadly lacking.'

'You have a brother, don't you?'

He shook his head. '*Had.*' He drank some of his coffee. 'Vincent, I'm afraid, is no longer with us. He was killed by another inmate while doing his latest stretch inside. Stabbed in the neck. He bled to death before he was found by the screw— by the officers. They don't know who's responsible, and I don't personally care very much. If that makes me a bad person, so be it.' He cleared his throat.

'I'm sorry.' I wasn't really, since I didn't know the man, and what little I had heard didn't incline me to like him, but conventionalities exist for a reason and ought to be observed.

'Don't be,' Briggs said. 'He took after our father. His prospects were poor and unlikely ever to improve. Frankly, death was probably the kindest thing that could happen to him.' He sipped his coffee delicately, like a cat. 'No, as regards Noreen, by we, I meant my wife and myself. And to a lesser extent, our two sons, who never met her.' He sighed again. 'Poor Noreen. She didn't have the upbringing she deserved. None of us did, I suppose, but she was cleverer than either me or my brother. She had an enquiring mind, should have had a bright future ahead of her. This book she'd written . . . about the Italian artist . . . has been having excellent reviews, or so I read.'

He reached into his jacket. I was instantly alert, remembering his past. As if he was aware, he half-smiled, held up a hand. 'I'm just getting out my business card,' he said.

He gave me a rectangle of pasteboard card decorated with a sheaf of white lilies and a single autumnal maple leaf drifting down. Very tasteful. TERENCE BRIGGS & SONS, I read. INDEPENDENT FUNERAL DIRECTORS, with an address in Leytonstone.

'My sister got out through her artistic abilities,' he said. 'I got out in a different way. Luckily I married my childhood sweetheart, a girl who was as determined as I was to give our sons a better upbringing than either of us had.'

I nodded.

'Respectability, Miss Quick. That's what it's all about. It's a bit like money. People such as yourself, who are born with it, don't have the faintest idea how hard it is to achieve if you don't automatically have it. You have to work for it. Cut ties with people who were once friends or even family. Remodel yourself.'

'So what exactly do you want from me?'

'I regret to say that my sister and I had been out of touch for a while, but I would like to hear details of her demise, should you be prepared to tell me, if only, as I said, to establish some kind of closure.' His speech was measured and precise. Sober. Very different from the image I had built up in my mind following my lunch with Lev Goldsmith.

I described for him the scene which had greeted me in Helena's bedroom, making it as wholesome as possible. Reliving it, again I had the teasing sense that there had been something present at the scene (or not present, its absence making it remarkable) which might make it clearer who was responsible. But it was Helena's room, not Amy's: why should there be any clue to Amy's death?

He nodded slowly when I had finished talking. 'She was a clever girl . . . too clever, really. I don't know where the genes came from, because there were certainly no signs of it in either of our parents. In fact, my father was illiterate. Poor Noreen . . . I don't blame her for cutting communication as soon as she could, getting right away from it all. It took me a lot longer, of course, but I've achieved what I wanted.'

'Good . . .' I couldn't think what to say.

'As I say, if you haven't got it, but want it, it's not the easiest thing in the world to find.'

'When did you last see your sister?'

'See?' He thought about it, frowning slightly above his rimless specs. 'Several years ago now. But seeing's not the same as talking to, or having any kind of relationship with. That's how she wanted it, and I respected that.'

'So you couldn't suggest anyone who might have wanted to kill her?'

He shook his head. Gave an undertakerly sort of semi-snort. 'Though from what I've heard, she seems to have got on the wrong side of most people she came into contact with.'

'I've heard that too. But it's a big step from dislike to murder.'

'That it is.'

'So where did you last catch up with her?'

'As I said, quite a few years ago I took my wife to New York for one of those short breaks they advertise – Shop Early For Christmas or something, take advantage of cheaper prices, I'm sure you know the kind of thing – and read about her in one of those gossip magazines. She'd been widowed, and my wife said that since we were more or less on the spot, we should at least deliver our condolences.' He paused.

'And did you?'

'Well . . .' Another pause. '. . . I saw her in a restaurant, one evening.' He frowned. 'Somewhere small, insignificant. Italian – I think it was called Mario's. Near our hotel. Perhaps she was looking for anonymity, choosing a place like that where no one would recognize her. That we were there is just one of those strange coincidences that life throws at us sometimes.' He looked away from me, and I could see he was having difficulty bringing out what he wanted to tell me.

'Yes?' I said encouragingly.

'She was . . . well, in short, she was with a young man. A much younger man than her. So much so that I wondered at first if he was her son. Except that she wasn't so much *with* him as draped all over him. It was a disgusting exhibition. In public, too. I was too embarrassed to point her out to my wife – it seemed unseemly, to say the least, to be behaving like that with her husband barely cold in his grave.'

'I don't suppose you knew the boy.'

'Not at all. No reason why I should. Young, as I said. Dark hair, dark eyes. Thin, nervy-looking lad. Very intense. If I had to give him a nationality, I'd have said Spanish, or Italian.'

'And was he reciprocating?'

'Enthusiastically. Not to put too fine a point on it, the two of them might just as well have been in bed together for all the notice they took of the other customers.'

'So in the end, you didn't get in contact with her.'

'I'm afraid not.' He gave another of his funeral-director sighs. 'But now I wish I had. We know not the hour nor the day, isn't that true? But if I'd had any inkling of her own death coming while she was still so relatively young, I would certainly have done so.'

'And no idea at all who the young man was?'

'At one point, I think I heard her call him Danny Boy. But I could have been mistaken. Or it might have been some sort of private joke . . . maybe that dark colouring of his was Irish, not Mediterranean. Who knows?' He lifted his shoulders and dropped them again. 'If you take the long-term view, what does it matter?'

'Nonetheless, as you said, strange behaviour for a widow.'

'I took the trouble to investigate a bit further – I have a few business contacts over in the States – and discovered she had quite a reputation on the social scene. Even while her husband was still alive. I believe that once she moved to New York, she went back to art school to study some more. I imagine that's where she did the research for her book.'

'I wonder who the young man was, and how we can find out.'

'I understood from my enquiries that she was always involved with one or other of her fellow students – the male ones, that is.' He spread his hands and made a rueful sort of face. 'At least she changed her name, so it didn't besmirch my company.'

Besmirch . . . nice word.

He got to his feet. 'Thank you for telling me what happened, Miss Quick. I hope they find the culprit soon, and we can all get back to our everyday lives.'

I watched from the window as he emerged from the front door of my building. There was a smart black Daimler car outside, with two young men in black suits standing in front of it, hands folded across their crotches in the way that undertakers – and footballers – do.

When they had climbed into the car and progressed in stately fashion across the parking area and out of sight, I did something I should have done much earlier. Looked up Dexter Morrison, now deceased, on the internet. Dexter had been very rich, wealthier even than the Lamonts, thanks to an adhesive developed by his father and perfected by himself. This adhesive was strong enough to temporarily weld together the damaged components of cars, bicycles, ships and other vehicles, even underwater, enabling them to be safely used until they could be brought in for repair without disrupting their usefulness. In time, Morrison's adhesive was superseded by other products, but by then Dexter and his brother had not only amassed enormous fortunes, they'd also diversified into other fields, from confectionery to a revolutionary hospital bed. Dexter had been married twice before he met Amy Lardner (as she was calling herself) at a fund-raising dinner in London in aid of limbless war heroes, a charity of which he was the patron, but that marriage had lasted until his death at the age of ninety-two.

Which should have left Amy absolutely rolling in it. But no. The Will, which left her a substantial fortune, had been contested upside, downside and sideways by Dexter's daughters, despite the fact that they too had been left mind-bogglingly huge inheritances. Reading between the lines, it seemed that they were more interested in preventing Amy from benefitting from their father's money than in gaining more for themselves. There was wild speculation in the gossip columns and celebrity trash-mags. Faux-sober articles about her behaviour. Accusations of sexual shenanigans. Lovers and would-be lovers jumping on the bandwagon to give sordid tales of their encounters with her.

There were many pictures of Dexter prior to his death attending black-tie dinners, accompanied by his glamorous wife in a variety of sumptuous dresses and jewellery. He featured in long articles about his charity work and was known for his generous contributions to other charities than his own. And always, be it dinners, congresses, speeches, there was Amy at his side.

The article mentioned a scandal which had overtaken the couple when one of Amy's fellow students committed suicide. There were accusations that Amy had been responsible for the young man's death, but other students attested that the boy in question, Marco Daniel Vendamo, had been 'a bit of a weirdo' and a 'nervy sort of kid'. 'Very intense,' one girl said. Was this the 'Danny boy' that Terry had mentioned?

I scrolled down through more photographs. Something caught my attention and I scrolled back until I found what it was. A group photo of the great and the good of New York at some charity function. There was Dexter, there was Amy beside him, glamorously begowned and bejewelled. There were milk-white shirt-fronts and solemn black ties. And there, at the back and to the side, unmistakably, were Bob and Mercy Lamont. He had a lot more hair, then. And hers was longer than now, blacker, piled up on top of her head. She looked impossibly elegant. Her face was fuller than it had been last time we met.

So the Lamonts and the Dexter Morrisons were friends. Or at

the very least, moved in the same social circles. That had to be significant. I needed to think about what it could mean.

I got my car out and started to drive to my parents' house. It was raining, lightly at first, then more heavily, turning into sleet and then heavy snow, so dense that my wipers could hardly cope. I peered through the windscreen into a swirling world of white flakes and dark skies. Perhaps I ought to have turned back, but I didn't want my parents to hear about Helena's death from anyone else. The snow lit up the darkness, catching further light from street lamps and houses where the curtains weren't drawn.

There were lights on in the house when I finally pulled up in their drive. Cosy glows from the kitchen and the sitting room. An upstairs bedroom illuminated. Smoke from the wood-burning stove being madly tossed about by the wind.

I ran to the front door, opened it, shouted out. No answer. I went into the kitchen and found Mary sitting at the table, reading *The New Yorker*, which must have been in the accumulated mail waiting for their return. There was a glass of white wine in one hand.

'Hi,' I said. 'Have a good time?'

'Very good, thank you.'

'Do a lot of sightseeing?'

'At our age, it's more about revisiting old favourites than searching out new places.' She took off her glasses. 'Did you come over while we were gone?'

I was – thank God – too old to be intimidated by her disapproval. 'Yes.'

'Why, when I expressly told you not to?'

'Precisely *because* you told me not to.' I got myself a glass and poured some of her wine into it. 'You have never, in all our shared years, either told me when you were going on holiday, nor that I was not to visit the house in your absence. Naturally, being of an enquiring turn of mind, I immediately drove over to see what was going on.'

'And what did you find?'

'Th-that you had a g-guest staying.' I picked up my glass and drank it down. 'Helena, in point of fact. Why didn't you tell me? You knew how worried about her I was.'

'For the very good reason that she begged us not to tell anyone.

Not even you. As she will confirm for you as soon as she comes back.'

My parents didn't know!

The enormity of what had happened to Helena suddenly welled up inside me like a tsunami of grief. I started to weep in a way I had not been able to since she died.

'My dear child . . .' Mary said. She stood up. 'What on earth is it?'

I went and stood next to her. Buried my head against her shoulder and sobbed. Longed with all my heart for an apple-pie-and-cookies mom, however temporarily. And like a necessary miracle, felt her arms come round me and hold me tight. The last time she had hugged me was when I lost my child. 'It's Helena.'

'What's Helena?' Her body braced itself for bad news.

'She . . . she's dead, Mary.' I explained the circumstances, gave her such details as I knew, said I had identified the body. 'I really . . .' I choked slightly. '. . . don't know if I'm going to be able to go on without her.'

Instant briskness. 'Of *course* you are.' She sat down again, reached for a pad of paper and a pen. 'And you say they found her in the river?'

'Just a mile up the towpath from here. The police are trying to say it was an accident or suicide.'

'That is complete nonsense.'

'So I told them.'

'Not only did Helena hate water, she also hated the cold.'

'And any form of exercise.'

'There is absolutely no way on earth she would have gone out in the cold to walk for a mile and then throw herself in the river.'

'Exactly.'

Mary refilled both our glasses. 'This is sad news for all of us,' she said. 'She was originally your friend, I know, but Edred and I were so fond of her.' She looked over at the door of the kitchen. 'Your father is going to be most distressed.'

Strong words from a woman who rarely showed emotion. As always, the two of them seemed almost disengaged. I wondered if they knew that Helena was a murder suspect, though I doubted it would change their opinion of her.

'As am I,' she continued.

'You'll have to tell the police that she was here,' I said. How long might it take before they got around to seeing my parents? The connection between them and Helena was not immediately obvious.

'I know.' She rested her head on her hand. 'Oh dear.'

'A DI called Alan Garside is in charge. You might want to emphasize Helena's hatred of cold, exercise and water.'

'Yes.' Mary looked out of the window. 'It's snowing hard. You'd better stay the night.'

NINETEEN

'Fliss,' I said, when DI Fairlight answered her phone. 'What was Helena Drummond wearing when she was found?'

'Uh . . . you do realize that this is Garside's call, not mine, don't you?'

'Yes, but—'

'Luckily some sixth sense warned me that you would be doing your stray dog act, hanging round for more scraps, which is why I've got a copy of the case file right here in front me. So what do you want to know this time?'

'What Helena was wearing when they found her.'

'Um . . . let me see.' Papers rustled. Fliss sniffed lightly. I waited. 'Ah, here we are. She was wearing a navy corduroy skirt, two under-vests, one green, one black, a pair of purple tights, a leather coat, green ankle boots, a big red scarf round her neck. Golly,' she sniffed again, 'talk about a riot of colour!'

'Sounds fairly restrained for Helena. And she always hated the cold.' I tried to laugh, picturing my friend, alive and vital, but other drowned faces I had seen over the years kept getting in the way.

'Plus, of course, that ethnic bag and—'

'Whoa,' I said. 'Back up a minute. You said a leather coat?'

'That's right. Dark brown, with big flap pockets. New and very expensive, according to this list.'

'But she hasn't got one,' I objected.

'Maybe she tried a spot of retail therapy and bought one. Or was given one by an admirer.'

'No. She would never buy anything new. Except for shoes. She went to charity shops. It was an ideological thing as much as a financial one. And I very much doubt that she was seeing someone who could afford to give her a leather coat, even if she would have accepted it. And when I went into her house and found Amy Morrison, I can assure you there was no leather coat hanging in the hall.'

'Maybe she'd hung it in her wardrobe, seeing as it was new and all. Or maybe she wore it when she went out with her friends the evening before.'

'Hanging in wardrobes wasn't Helena at all. But we can easily check with the folk she went to the concert with.'

'Be that as it may, that's what she was wearing when they fished her out of the water. With the pockets full of stones, big ones. And more of them in that woolly bag thing, as I told you.'

'What did she actually die of?'

'Not sure. But not drowning. According to the ME, she was dead when she went into the water.'

'Though you were obviously meant to think that she had gone in willingly, after filling her pockets with stones. So what *did* kill her?'

'A massive blow to the side of the head, made by one of the bigger stones. They found it in her bag, still with blood on it.'

'So unless they think she stood on the bank, decked herself on the head with a stone and managed to put the weapon back into her bag before falling dead into the water, presumably they've ruled out suicide.' A slip-up by this very competent murderer, I thought. Who had gone to the trouble of bringing a coat with him and filling the pockets with stones. Especially in buying a new and expensive one, not realizing it was the sort of thing Helena would never have bought.

'They've also ruled out accident,' said Fliss.

'So they recognize that despite the stones, it's officially murder?'

'Right.'

'Anything else I might find interesting?'

'Well . . . no prints, obviously. The ground was iron hard. But apparently there's some slightly mushy kind of grass and mud at the edge of the towpath, the remains of a dried-up puddle where the ground is sheltered by a small area of trees and undergrowth.'

'I know the place.'

'They found traces of tyre marks. Or *a* trace, at any rate.'

'You couldn't get a car along there.'

'Sorry . . . traces of a bike tyre.'

'What sort of bike?'

'A motorbike, fairly new and top-of-the-range, according to our experts.'

Ding! Likewise dong! Motorbikes went together with Laurence Turnbull the way maggots went with a corpse. And a neighbour of Helena's had mentioned a motorbike being revved outside her house the night Amy was murdered. On the other hand . . . I could understand why he might have wanted to kill Amy (I was sure there would be a connection between the two, via art college), but what possible beef could he have had against Helena? Unless she was behind him leaving art school without completing his diploma and he had been thirsting for revenge ever since.

'What about the first murder? Amy Morrison's.'

'So far, almost nothing. The usual crop of out-of-town sightings, the usual nutters claiming they saw her being eaten by aliens or abducted by their son-in-law in Newcastle.'

'If she was eaten or abducted, how do they explain her body being discovered in Helena's house?'

'They don't. Logical explanation isn't part of the brief. You know that.'

I terminated the call, then pressed in the numbers for Paul Sandbrook, owner of the antiques shop in the town. This time he answered himself. 'Yes?'

'Quick here,' I said. 'Alex Quick.'

'Remind me.'

'We spoke a few days ag—'

'I remember, Drummond & Quick. Of course. And now poor Helena . . .' His voice tailed away.

'Last time we spoke, you mentioned some former student of hers who was eating in the same restaurant as you and your party.'

'That's right.'

'Who came over to speak to Helena.'

'Yes. Helena tried to give her the brush-off but the woman refused to take the hint. Just kept swaying about and giggling. She must have been either drunk or high.'

'Did Helena say who it was?'

'No. In fact she was uncharacteristically tight-lipped about her.'

'Could you describe her?'

'I've already done so, to the police. The *real* police,' he added pointedly.

Undeterred, I said, 'I would really appreciate it.'

'Blonde ringlets. Early forties. Quite good-looking.'

'Clothes?'

'A black dress, lacy round the hem. A bit too much bosom on display. Heels.'

'Any jewellery?'

'A necklace made of interlocked gold rings. Diamonds on her fingers. No earrings.'

Amy Morrison, without a doubt. 'Was she dining alone?'

'No idea. I couldn't actually see her when she was sitting at her table. But I shouldn't think so, would you?' He paused a moment. 'On second thoughts, when she went back to her own table, maybe there was someone. I couldn't see clearly and he could have been at another table.'

'Can you give me any details, supposing he *was* with her?'

'Younger than she was. Bright hair. That's all that registered.'

I waited but he didn't say anything more. In the end, I said, 'One last question, if you don't mind: was Helen wearing a coat that night?'

'She'd be pretty silly not to, wouldn't she? In those sub-arctic temperatures.'

'Is that a yes?'

'Yes.'

'And do you have any recollection of the coat she had on?'

'It was one of those weird garments Helena used to wear. Quilted. Red. Knobbly, in some way. A Chinese-style ideogram on the back.'

'But nothing leather?'

'Leather? Definitely not.'

'Thank you, Mr Sandbrook. You've been most helpful.'

He grunted and cut off the call.

I knew the coat he was referring to, a thickly padded long jacket from somewhere like Outer Mongolia. Knobbly, as he said, with knots of cloth hanging from it, wild buttons. Helena had found it on some stall at Brick Lane market.

So, I thought. Amy was in Canterbury on the night she was murdered. Obviously. Was it just chance that took her to the same restaurant as Helena and her friends? And chance or no chance, what led her to Helena's house? And since Helena spent the night at Peter Preston's house, she wouldn't have been able to let Amy in. And given that her portfolio still lay on the back seat of her old car, it looked as if she had never set off for the meeting with Clifford Nichols.

Were there signs of a break-in? I examined the possibility of a scenario in which the killer in some way kidnapped or disabled Helena after her meeting with friends, took her keys, got into her house, waited for Amy to show up (having arranged a rendezvous there beforehand?), and as soon as she did, pulled her inside before she could escape, got her upstairs and proceeded to brutally kill her. I wondered if there was evidence of sexual activity prior to that. Perhaps Amy was aroused by the whole set-up.

Which set me thinking. Since the body was almost naked, I had assumed that sex had taken place, but perhaps it hadn't. Did I dare ring Inspector Garside and ask? Of course I did.

'Why do you want to know?' he said, when I was put through.

'Just wondering,' I said. 'When I found Ms Morrison's body, it looked as if she had been in the middle of some hanky-panky and it was after that that she was . . .' I shuddered, thinking that unpleasant as the woman had been, nobody could have wished her to still be alive when that implement was driven into her eyes.

'Mmm,' he said, giving nothing away.

'Any signs of a break-in?' I was pushing my luck, I knew. On the other hand, I was an ex-copper myself, so I knew he was unlikely to be divulging details of the investigation which the police were repressing for the time being. And besides, I could always get into the house with a legitimate excuse about work or papers, and check for myself.

I could feel him considering all these points. Then, grudgingly, he said, 'No.'

'Thanks.' This was information which bore out my suppositions. Unless Helena had simply left the door unlocked when she set off for her evening out. Which still left the question of why Amy would have appeared at the house of someone she knew disliked her, especially late at night.

I called Paul Sandbrook again. He gave an exaggerated sigh when I identified myself. 'What now?' he said. 'I'm really frightfully busy.'

I ignored him, knowing perfectly well that he spent most of the day sitting at the back of his shop, drinking tea and reading Mills & Boon romances, of which he had an extensive library. 'Do you know who picked Helena up on the evening of the concert and drove her into the city?'

'That neighbour of hers, I believe. He lived in her village, name of Peregrine or some such.'

I longed to ask if Awesomesuch was the neighbour's name, but guessed it wouldn't go down too well. 'But this guy didn't join you for the evening?'

'Apparently he runs evening classes twice a week. Aromatherapy and massage, body-painting, poncey stuff like that.'

'Is that how he earns his living?'

'I think he's in the art department of the university, actually. Or associated with it in some way.'

Peregrine . . . aka Perry. Perry Nutley. I'd already met him. 'Got an address?'

He gave me one and ended the call.

'So do you know how, or indeed *if* Helena got home that night?' Trying not to make a face, I tasted the coffee Perry Nutley brought me. It had not improved since my last visit. I knew the answer, of course, but did he?

'Is that the same night the . . . uh . . . person was . . . found dead in her house?' he asked. He laid one of his delicate but manly hands on my arm. 'It must have been ghastly for you.'

'It was pretty awful – but it was the following day that I was there. Helena's car was still outside her house, but there was no sign of her and I wondered if you knew where she went after she ate out with her friends.' I had gone to his address, just round the corner from Helena's place, but there was no answer. I had tracked him down at the university.

'I'm not sure. I usually brought her back on these occasions, but that particular night she said she would be late and I wasn't to wait for her. So I didn't. In fact, I know perfectly well that she went off with Peter Preston, classy car salesman.'

'Did you notice anything different from other nights that you gave her a lift into town?'

'Not really.' He wrinkled his smooth brow. 'There was that idiotic motorbike, mind you. Kept behind us all the way, wouldn't overtake even though I slowed down where I could to let him by.'

'Did Helena say anything?'

'Started babbling on about a stalker!' He smiled. 'So ridiculous.'

'Yeah.'

'Dear dear Helena. I love her – *loved* her – dearly but she was always such a drama queen.'

'Wasn't she, though?'

He stopped being so dismissive in tone. 'Though come to think of it . . .'

Another of my brilliant notions hit me. I could so easily see the motorcyclist following Perry and Helena into Canterbury, hanging about the cathedral precincts while they attended the concert, maybe even going inside to listen as well, then tracking Helena and her friends to the restaurant afterwards. More than that, I had a good idea who it might be.

And after they emerged from the restaurant . . . what then?

I was beginning to get a reasonably clear idea of the course of events in the twelve-hour time span during which Amy must have died. It was all just feasible, though I still needed to work on the finer details. Such as why he was in town that night. And, of course, establish the identity of the stalker/murderer with enough credibility to present a case to Inspector Garside.

A man came hustling through the swing doors of the studio where we were sitting. 'I'm looking for Professor Nutley,' he said. His deep antipodean tones rang round the studio.

'And you are?'

'I believe he's Helena's former husband,' I said. 'Professor Liam Hadfield.' I surveyed the newcomer. Tall, fit, sunburned in that bone-deep way Australians have. Wearing one of those full-length, rust-coloured Drizabone raincoats. And very good-looking. No wonder Helena had fallen so heavily for him – and got out so quickly when she realized what a sod he was to live with. You only had to look at him to see it. It was obvious that Perry wasn't impressed.

'She's not here,' he said.

'For God's sake, man, I know that,' said Hadfield impatiently. 'She's dead.' He swung round to me. 'Do I know you?'

'We've never met, if that's what you mean. I'm Helena's partner. Alexandra Quick.'

'Partner? She hasn't gone over to the other side, has she?' His rich voice resonated. His face sneered.

'How do you mean?' Perry asked politely. His fists were clenched. I admired his self-control.

'Gone lezzy on us. Turned queer. Started hanging out with the

arse bandits and muff divers. She was never picky about the kind
of riff-raff she shagged—' The man was an impossible boor.

'We have a thriving LGBTQ group here at the uni,' Perry said,
his voice even but quivering with rage. 'Maybe you'd like to have
a word with the President of the society. I happen to know she's
on campus at this very moment. I'm sure she would be very interested to meet you and hear your antipodean views.'

'I didn't come here to discuss sexual deviants,' Hadfield said.

'So why did you come?'

'I'm giving a talk on Homer's Influences to the classics faculty.
Thought I'd stop in and say g'day to Helena's colleagues. Least I
could do, given the circumstances.'

'Expecting a large crowd this afternoon, are you?'

Hadfield gave a smirk. 'Given that I'm quite well-known in my
field, I would anticipate that a fair old number would show up, yes.'

I could see from the glint in Perry's eye that the chances were
slim of more than half-a-dozen brave souls getting through the
LGBTQ picket line he was undoubtedly planning to organize in the
lunch hour. I wondered whether I might not even join them.

'Where were you last Monday?' I asked.

'Last Monday? Almost certainly in Oxford, fast asleep, catching
up on the jet lag. I'd only arrived the evening before after a long
journey from Sydney.'

'Can anyone vouch for you?'

'If you mean was I sharing my bed with some Anglo-Saxon
beauty – or any other kind, for that matter – unusually the answer's
no.' Another complacent smirk. His macho self-satisfaction was
beginning to grate.

'So,' said Perry, 'you can't have had anything to do with Ms
Morrison. But how about Helena, your former wife? You hated her,
I bet. She had the audacity to discard you—'

'And who could blame her?' I murmured.

'—and you couldn't forgive her for the humiliation. So when
you were offered the chance of a semester in Oxford, you jumped
at it, seeing an opportunity for revenge. Is that about the size of it?
Hmm? Hmm?' He squared up as though he was about to land one
on the prof's nose.

Hadfield and I stared at him in astonishment. 'What?' spluttered
the Aussie. 'Have you gone stark raving bonkers?' His sunburn had

turned greenish. 'Kill Helena? You shonky little shithead, why would I kill her? I *loved* her . . .'

All of which I found intcresting. And, reluctantly, credible.

Back at home, I had no sooner sat down at my desk than the phone began jittering around on the desktop in front of me. It was Bob Lamont.

'Hi, there,' he said. 'I'm calling to ask if you've had any further thoughts about the proposition which my wife and I put to you last time we met.'

'I haven't really had—'

'I understand. After Doctor Drummond's death you must be in a state of total shock.'

'I am rather.'

'And Christmas is nearly on us, as well.'

'I'll be spending it with my family,' I said. 'I can't do much until after that.'

He laughed. 'We Yanks always find it kinda strange how England closes down for nearly two weeks over the holiday season. Lord knows what it does for the economy. But be that as it may, my wife and I would very much like to talk to you further, iron out any problems you foresee, look at details and so on. Then we would draw up a contract, have it delivered to you and wait for you to send a signed copy back.'

'Sounds good.' Obviously I would need to discuss with the Lamonts the fact of the three-book contract from Nichols. It would mean a great deal of work on my part for the next three or four, even five years, but that was probably a good thing.

'So is there any day in the near future which would suit you best?' In the background, someone murmured at him. 'Oh yes, there is one small snag. My wife's just reminded me that I'm booked to fly to the States on the sixth of January.'

'I can't possibly get up much before . . .' I looked at the new leather-bound desk diary which had been a gift from my sister Meghan. '. . . January ninth at the earliest.'

'Pity. But you can talk to Mercy on her own, can't you? She's just as savvy about the terms and conditions of the operation as I am – if not more so – and she won't be leaving London for at least a week after I do. Would that work?'

'It sounds very workable indeed.' I almost slavered at the thought of standing in front of some of the Lamonts' paintings again. That Feininger, for instance. The small Cranach. And I would love to see their Ainslie Gordons, if they kept them in the London flat. 'Yes, give me a date which would be good for her.'

We settled on a time and day in the early part of January. Truth to tell, I was rather glad that Bob wouldn't be present at the meeting. Despite the fact that I liked the man, I found him rather disconcerting, though I couldn't have said why. He was charming and positive and obviously an extremely competent businessman. And I had a warm and exhilarating feeling that we would be working together on a lucrative deal over the next years. If I accepted their offer (and why on earth wouldn't I?), I might even find myself lifted out of my financial slump at last.

TWENTY

For nearly a month, I seemed to have been simply chasing shadows. But now it was Christmas; hard as it was, I had to put all thoughts of Helena out of my head, though my heart mourned. She'd spent last Christmas with us. This year, Hereward and Lana, plus Anton, came down to my parents' house, and I joined them. Meghan and Leo flew over from Rome for three days along with their children. We played Charades and Monopoly and Consequences. We ate roast beef and clove-studded ham. My uncle, Sir Aylward de Cuik, sent down a whole salmon fished from his own stream in Scotland, which we simmered in orange juice for four minutes, two on each side, and ate with Mary's lemon and garlic mayonnaise, almost the only thing she could make.

My other uncle, Hengist Dee Quick, as he styled himself, who was an attorney in Tennessee, (he was what he called a Love Refugee, married to a girl from Memphis who wanted to stay close to home), sent his annual care package of maple syrup, Oreos, peanut butter, vacuum-packed Cornish game hen, canned clam chowder, blue cheese dressing and other assorted American goodies. None of us had the heart to tell him that all these items were now easily available in England, at Harrods, Fortnums or even on the shelves of supermarkets.

We sang carols and opened stockings. Father Christmas turned up, shouting 'Ho, ho, ho!' at frequent intervals, and handed out presents. We took Anton for long walks. With the turning of the year, these were the family customs which had evolved over all our childhoods, the perfect way for me to try and restart the life, both personal and professional, which had stopped so abruptly with the murder of Amy Morrison. The evening before she and Herry returned to London, Lana told us they were expecting their first child, scheduled to arrive in May. A good end to a bad year.

I tried several times to get my parents alone, in order to ask them about Helena, but it proved impossible. Too many people there. Too much going on. Too many interruptions. Or were they deliberately avoiding me, knowing what I wanted to talk about? I would have to drive over, take them by surprise.

Now, with Christmas and the New Year over and a new beginning ahead, I decided that the best thing I could do for Helena was to continue with *Ripe for the Picking*, just as if she were still around, since between us we had already done ninety per cent of the work.

Sitting at my desk a week later, I telephoned Clifford Nichols.

'I heard about Doctor Drummond's tragic death,' he said, before I could say anything more than my name. 'I'm so very sorry.'

'It's terrible,' I said. 'But unfortunately life has to go on. So at the risk of sounding mercenary and uncaring, I have your contract right here in front of me, and want to know if you are willing to let me carry on as planned, but from now on as a solo effort.'

'Elaine and I were just talking about this. We both feel that you're more than competent to produce the anthologies on your own. After all, you did *Baby, Baby*, and *Tell Me a Story* before you even met Doctor Drummond.'

'So you're happy for me to sign the contract and send it back to you?'

'More than.'

Standing in the kitchen, waiting for the coffee to finish gulping and burping in its glass cylinder, I watched a heavily-built runner plodding into the wind along the seafront. I felt guilty that I wasn't running too. Remembered my new year's resolution to get out there and go jogging more often. Especially when the guy glanced up at my window in an almost accusatory manner. I shivered. Told myself that tomorrow I would definitely do it. Run to the railway bridge almost two miles away. Run back. At least it would be away from the north-easterly wind currently driving white-capped waves fiercely towards the shore.

The afternoon wore slowly on. Any light in the sky began to merge with the heavy grey cloud cover. I wasn't ready to settle down for the evening. Maybe I would get myself into a jogging frame of mind by walking briskly down to Willoughby's Books. I wrapped up warmly with a scarf, gloves and my full-length quilted coat. Which immediately reminded me of Helena. As so many things did. Where would she have acquired a leather coat? Or to put it another way, how had her killer persuaded her to put on a leather coat, which he must have brought with him. Again, my mind flew towards motorbikes and studded leather jackets and shiny leather trousers. New and expensive, DI Fairlight had told me. Which strongly implied that he had bought it specially. And if Helena had been hiding out with Edred and Mary, how had her killer discovered her? Was it pure coincidence? I very much doubted it: this killer was both meticulous and organized.

Neither of them were attributes I would have connected with what I had so far seen of Laurence Turnbull. Nonetheless, he seemed to be a ripe candidate for the crime: he had means, motive and opportunity.

I walked through the town, eyes closed into slits against the by-now driving snow. In the falling darkness, shop windows glowed, still hung with Christmas baubles. Even the austere woman who owned Hinton's Shoes had unbent far enough to add a few shiny glass balls to her display of fur-lined Ugg boots and thick-soled ankle-high walking shoes. I passed the Polish guy selling the *Big Issue*, the Salvation Army lot rattling tins, the local volunteers collecting for the lifeboats. I dropped a pound coin into each box. Didn't take a copy of the *Issue*.

In the wine shop, I could see Edward Vine sitting on a high stool at his counter. His impressively bald dome of a head shone like a low-lying sun. A couple of bottles and a few glasses stood in front of him. When I walked in, he looked up and smiled.

'Quick! How are you, my dear?'

'Just fine, thank you.' I pointed to the glasses in front of him. 'You look like you're enjoying yourself.'

'Enjoying myself? Are you joking, madam? This is hard work. I'm tasting samples from a mixed consignment I purchased recently. Chilean wine. Some of it is excellent, at least as good as a grand cru. Other stuff is only fit to clear the drains with. Want to try a glass of the good stuff?'

'Love to.'

I sat down on the customer chair on the shop side of the counter. He poured me a glass. I did all that wine expert stuff: sniffing and swilling and slapping against my palate. I couldn't bring myself to spit it out: it was far too good. 'I'll take a bottle of that,' I said.

'Are you sure?' He told me the price.

'On second thoughts . . .' I said.

We exchanged chit-chat about Christmas and how we had occupied the holidays. Edward had passed five days with his mother, former model and gifted narcissist. 'It was even more ghastly than I'd feared,' he said. 'Talk about Sunset Boulevard. And eating overdone turkey with four of her former lovers, dentally challenged to a man. I could scarcely hear myself think for the clattering of ill-fitting false teeth.'

'We had roast beef,' I said.

'Oh please. Don't make me weep.' Edward lifted his glass and then looked across at me. 'Do you know, I absolutely hate turkey. With or without cranberry sauce. I swear my old bat of a mother buys it especially because she knows I loathe it.'

'And home-made Yorkshire pud,' I continued meanly. I knew Edward's views on Yorkshire pudding.

'Stop at once or I shall have to kill you.' Edward laughed and then looked stricken. 'What a very ill-judged joke,' he said. 'I apologize.'

'Don't worry about it. I have to go on without Helena. I still have a living to earn. And there are several commissions in the offing.'

'Still no idea who . . . um . . . who was responsible for the . . . uh . . . the demise of Doctor Drummond?'

I'm always amazed by the way even highly intelligent people like Edward tend to sidle up to and edge around the fact of death rather than facing it directly and going straight ahead, 'None at all. Just one or two theories,' I said. 'We'll see how they develop. Meanwhile, I'll have one of your burgundies, please. You choose.'

I took the wrapped bottle next door to the bookshop where Sam was selling a box of Cluedo, two packs of cards, Scrabble and Pictionary to a harassed woman who was crossing things off a long list. 'At least that's my sisters' children done,' she said thankfully, as I walked behind her to the crime fiction shelves, always my favourite section. Did she not realize that Christmas was over? She saw the look that passed between Sam and me and laughed. 'Believe it or not, my sisters have four children between them, all with birthdays in the middle of January. It's a nightmare, coming so soon after Christmas.'

'Let me offer you a glass of wine as partial compensation,' said Sam.

'I'd love to, but I'm driving. Thanks anyway, dear Sam.' She blew him a kiss and went out.

'Dear Sam, eh?' I raised my eyebrows at him, ignoring the tiny flame of pique which spurted inside me. After all, he wasn't my type. And I had already rebuffed several of his tentative efforts to move our friendship on to something warmer. 'And a kiss, too. Well, well, well . . .'

'We were an item for about five minutes,' he said coolly. 'And then she met my best friend. They've been married for ten years. I'm godfather to their eldest boy.'

'Right,' I said. 'Fine. Excellent.' I felt like a fool, letting him get the impression that I gave a toss. Because I didn't. Really.

'So,' he said, and to my annoyance, I could see he was repressing a smirky grin. 'What can I do for you?'

'I wanted to run some things by you, when you've finished for the day. But if you're too busy flirting with former girlfriends and the like . . .' Hell and damnation! Why did I say that? I mean, as if I cared.

He looked at his watch. 'Give me ten. Alison isn't in today so I'll have to do the cashing up and general bookkeeping and so on. After that, Alexandra, I'm all yours.'

He gave me a meaningful look. I realized that in some indefinable way, our positions had been reversed. I had lost whatever advantage I might once have had, though it seemed an odd way to look at our relationship, whatever that was.

Twelve minutes later, he came over to where I was leafing through the latest Pierre Lemaitre. 'I'd like to buy this,' I said. 'The first two of the trilogy were brilliant.'

'I'll give it to you,' he said. 'I've closed the till for tonight.'

'I'll give you this in exchange.' I handed him the bottle I had just bought next door.

He went over and turned the OPEN sign to SORRY WE'RE CLOSED. He took two glasses from underneath his desk. Came over and put them on one of the four tiny café tables squeezed into a corner.

'Sit down and tell me what's on your mind.' He removed the cork and poured a little wine into each glass.

'Okay.' I took a sip. Took a breath. Began. 'The more I examine it,' I said, 'and ruling out the legendary rapist and notional psychopath, the more obvious it seems to me who must have been responsible for killing Helena. And if he killed Helena, one must assume the same guy murdered Amy as well. He had motive, means and opportunity.' I outlined the facts as I knew them. Helena's role in getting him kicked out of art school. The motorbike which had been mentioned by several people as being at the scene or scenes of crime. His presence here in England at the relevant times – 'I bet we find when we check, that Ainslie Gordon sent him over to England for fresh paint supplies or canvasses or whisky or something. And don't forget the fact that he's already proven to be a conscienceless killer.'

Sam's eyebrows rose sharply as I expounded. 'Specious,' he said.

'And I'm quite sure that if we look into it further, we'll find that he had some kind of an affair or involvement with Amy Morrison when he was still at art college,' I finished. 'Maybe it was him who was having dinner with her at that restaurant after the cathedral concert.'

'Very neat,' Sam said judiciously. 'Very clever. Very well-thought-out. Unfortunately, you don't have a single scrap of evidence to support your thesis. So, I'm sorry, but I don't buy it. At least, not without a great more solid fact. Just for a start, while I can see Doctor Drummond taking advantage of a spin on a fast bike, if one was offered, how come she didn't go to the police as soon as Morrison's body was found in her house?'

'Because obviously she didn't go home that night.' I repeated the information I had received directly from the mouth of the car salesman, Peter Preston.

'So how did she progress from the man in the restaurant onto the back of the murderer's bike?'

'That's fairly clear, I'd have thought. Turnbull takes Amy back to Helena's house, loves her up a bit, kills her, and races back to the restaurant, where Helena is still sitting, or just settling the bill or whatever. Follows her to the house of the guy she's planning to spend the night with, waits until she eventually emerges in the morning. Possibly looking at her watch in a worried fashion, as one who is running late. Offers to run her home, takes her somewhere isolated instead, and tries to kill her too. She gets away, makes for my parents' house, knowing that if she goes to her own home, he could easily try again. Wants to call the police to report the attack, not realizing that by now I've found the body of Amy and called the police, only to discover in the morning's newspapers that she is their prime suspect for Amy's murder.'

'He's a busy lad, this stalker-cum-murderer. And frankly, I don't see Doctor Drummond as too chicken-livered to report the attack on her. And why didn't she come to you, rather than your parents?'

'Because knowing how close she and I were, it would be the logical place for him to look for her – if she's not at her own home – in order to try again. Whereas nobody would immediately think of my parents.'

'Sorry, Alex, but it's very thin. And how did he eventually find out that she'd gone to your parents?'

'He followed the taxi she took – or bus or train, whatever means she used to get to Edred and Mary's place. Then he waited, knowing she'd have to emerge eventually – even though my parents then went on holiday, in the hope of putting anyone trying to find her off the scent.'

'And how does the leather coat fit into this fairy tale?'

'He brought it with him.' Annoyed, I explained my reasoning on that point. 'Then he waited some more . . . lurked would be more apt.'

'He does an awful lot of waiting. And why didn't she call you? You were the obvious person to tell.'

'Then he abducted her, knocked her on the head with a stone and pushed her body into the river.'

'It's all suppositious, based on nothing more than wishful thinking.'

'You're not very supportive.'

'I was asked for my opinion, Alexandra. And accordingly, I'm giving it.'

'So you would say I don't have anything like enough to go to the cops with?'

'I would say that you have manufactured a case more or less out of thin air, combined with extreme prejudice against the party under discussion, and you are now desperately trying to make the very few facts at your disposal fit your theory. I would also say that in my opinion, were you to advance it to the police, you would become a laughing stock among your former colleagues.'

'Well,' I said, more than a little irritated. 'You can't say fairer than that.'

'I would also say that I would love to take you out for dinner. Maybe ask Edward next door to join us.'

I tried to receive this invitation with hostility, but couldn't quite manage it. 'All right,' I said, sounding sulky. 'Why not. Could be fun, I suppose.'

And it was.

I slept well, despite previous apprehensions about a possible intruder. By now, the locks on my doors had been strengthened and underpinned with secondary locks, loose windows had been reinforced and an alarm system installed. All at vast expense, paid for by my insurance company.

The next morning, I lay snugly in bed and watched snow swirling outside my window. Even with the double glazing, I could hear the waves crashing on to the shingle. Do it, Alex, I told myself. Just *do* it. But I couldn't bring myself to get out of bed and go jogging. 'I'll work hard all day and go this evening,' I said out loud. 'I absolutely will.'

I turned over and went back to sleep.

Although the sea was calmer by the evening, the wind was blowing more strongly now than earlier. I shut down my computer and considered my options. *To thine own self be true . . .* I'd said I would go for a jog, ergo I must. I put on my warmest layers, zipped my windproof jacket tightly closed, laced up my running shoes. Stepped out through the doors to the outside. Turned inland away from the sea.

Was this really wise? The sky was already darkening. As I reached the small wood which marked the edge of town, the air movement grew stronger, full of noise and debris: broken twigs, dead leaves swirling in the gutters, a creak of tree branches, and the piercing squeal of air rushing through overhead telegraph wires. I decided I would go to the top of the hill where the bridge went over the railway line, then turn back towards home, down the track, into the wood and out again, along the road, hang a left towards the sea and thus into The Strand, my own road. Rain spat at my face as, head down, I jogged up the hill. At the top I paused, bent over for a moment to ease my muscles. The world seemed empty of people, apart from a lone figure flogging along the wet track towards me. I promised myself a nice hot bath when I got in, scented candles in the bathroom, a slug of brandy for inner warmth, maybe a triangle of eighty-five per cent chocolate, followed by a slather of the expensive French body cream Herry and Lana had given me for my last birthday. I might even go to bed early with a tray of something light and a book. Sometimes there are compensations to living alone.

I leaned for a moment on the flat pimpled top of the bridge, its grey paint gleaming dully in the fading light. As a child I had loved to come up here with Edred to wait for the train to pass beneath us, rushing onwards like a glossy steel caterpillar towards London or the West. I had been small enough then to peer between the criss-crossed girders (*'hold tight, darling, don't want you to fall through'*) at the rails below, gleaming into the far distance. I still remembered that delicious frisson of fear – despite the firm grip of my father's hand on the collar of my coat – as the train thundered below and I imagined my body cartwheeling down to thud onto the rushing roof beneath me.

The storm was building in intensity. The ends of my scarf had come loose and were flailing manically in the wind, snapping at the edge of my jaw. The air vibrated. I lifted my face to the lowering clouds above me, the shouting trees: this was definitely as far as I was going tonight. The oncoming jogger had his head bent against the wind, going more slowly now. I turned and ran down the hill towards the tossing branches of the little wood; beyond them, I could see the street lamps along The Strand, parked cars, the lights of the little corner shop, people carrying paper-wrapped parcels from the chippy next door to it.

The air was less turbulent under the trees, though wind filled my mouth and my eyes streamed with cold-induced tears. Suddenly, out of the windy darkness, without the slightest warning, an arm wrapped itself round my throat. The attack was so swift and sudden that I didn't even have time to scream. I felt the warmth of another body, heard the faint squeak of leather gloves, my frantic fingers clutching ineffectually at the constriction round my throat. A fist slammed into my face, once and then again.

How many seconds were there before I fell? Two, maybe, possibly three, before the massive terror dissolved into mercifully cut-short agony. My head hit the ground with the force of a sledgehammer. Lights wheeled and circled behind my eyelids. I knew I was on the edge of death. There was no time to wonder, to protest that it shouldn't end like this, alone in a dark wood. No time for regrets or thanks. Maybe a fleeting image of Jack Martin flashed through my terrified brain, maybe I saw the navy-blue PVC raincoat I had worn aged four, with its matching sou'wester, maybe I remembered a pink rose from my mother's garden, or Sam Willoughby's smile. Then nothing.

Voices swelled around me, though I couldn't make out what they were saying. My body seemed completely constricted, as though I had been mummified, so that I was only able to move my fingers. I couldn't shift my head to either side. When I tried to swallow, the pain was so intense that I started to choke, which was even more painful. Somebody held a glass of water to my lips. Above or to the side of me, voices heaved and retreated, hollow, like the sound of the ocean when you hold a seashell to your ear. I tried to work out why I was lying there, whether I was in a bed, where I was. Who I was. Whether I was in some kind of danger.

I remembered jogging through the woods. The grey-painted buttons on the iron railway bridge. The buffeting wind. In the distance, a lone figure battled on towards me, standing on the summit of the overpass, on and on, yet never coming any closer. I saw him there, clear as a signpost, but couldn't remember any details about him. Was he the one who had flung an arm like a steel tendon around my neck? I tried to move an arm to ease the pain in my throat but couldn't. Someone touched my shoulder briefly. Someone spoke, but I wasn't able to make out what they were saying, or whether they were standing right beside me, or talking from the next room. My eyes would not open. I thought I was going to throw up. And still the black figure came pounding towards me, black feet on the black path, head down, elbows swinging, feet rhythmically hitting the cindered path, over and over.

There had been menace somewhere recently. The plots of a hundred crime thrillers flitted like wisps of fog through my incapacitated brain. Trussed up like this, was I in danger from some perverted thrill-seeking maniac? It was a coherent thought, the first since I had become aware of lying there on my back. Danger . . . why would I think I might be in danger?

'Pulse . . .' someone said, the voice swaying like a cobweb in a breeze. '. . . examined but there was . . .' A conversation swinging above me. 'Doctor Fitz . . .' A hand was laid on my chest. Heavy, so heavy that I thought I might pass out. Then I managed another thought: I already was passed out, wasn't I? It seemed amusing, so amusing that I would have laughed aloud, had I been capable of it.

My eyelids seemed to have been glued shut; if I tried any harder to open them, I was afraid I would rip them apart.

'Quick?' someone said. 'Alex?'

And I said 'Yes?'

There was the sound of relieved laughter. 'She's there, she's back,' someone said, the words retreating into the almost-solid fog of conversation going on all around me.

There had been hands round my throat. Reflexively, I tried again to move my arm upwards, and this time was able to complete the movement. Under a layer of bandages, my neck felt tender and sore.

'Alex?' someone said again. Who was it . . . parent, friend, doctor, nurse?

'What?' I managed, then gave in to a sudden overwhelming desire to sleep.

When I woke up again, someone was holding my hand. It was a hard hand, a calloused one. A hand I recognized. 'Mary?' I said. I opened my eyes.

My mother bent over me. 'Oh, Alex . . .' I could hear her perfectly well. Plus the faint drip of a tap, footsteps heel-and-toeing along the polished composition floor outside the room, a man's cheerful voice, the squeak of rubber wheels.

'What happened?' I asked, sounding like a rusty gate.

'Someone attacked you while you were out jogging. I think they meant to kill you.'

My father's voice. 'God, Alex, what would we have done if he had succeeded?'

What *do* people do in those circumstances? They survive. 'But he didn't,' I croaked.

'It's a miracle,' Mary said. 'Someone was walking their dog, saw you, and then some other guy came running up behind you, jumped on you. So this guy, the one with the dog, started shouting, and the guy – the one who attacked you – leaped to his feet and took off in the other direction. Luckily, the guy had his cell—'

'I'm confused, Mary.' Despite her analytical brain, my mother never could tell a coherent story. 'Which guy had the phone?'

'—and called the cops. You were brought in here, to the hospital. Someone got hold of us – not sure how – and we came racing over to be with you.' Her grip on my hand tightened. 'Oh, Alex . . .'

This was all wrong. My parents didn't do emotion. They never betrayed distress, particularly where their children were concerned. Yet here they were, emoting. Perhaps they were mellowing at last.

'No,' I said. 'No idea at all who it could have been.' I was still a little woozy from painkillers, and my throat was definitely unfit for purpose, but otherwise I was fine.

My parents had gone. Edward Vine and Sam were sitting on either side of me. 'None,' I repeated. I looked from one to another. 'How long have I been here?'

'This is the third day,' Sam said.

Three days! It didn't seem possible. 'I can't have been that badly hurt.'

'Concussion, dear,' said Edward. 'They wanted to keep you in for observation.'

'When can I go home?'

'Some time today. They'll be in to tell you when as soon as they've come to a decision.' Sam patted my hand. 'And I'm standing by to drive you home.'

'You're a star,' I said.

'Why would anyone want to attack you?' he said.

'If it's just your average maniac, there's no answering that question. It could have been entirely random.' Edward frowned. 'But if it's someone who specifically targeted you . . .'

'Why? What have I done?'

'Maybe he thinks you have information that could endanger him in some way.'

'How many of those are there likely to be?' I started to shrug, then changed my mind as my shoulders protested. 'I don't have any information about anything.'

'Maybe he thinks you have.'

'Well, I haven't.' I could feel my face drooping.

'Maybe you should take an ad out in the paper, stating so,' Sam said, trying to make me laugh.

It didn't work. I fell asleep again.

I was allowed to leave the hospital later that afternoon. Sam agreed to take full responsibility for me. I have a feeling he implied that he was my fiancé and we lived together. As promised, he took me home, treating me with the tenderness he might have shown to a newly discovered Shakespearean Folio One. Or a first edition of Chaucer. He made us some supper. Announced firmly that he would be staying the night, had indeed sworn to both the hospital and to my parents that I would not be left alone. He made up a bed for himself on the sofa. I had insisted that I was fine, thank you, getting better by the hour, but pain is tiring, and I fell asleep before Sam had even left my room. I woke at seven the next morning, feeling more or less back to normal, apart from a few aches here and there.

Sam said he would have to go down to Willoughby's Books, but wouldn't be more than an hour. He assured me that Alison was more than capable of handling things; he was simply going to pick up some paperwork and then come back. Before he left, he went round the flat, locking doors and windows. 'Do not open the door to anyone,' he ordered me. 'Not even if it's Edward. Not even if it's your parents. No one.'

'That's a bit melodramatic,' I protested.

'Nonetheless, you must promise.'

So I did.

By the time he came back, I had, with some difficulty, and a lot of yelping as my bruised muscles came into play, managed to take a shower and dress myself in a flowing kaftan thing I found in the wardrobe, bought years before in Marrakesh, God knew why. It didn't touch my body at any point except my shoulders, and by the time the painkillers supplied by the hospital had kicked in, I felt so invigorated, I could have scaled a mountain. Or at least a low hill.

Sam found me drinking coffee at the table in my kitchen, trying to recall the slightest feature about the attack which might help to identify the man responsible. But I could not. They had warned me at the hospital I was suffering from a temporary amnesia, though almost certainly my memory would eventually return. I wasn't all that convinced I wanted to bring it back, knowing I could be doomed to relive the incident again and again. I wondered what thoughts had raced through Helena's mind as her killer slammed the rock against her head. A favourite painting? Ainslie Gordon? A Fu Dog? Me? I'd never know. I just hoped she'd not had time to be scared.

TWENTY-ONE

I woke to the ringtone of my iPhone and groped for it without opening my eyes, wincing at the stab of pain the movement caused in my shoulder. 'What?' I gruffed.

'Wake up and listen good.' DI Fairlight sounded unusually excited.

'I'm listening.'

'We've got him! Or rather CID has. And before you say "Got who?", which I know you were about to, I mean that we've got the guy who killed your friend Doctor Drummond.'

'You have? How? Where? Above all, who? Tell me all.' I piled the pillows against my back and sat up.

'Caught him boarding a cross-Channel ferry, picked him up in Calais and brought him back to Dover. Denying it loud and clear all the way, of course.'

'Well, he would, wouldn't he?'

'Tried to get away several times. He's a stroppy little sod, from what I hear.'

'What put them onto him?'

'As so often, a combination of good solid detective work and luck. One of the investigating officers had noticed the number of mentions there'd been of a motorbike in witness statements. One person had also said that they'd seen a machine with foreign plates. And we caught some CCTV footage of a bike fitting the description and the owner.'

'And who *is* he, Fliss? Tell me before I explode.'

'Guy called Laurence Turnbull,' Fliss said.

'I *knew* it.' I punched the air. 'But how did they connect Helena with Turnbull in the first place?'

'Someone in Doctor Drummond's village – the usual invaluable dog-walker – was able not only to place him right there, at the time Morrison must have been killed, but actually saw him exiting the Drummond residence. And Garside now likes him for both homicides.'

I thought of Sam's lukewarm response to my hypothesis a few

nights before. This would show him! I could hear him moving about downstairs and the faint purr of the kettle. 'But that doesn't mean he killed her,' I objected. 'She was found over in Dovebrook.'

'An astute WPC did some cross-checking. Helena Drummond plus Alexandra Quick plus Dovebrook plus Edred and Mary Quick plus an artist guy living in southern France, added up to connections which were followed up and led in a more or less straight line to Turnbull.'

'Brilliant.' I thought a moment. 'Fliss . . . does the name Turnbull ring any bells?'

'Funnily enough, it does. Why is that?'

I explained about the two little girls Turnbull had ploughed into and killed, the third one confined to a wheelchair for the rest of her life. Another one doomed to wear a colostomy bag until they could find a way to repair the poor child. The bastard.

'Of course. I remember now. And the bugger got off with a caution, after all the work we put into the case.'

'Justice being done,' I said. 'No question of him getting off this time, is there?'

'Garside seems to think he's got him nailed, inside out and upside down.'

'Good. Excellent. The mills of God grinding.'

I heard Sam knocking gently on the bedroom door.

'Gotta go, Fliss. Thanks for keeping me in the picture.' I pressed the Off button. 'Come in.'

Sam came in with two cups of tea on a tray. Gave me one. Sat on the edge of the bed while I told him the gist of Fliss's phone call.

'Thank God for that,' he said. 'Presumably he's also the one who attacked you.'

'I think so, though I don't know what I've done to make him want to eliminate *me*.' I remembered again the faintly acrid smell which had come off both my attacker and the intruder into my flat, and this time I recognized it. Turps! Which a man who spent his time with paints and brushes would be in contact with daily. I'd smelled it in Ainslie Gordon's house as well. I'd pass the information on to Garside. One more nail in Turnbull's coffin. It would mean a police search of my flat some time, in case DNA had been left behind from the break-in, but I could put up with that.

'Sam,' I said, after I'd got him up to speed. 'Tomorrow I have to go to London.'

'No.' Calm but firm.

I eased my arms, sucked up the discomfort. Flexed my shoulders. 'I've got an important appointment.'

'No,' he said again.

'I can't afford to miss it, my whole future could be jeopardized.' I tried to match his firm with my firm, but his was better.

'No.'

'It's got to be tomorrow because she's going back to the States very shortly.'

'Are you talking about Mrs Lamont?'

'Yes. She and her husband are talking about an extremely lucrative offer, Sam.'

'So?'

'So if I don't show up, it not only looks very unprofessional, I also risk losing what could be a huge boost to my career. I simply cannot afford to miss this opportunity.'

'Listen, sweetheart, you're not going anywhere. Not yet. You've just spent three days in hospital after a nasty mugging. And there's no point in jutting out your jaw and looking obstinate. Give the woman a call and explain. She'll understand.'

'Even if she would—' I thought quickly. I raised an arm, and winced. Deliberately. Tried to rotate my head on my neck and winced again. For real, this time. 'Oh God, perhaps you're right. I damned well hope so, at any rate.'

'What time's the appointment tomorrow?'

'Eleven thirty,' I lied. The man was acting like a bloody Rottweiler. If he thought I'd cancelled, he'd relax, be off his guard. Might even go to the bookshop for an hour or two, leaving me on my own. At which point I would immediately head for London and hang about until three thirty, the time I'd arranged last week with Mercy. 'I'll call her later this morning, when you've gone to work. And no, I won't let anyone in until you come back, though now they've got Turnbull in custody, I should be perfectly safe.'

'There are a couple of things about the death of Ms Morrison still bothering me,' Sam said. 'One is, why would Turnbull roll up several pages of the woman's manuscript and stick them up her . . . ahem? And where would he find them in the first place?'

'Amy's book was on the night-table beside Helena's bed,' I said. 'And like I said yesterday, I'm quite sure that the police will find a connection between them. And sticking the pages where he did was probably just an act of spite.'

'But the pages weren't torn out of the book, were they?'

'No . . . they were typescript. Or proofs.'

'Another objection: if your theory is correct, and he had to race back into Canterbury to lie in wait for Doctor Drummond, why spend time on psychopathic little acts like that one, let alone sticking an implement through Amy's eyes? An implement he would have had to waste time in going to find among Doctor Drummond's tools, since I can't believe he brought it with him.'

I yawned again. 'There'll be some kind of explanation. Meanwhile, I'm going back to sleep. Those hospital meds are doing my head in.' In actual fact, I was weaning myself off them, terrified of becoming too dependent. The medicine cabinet in my bathroom already contained more than enough OTC painkillers.

Sam got up. Took my empty mug of tea. Leaned over and dropped a kiss on my forehead. 'Sleep tight, Alex.'

Some impulse urged me to pull him closer. Undo the belt of his dressing gown. Snuggle him into bed with me. I resisted it. Instead, I hunched myself down under the covers. 'See you later. G'night.' I produced another yawn, to add some verisimilitude.

When I'd heard him close and lock my front door, and the sound of his car pulling away from the parking space in front of the building, I got out of bed. After a long hot bath, I did some exercises, stretching and lifting, running on the spot, crunches. It hurt, but after a while I was through the pain and into a mini workout. I felt really good. By the time Sam reappeared, three or four hours later, I was in bed again, looking wan, eyes half-closed as though I was all dosed-up.

'Did you make that phone call to Mercy Lamont?' he asked, soon as he was through the door.

'Yeah. She understood. Said it wouldn't make any difference, in terms of her and Bob offering me work.'

'Good.' He removed his jacket. 'And how are you?' He sat down on the edge of my bed and took hold of my hand.

'Fine. Tired. But beginning to feel better, at last. The medication from the hospital really knocks you out.'

'What about something to eat?'

'I don't know,' I said weakly, although I was absolutely ravenous. 'A cheese sandwich, maybe. Or some soup. Something light, anyway.' I smiled up at him. 'Thank you, dear Sam.'

We followed the same routine the next morning. Sam waited until there was no chance of me getting up to London in time for an eleven thirty meeting, just in case I had been extremely economical with the truth the day before about cancelling my appointment with the Lamonts. I found his lack of trust in me very disheartening, but then, of course, it was understandable, given that I had been lying through my teeth for most of yesterday, though I hoped he hadn't realized. Perhaps he still hadn't.

As soon as he left for the bookshop, I got out of bed, trying not to groan. I certainly felt stronger than yesterday and was in much less discomfort. I did some more stretching and loosening-up exercises. Took a deep breath. I needed it, to get myself into some reasonable clothes in which to conduct an important business meeting.

I ordered a taxi to take me to the station and tumbled into the nearest carriage when the train stopped in front of me. I leaned wearily against the blanket-like upholstery of my seat and closed my eyes. And there he was again, the black figure, pounding towards me, head down, elbows working, running, running towards me over and over again . . . I opened my eyes with a start. I leaned back again and closed them. Was it Laurence Turnbull? Or some as-yet-unnamed bogeyman?

We pulled into Victoria and I got out. Found another taxi which took me to Eaton Square. The doorman let me in and I took the lift up to the second floor, prepared to walk along the passage to ring at the Lamonts' front door. But Mercy must have heard the lift because she was standing at the open door of her apartment, waiting for me.

She air-kissed me on both cheeks, in the Continental manner. 'Dead on time,' she said. 'I like that. I believe that punctuality is one of the great social arts. So many people these days seem to think it doesn't matter if you show up early or arrive late, as though specifying a time is purely arbitrary. Come on in.' She led me into her apartment, which already had the dispossessed air of a place about to be vacated by its owners. But the paintings were still in place. She saw me looking at them. 'The men come in the day after tomorrow to take the pictures into storage until we come back later in the year,' she explained.

I tried very hard not to wince as I eased out of my coat, but she noticed anyway. 'Are you all right, honey?' she asked.

'I had a bit of a fall the other day,' I said. The train ride seemed to have set my bones aching again.

'Oh dear. It's good of you to come, in the circumstances.'

'With you returning to the States, I didn't want to miss the opportunity to discuss your proposals,' I said. 'It's so much easier to go through the nitty-gritty detail face to face than by email or phone.'

'Very true. Now, come and sit down in the office. I'll get the housekeeper to bring in some coffee – unless there's something else you'd rather have.'

'Coffee's fine. And if you had some kind of mild painkiller . . .'

'Sure. I'll go and find something.'

While I waited, I glanced around. The room was lined with wood-fronted cabinets which held, I guessed, filing cabinets, shelving, cupboards, storage space, a TV. A big partners' desk took up about a third of the floor space, but there was still room for a sofa and two club chairs in maroon button-back leather, and a gas-fired stove designed to look as though it was a wood-burning model.

A number of photographs hung above the cabinets. Mercy and Bob appeared in various incarnations. Sailing, lying by a swimming pool, sitting at a table under palm trees with big umbrella-crowned drinks in front of them, hiking in the hills. Sometimes there were two kids with them, sometimes only one, sometimes there were six or seven, seated round a table or crowded together with ice cream cones in their hands and the sea behind them. And of course, numerous black-tie functions, some of which I'd seen in the magazines Sam had produced. In several of the latter, Mercy wore the gold-linked necklace. In one or two, she was being escorted by a handsome man with dark hair and eyes.

She returned and handed me a blue pill and a glass of water. 'It's not prescription medicine or anything of that kind, so it's not all that strong, but I find one of those usually sorts things out for me.'

I swallowed the pill and gestured at the photographs. 'Is that your family?'

'Yes.'

'They look like a pleasant crowd. Happy.' But then doesn't every-body look happy, in these kinds of photos?

'They are,' said Mercy. 'Or were.'

'Were?'

She shrugged, her face rueful. 'That's the way it goes. I always urged my son to live life to the full, since the difference between death and life is never more than a hair's breadth.'

'And one of those is your son?'

'Dante. Yes.'

She nodded as a smart young woman appeared, carrying a tray. 'Thank you, Cathy.' She was the same housekeeper Sam and I had met last time we were here.

'If there's nothing else,' Cathy said, 'I'll be on my way.'

'Good. I'll see you on Monday. Have a good weekend.'

'You, too.'

Minutes later, I heard the front door of the apartment closing. 'Cathy's a real treasure,' Mercy said. 'Much too smart to be acting as our housekeeper. She's got a university degree in law, but with two small children and a husband who's gone off with another woman, she likes the flexibility of the job, and the fact that we pay her a retainer even though we're not here all year round.'

She pulled some papers towards her, pushed others towards me. 'Before we begin, tell me about this accident, this fall you had.'

I explained.

'And you've no idea who or why?'

'None at all. Just a random nutter, I suppose.'

'You were fortunate that there was someone around to call the emergency services.'

'I know.'

'Well, as long as you think you're up for it . . .' she said doubtfully.

We settled down to look at the proposals she and Bob had drawn up. They all seemed fair and above board. And very generous. There didn't seem to be any hidden pitfalls, either, though after a while, I had to acknowledge that my concentration was beginning to slip. I hated to admit it, but I began to wonder if Sam had been right, and I wasn't yet recovered enough from my concussion to have undertaken the journey up here. I tried to concentrate, desperately resisting the urge to put my head down on the table and go to sleep. Across the desk from me, I could see Mercy's look of concern.

After a while, she reached across and said, 'Would you like to lie down for a while? I have plenty to be going on with, so I wouldn't take offence or anything.'

'Well . . . let's see how I go.'

'If it's anything like the way you've been going for the last ten minutes, my dear, I would say taking a short nap is the best thing you could do.'

I argued a bit, but in the end I agreed to go and lie down in one of her spare bedrooms. 'Just for half-an-hour,' I said. 'I need to get back home reasonably soon.' It was already getting dark; the lamps around the Square had come on, and the bare black trees were casting sinister shadows across the grass.

I wondered what Sam had done when he'd discovered I'd given him the slip – which was what it amounted to. He would be furious, I knew. And I also knew I shouldn't have come. He was right: I wasn't ready.

Gratefully, I took off my shoes, lay down on the bed and let Mercy cover me with a cashmere throw. On the wall facing me was a Blue Period Picasso painting, three painfully thin women embracing each other at the edge of an ocean. The Three Graces, I wondered. Or the Fates? Clotho, I told myself. Or was it Thalia? Euphros—

I had no idea for how long I slept, but when I awoke, the sky outside was black, and there was almost no sound of traffic. So was it late, or did the Lamonts have really efficient double-glazing? I tried to open my eyes in order to check my watch, but they felt unreasonably heavy, as though they had been glued shut. All I wanted to do was go back to sleep, but I was already embarrassed enough at having brought an untimely end to the discussions I had come here for.

Somewhere down the passage from the room where I lay, there was the sound of some kind of disturbance. Knocking and banging. A doorbell pealing non-stop. Mercy shouting, telling someone to go away. Her voice sounded very different from her usual well-modulated tones. More like Madame Montras behind her fish stall in the Dordogne.

I could make out muffled yelling. More banging. A voice that I vaguely recognized. Mercy screeching.

It occurred to me that I should get off the bed and see if she needed help. On the other hand, my arms were refusing to obey my brain and fling off my coverlet. Nor could I swing my legs over the side of the bed to the floor. What was wrong? Had I been struck with paralysis? Was this what captured flies felt like, cocooned in silk thread, ready to make a gourmet meal for some hungry spider?

'Help!' I cried. My voice sounded pitifully frail, a squeak rather than a shout. With an enormous effort, I opened my eyes. The room seemed the same except that while I slept, a small cinema screen had been erected on the wall at the foot of my bed, and a blue image came hurtling towards me and then was drawn back before hurtling again.

I tried to lean on my elbows, but couldn't. 'Lachesis!' I exclaimed in a faint mouse-whisper. It was the Picasso, but something terrible had happened to my eyes.

I made another supreme attempt and managed to lift myself up so that I was half-sitting against the headboard. Which was when I realized that although my hands were free, my arms had been bound to my sides with gaffer tape, so that in effect, I was trussed up like a Christmas joint.

What? Why? How had that happened?

Feebly I pushed with my upper body, trying to shake off the throw which Mercy had put over me before I went to sleep (minutes, hours, weeks ago?), and discovered that my legs too were immobilized in the same way. Who had done this? I'd work that out later. Meanwhile, there was Mercy. She needed my help and I must get out of this room and go to her.

Beside the bed was a carafe of water with a glass over the top. I wanted it. I *needed* it. My throat was parched, and thirst had spread like a virus throughout my body. I had to have that water or I would die. Grunting with effort, I managed to move my body round, inch by inch, until my bound legs swung like a single limb to the floor. Which was now covered in a large piece of heavy plastic sheeting. Big enough to hide a body in, one part of my brain thought idly. And then thought it again, very much less idly.

Speed was not just of the essence, but absolutely vital. I gazed round the room: was there anything I could use to slice through the tape and cut myself free?

I heard Mercy shrieking. I heard police sirens in the street below. I thought I heard my own name.

Getting free was paramount. I presumed that art thieves, whether a gang or a couple of individuals, had deliberately targeted the flat to coincide with the upheaval of removing the paintings into storage. They must also have been aware that Mercy's husband would not be there. The carafe on the night-table gleamed with thirst-quenching water, its bulbous body reflecting the rectangle of dark window, like one of the Dutch flower-paintings I had collected to include in *Ripe for the Picking*. My dry throat yearned for the water it contained. Using my fingers, I inclined my upper body towards it, flapped my fingers and knocked it to the floor. The damn thing landed on the plastic sheeting but didn't break. Water spilled over my feet.

I sat back on the bed then brought my legs down hard on the drinking glass. And again. The third time, the glass smashed. I bent down, scrabbled around with my fingers, found a good-sized shard. Awkwardly, I began to slice through the tape which bound my legs together. Gaffer tape is not duct tape. It's basically a sort of coarse cotton cloth which has been heat-treated with a strong adhesive. It is not easy to cut through, especially by someone whose movements are restricted. I managed it in the end, my nerves screaming with impatience. My legs were bleeding from various cuts and nicks made by the piece of glass I'd been using, but at least they didn't hurt. Not yet.

Afterwards, I was to ask myself why I felt so little fear or apprehension. But at the time, I believe I must have segued immediately from anthologizer into senior police officer mode. There was a job to do, and I was the only one who could do it.

I used my right hand to hack clumsily at the tape binding my left arm to my body. I'd never be able to wear my expensive cardigan again, but that was the least of my worries. The adrenalin racing through my body meant that I felt none of the muscular pain from the attack on me. My left arm released, I did the same in reverse.

Finally, I was free. I bent down and pulled off my wet tights. Sucked at them, for the moisture. Slipped my feet into my shoes. I ran, as quietly as I could, to the bend in the passage. Mercy stood there, her back to me, staring at the front door, which shuddered under the blows from the other side. She was screaming silently, her head arched backwards. Veins stood out on either side of her neck.

'I'm here, Mercy,' I said. 'The pol—'

She swung round. 'What the fuck?' she snarled. 'How the hell did you manage to . . .?'

I took a step back. The change in her was astonishing. Her face was mottled red, her eyes glared, her lips were pulled back in a ferocious grimace. She looked like a wild animal. She was clearly insane. I backed away from her as she came towards me. It was hard to reconcile her with the sophisticated blue-blooded art collector I was familiar with. Terror can do that to a person, I thought. And then I saw the gun in her hand.

A gun? Mercy Lamont? What was going on? And then, like beads on an abacus click-click-clicking precisely into position to produce a grand total, everything fell into place. 'And now it's your turn,' she snarled. 'You've ruined everything with your probing and suspicions.'

'They'd have caught you eventually,' I said, as calmly as I could.

She gave a scornful laugh. 'Bob would have arranged things.'

'Paid the police off, you mean?'

'He always has in the past.'

'This isn't the Deep South, you know. This is England.'

'Money talks just as loudly here as in the States.'

There was more banging on the door. A voice shouted, 'Police! Open up.'

'They'll never get through that door,' she said, sounding quite rational. 'It's steel-reinforced.'

She looked at me again. I didn't like the way the gun shook in her hand. Nor the way her fingers seemed to be flexing.

'Give me the gun, Mercy,' I said, holding out my hand, but she jittered away from me like a nervous horse. One of her eyes began to twitch, as though a fly was trapped beneath the skin.

'Keep back,' she said.

Another voice shouted, 'We have reason to believe you are holding a hostage. Please release her immediately and we can negotiate a peaceful solution to this situation.'

'Peaceful?' She gave a bitter laugh. 'There is no solution. Except death.' She raised the gun higher and pointed it at me.

'What on earth good would it do to shoot me?' I knew that in these circumstances, the longer you kept the perps talking, the more likelihood there was of a positive outcome. But my body was filling with apprehension as I realized that I was unlikely to survive the next few minutes. Like Macbeth, she was in blood, stepped in so far that one more victim wasn't going to make much difference. I had been so fixated on Laurence Turnbull that I had failed to see the signs right under my nose of who the killer really was.

'That bitch,' she said, her voice rising. 'That vile callous *wicked* bitch.' Her gaze seemed to turn inward, as if she were seeing some other place, not a London hall with the police outside the door. 'I want you to know that I'm glad I killed her. Glad that she knew it was me, glad that she was terrified and in agony as I gouged out her eyes, smashed her beautiful heartless face. It was all I could do for my boy.'

The primeval sound she made was chilling. Just so had bereaved mothers expressed their grief and loss through the centuries. Just so did they still mourn, beating their breasts, plucking at their hair, weeping in despair. The desolate look I remembered from our first meeting had taken over her face.

'What happened to him?' I asked. *Keep her talking while the cops figure out a way into the place.*

She turned those unseeing eyes on me. 'The bitch killed him,' she said.

'Amy Morrison killed your son?'

'She stole his heart, then his work, then his book. The book he had worked so hard on. The book which would have made his name. It killed him. So I killed her.' She produced a mirthless grin which reeked of death and murder and heartbreak. 'Tit for tat.' She gave an ugly snorting laugh. 'And an eye for an eye.' Those punctured eyes. That missing nipple – I didn't want to go there.

'Book?' I said quickly.

'*The Magic of Illusion,*' she said. 'And if ever there was an illusion, it was that bitch of a woman. Fooling everyone into thinking she wrote it, when she had absolutely no right to it. And when I saw her being praised and feted for the work which my poor deluded boy had done, I just couldn't . . .' She shook her head.

Behind her, a door opened, so quietly that even though I saw it move, I didn't hear a thing. A man slipped through the gap. He was wearing black. He had a gun in one hand and a black-jack in the other.

'I'm going to have to kill you too,' she said. 'You can see I have no choice.'

'Why?'

'Because you knew it was me, didn't you?'

'Well, actually . . .' I coughed. My throat was so dry. 'Do you really think you'll get away with this?' I was praying that the man behind her didn't warn her in any way of his presence, because if he did, sheer surprise would tighten her finger on the trigger and I'd probably be dead.

'Killing the Bitch Goddess was one thing, but I was sorry about Doctor Drummond. She was a nice woman, and it wasn't her fault.'

'What exactly did she do?'

'It was more what she was *going* to do. As soon as she started to read the book she'd know it was me. She'd been Dante's supervisor at art school. She would recognize at once that she was reading Dante's work. She knew perfectly well that the Morrison slut hadn't written the Masaccio book and my son had.' I remembered Helena saying at the Masaccio launch party that she hoped when she got round to reading the book, she wouldn't recognize that she'd read it before. I remembered too, the annotated copy she had been reading at my parents' house, the exclamation marks and underlined words.

I was interested in the way her high-class accent had deteriorated from Manhattan to Brooklyn.

'Was that really a reason to kill her?' I calculated the distance between us and figured I didn't have a hope in hell of getting to her in time to wrest the gun from her hand before she shot me.

'Not really. Killing Amy Morrison should have been enough.'

'Agreed,' I said. 'So what do you have against me?'

She seemed surprised that I should ask. 'You must have known it was me,' she said. 'You had me down on the floor in your apartment, had your arms wrapped round me. You must have realized I wasn't a man.'

Slight, slender, wiry . . . just like Turnbull. My lack of recognition was understandable.

'Pretty unobservant of me, one way or another, but I didn't, actually,' I said. I kept my voice loud. The man behind her was moving with infinite care. He too was holding a gun.

'After my son . . . died, I looked for his thesis and then realized she'd stolen it. And then when I heard all the praise she was getting,

read all the reviews which should have been my son's, I just . . .'
She shook her head. 'It was too much.'

Behind her, a second man had crept into the passage. He was a
burly bloke, dressed in black like his colleague. I raised my voice
to cover any noise the two of them might make.

'Helena had absolutely nothing to do with any of this,' I shouted
at her. 'Who do you think you are, God or something? What gives
you the right to decide who lives and who dies? Such arrogance,
such contempt for others. Helena was a woman who contributed to
the world in so many ways, whereas you . . . you're just a rich
parasite. Sponging on society. Used to having your own way. Used
to buying whatever you want.'

For a moment her head reared back, as though I had punched
her. 'How dare you!' she screamed. She aimed the gun directly at
my head. 'How fucking *dare* you? I contribute in all sorts of—'

And as she spoke, the first man leaped forwards and drove Mercy
hard to the floor, landing on top of her. Beneath him, Mercy struggled, trying to shake him off. I could hear her gasping for air. The
second man joined him. He bent down as the first officer tried to
pull her arms out from under her and cuff them behind her back.
Before he could do so, there was a muffled shot. The three of us
stared down. Blood was slowly seeping along the floor. Mercy was
still.

'Hell's teeth,' said the second officer. 'She managed to pull the
bloody trigger.'

The two of them turned Mercy over onto her back. It was obvious
that she was dead, although between us we attempted to resuscitate
her. The bullet had gone straight into her heart. A lucky shot, I
thought. Lucky for her.

When we opened the front door, Sam Willoughby was standing
outside. He came in and took me hard into his arms. 'Don't ever
do that again,' he said, looking down at me. 'Not *ever*. You don't
know what nightmarish situations I've imagined you in.'

I relaxed against his chest. It felt good to let someone else take
charge.

TWENTY-TWO

'She married Luigi Vendamo when she was sixteen,' said Bob Lamont. 'Couldn't get a divorce, being Catholic. Had the twins – Dante and Cesare. Luigi was an alcoholic brute, and she left him when they were four. Luckily – or unluckily, depending on your point of view – he fell off some scaffolding two years later. She got compensation from his employers, which made things easier for her. She managed somehow. Then she met me . . .' He buried his head in his hands. 'Oh dear, oh God . . . this is all so terrible.'

Sam passed him a clean handkerchief so he could wipe his eyes. We were sitting in the Connaught Hotel, coffee in front of us, along with DI Felicity Fairlight. Neither Fliss nor I were particularly sympathetic. I simply sat. She had her arms folded across what was generally regarded as a formidable bosom. As she had kept reminding me, it wasn't her case, but we felt that Bob would talk more easily to her. All this, of course, was strictly unofficial, though I knew Fliss was hooked up to a discreet voice recorder.

He raised his head and looked at the three of us. 'She had a tremendous business head – it was because of her that we began to diversify, strengthen our position in the markets.'

And get richer and richer, I thought, remembering Mark and his desire to help people much worse off than himself.

'I was happy to give her whatever she wanted,' Bob was saying. 'Show her the world. She was like a sponge, soaking up painting and architecture and food and museums, all the things she'd never had access to. She was the one who started collecting paintings, researching them, her ancestors and mine. They were wonderful years. She fit right in.'

'And then what happened?' asked Fliss.

'Cesare was in his second year at Harvard and died in a car crash. Mercedes never got over it. Neither did Dante. He became doubly precious, was forced to become both her sons, himself *and* Cesare's stand-in. It was particularly hard because he was the absolute image of his twin. Mercedes had had so many plans, so many ambitions

for them both. And then Dante got himself . . . mixed up with Mrs
Morrison. Quite apart from the fact that she was married to our
good friend Dexter, she was a . . . sorry, but she really was a bitch.
Mercedes hated her on sight.'

'She sounds like the kind of possessive mother who'd have hated
any woman her son fell for,' I said. Did I sound aggressive? I
certainly felt aggressive.

Sam looked at me in surprise. I didn't care. So far, I wasn't
entirely buying into this sob story.

'And then,' Bob said, staring coldly in my direction, 'Dexter died,
and Dante thought that was it, the two of them would be able to
be together openly. But that wasn't Amy's plan at all. Once she'd
got her share of Dexter's money – or at least as much of it as she
could get her claws on – she dumped him.'

'*La Belle Dame Sans Merci*,' I said.

'Dante couldn't hack it. First his brother. Then his girlfriend. And
then, as he discovered later, his PhD thesis. Four years' work just
gone.'

'So he killed himself.'

'Hanged himself from a cross-beam in his Village apartment, while
the bitch went back to England,' continued Bob, 'and then eventually
produced the Masaccio book as though it was her own work. My
poor Mercy. It was just too much. She was already . . . well, unhinged,
by Dante's death. But I never dreamed she would . . .' He shook his
head.

'I almost feel sorry for her,' Sam said. I hoped he was being
sarcastic.

'I don't,' I said. 'She killed Helena Drummond without the
slightest compunction.'

'And when she didn't succeed the first time, she tried again. And
again,'

'The strange thing is how similar her background and attitudes
were to Amy's,' added Fliss. 'Both of them from lowly backgrounds.
Both ending up married to rich men—'

'I knew there was something off about that necklace and the bollocks
about the great-grandfather . . .'

'I had it made for her,' Bob said, sighing. 'Copied it from the
portrait, which she liked to pass off as a family heirloom. As soon
as she saw it, Amy said she wanted it, so Dante took it from his

mother's jewellery chest and gave it to her. I believe she was wearing it when . . . when my poor wife killed her.'

'Where did the motorbike come from?'

'It had been Dante's. She loved it. Rode it all over the place. Fast. I think it was a way of letting off some of her feelings.'

'You can understand her grief and rage, I suppose.' Fliss emptied her coffee cup. 'It's all rather sad, isn't it?' She stood. 'I must go.'

'At least she's at peace.' Bob stood up too. 'Thank you for listening.' He fixed his gaze on me. 'And I'm sorry, Alex. I truly am.'

I tried to smile at him, but my mouth simply wouldn't turn upwards. There was no way he and I would be working together on – what had he called them? – must-have books for the luxury crowd. But at least the offer from Cliff Nichols was still on the table.

When they'd gone, Sam held out his arms and I stepped into them. Tension flowed away from me. It was such a relief to relax against his chest, and know that the ball was now in someone else's court.

Lightning Source UK Ltd.
Milton Keynes UK
UKOW03f0738271116
288572UK00003B/56/P